BLACKOUT MAN

CHARLES CUTHILL

Published in 2020 by Daisy Dog Press, a division of the Sparky the Dog Entertainment Empire

ISBN (print version): 978-1-0882-0786-4

ISBN (e-book edition): 978-1-0882-0795-6

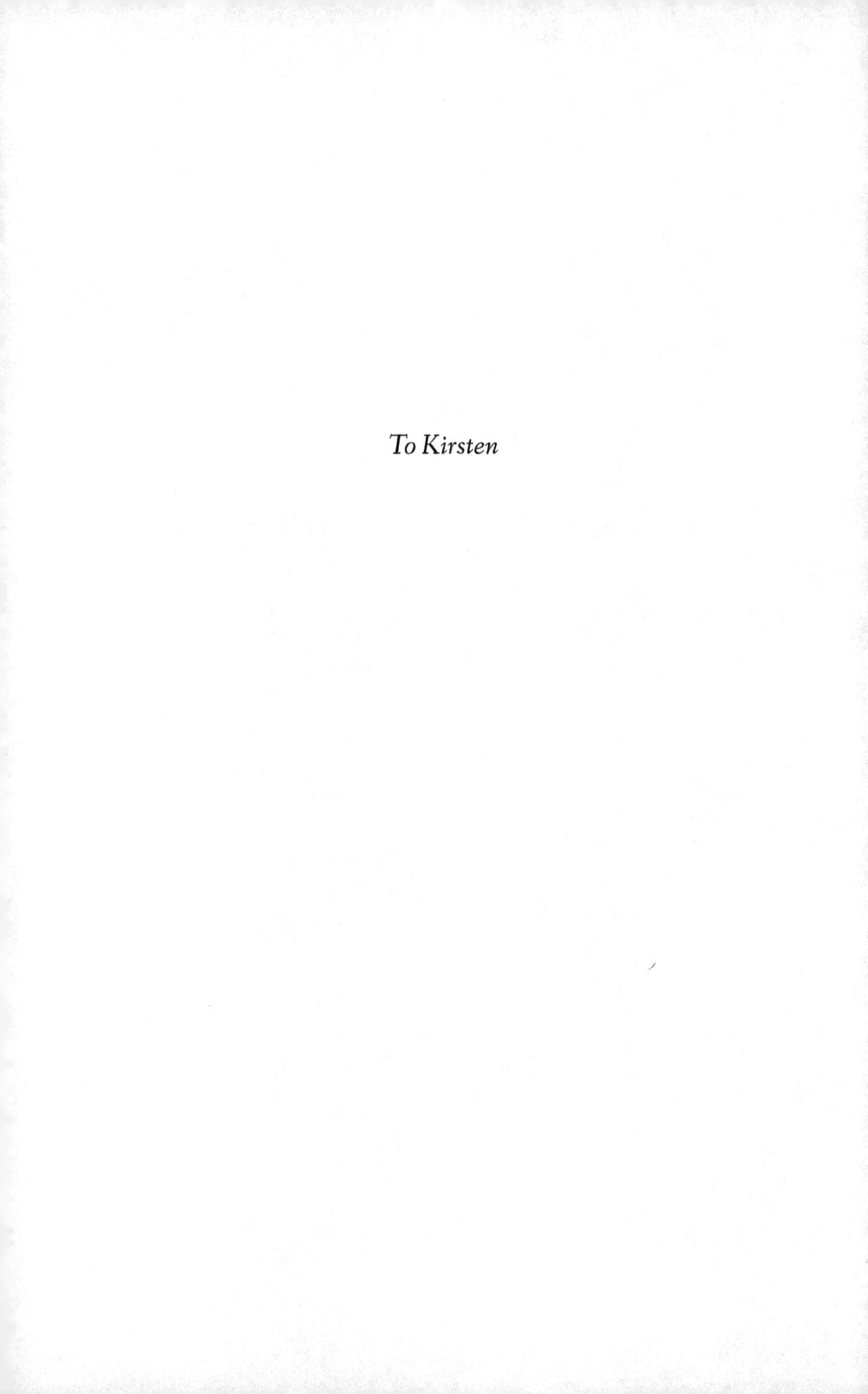

To Kirsten

PART ONE

All evils are to be considered with the good that is in them.
    –Daniel Defoe

For you, to do what I do, is not right—
    But, for me, it's not wrong
    –Robert Craig Knievel

CHAPTER ONE

Denver, Colorado
September 9, 1974

Beep, beep, beep...

Jack sat next to Wendy's hospital bed and moaned. She lay in a coma, under a ventilator—an artificial womb that kept her alive but oblivious to her burnt body.

Jack hated hospitals, the first and last stop on life's highway of misery. The sighs, the anxiety, the beeping cardiograms. And the nagging question: will my grandpa, my daughter...will my wife be all right?

Monotonous despair.

Beep, beep, beep...

And how life could change so suddenly, so randomly. The day's events, which had led Jack to this moment, were like pieces of a tragic jigsaw puzzle. This little white piece, part of an iceberg. A darker piece, the hull of a ship. Another piece, the captain asleep at the wheel.

He thought about the little pieces in his own life.

The brand-new TV set. The stunt. The antenna. The

storm. The lightning. It was as though the cosmos had ordered those things along with a slice of apple pie and a scoop of ice cream billions of light years ago, and now the pieces were assembling themselves.

No, not as *though*.

That's *how* it happened!

The Big Bang had dictated it and every other occurrence, large and trivial, from the start.

Neutrinos, bosons, quarks, combined into atoms and molecules and gasses and rocks and DNA, and collided in such a way that it would eventually put Wendy on a roof during a lightning storm. And maybe that's why his RCA-TV was invented in the first place. Maybe that was the point of the Big Bang: to put his wife in a coma!

But it really made no difference how this moment came to be. In the end, like everything else, these things just happened. It was saner to think like that.

Or, at least, it made one less crazy.

Only hours ago, Wendy was just fine. A picture flashed through Jack's head: Wendy in a summer dress—looking good, vibrant, handing him a hot dog. And he remembered her clenched teeth after he had thrown that hot dog against the wall. He remembered the red-hot blood rushing through her cheeks. He remembered a bottle of wine sailing through the air, just missing him, and smashing against the wall.

Cheap Merlot. All over his head.

Life.

Vitality.

Soul.

Not all those things could be explained by the Big Bang: not an enraged wife throwing a bottle of wine at her husband, not a stuntman on TV who turned cheating death into an art form.

Some things were just bigger than two-plus-two-equals-four.

Jack pushed his trucker cap over his eyes, trying to stop the movie reel from looping in his mind. The flash. The noise. The explosion. The fire. The smoke. The extinguisher.

And where the hell had he found that fire extinguisher? Right in the kitchen cabinet where it belonged.

At first, Jack had thought the TV was defective and that JD Stevenson had better return all his money. Every penny of it. Solid state? Chassis tubes never did that to him! Just another advertising conspiracy designed to separate him from his hard-earned four-hundred-and-fifty dollars.

All those thoughts had bubbled through his brain as he'd extinguished the flaming television.

And he remembered how he had finally put out the fire and gone outside, cleared the soot from his eyes, and looked at the roof.

"Wendy, get down here! The TV just blew——"

Then he saw it...

The horror.

Wendy's legs dangling over the side of the smoldering roof, the black thundercloud flashing above. He put two-and-two together. The TV hadn't blown up on its own.

The lightning had done it.

It had hit the antenna.

And it had hit Wendy!

...*beep, beep, beep*...

He looked at Wendy's bandaged hands. The door squeaked open and the room filled with a green fluorescent light from the hallway.

Dr. Vladik entered and sat beside Jack. He was tall and pale, and he had a beaked nose. His dark thin hair was combed back over his head.

Jack looked up. "Will she be okay?"

The doctor fiddled with his stethoscope and looked at his reflection in the cold, shiny chest piece.

"It is hard to tell, Mr. Hawks."

When the doctor said, 'Mr. Hawks,' it sounded more like, *Meestehr Hawkz*. Dr. Vladik was from Romania. He had a deep voice, steeped in an Old-World Slavic accent. He smelled of cigarettes. His deep-set eyes were those of a man who had seen too much. Sad black eyes.

Things didn't always end well in those ER rooms.

"What's so hard about it?"

"Well," he said, "some victims of lightning strikes come out okay in the end. And others—"

"Others? Others what?"

The doctor dangled the stethoscope around his scrawny neck and stared at the bag of saline dripping into Wendy's arm.

"Others not so well. They can become mentally ill. Their symptoms might become apparent right away, or they can take years to develop."

Jack leaned over the bed and listened to the EKG beeping to the rhythm of Wendy's shaky vitals. He rubbed his eyes and looked at Wendy's burnt, blistered, bandaged hands. He caressed her cheeks.

"Mr. Hawks," said the doctor. "Are you okay?"

"No," sobbed Jack. "Why did I let her climb up on that roof!"

"These things, they just happen. That is all I deal with every single day, one improbable accident after the other. Please, do not be so hard on yourself."

"Easy for you to say."

The doctor stood up. "But before I leave, there is something you should know."

"What?"

"She is your wife, correct?"

"We've been married almost three months."

"How do I put this? We did some tests."

"Tests?"

"Mr. Hawks..." The doctor put his hand on Jack's shoulder. "Your wife is pregnant."

"Pregnant? For how long?"

"About two months. It is amazing that she has not miscarried. But it remains a possibility."

Jack's steel-blue eyes misted, and he whispered into Wendy's ear, "Did you hear that? You're going to be a mommy!"

Dr. Vladik scratched his beak-like nose. "That goose is not hatched, yet. Anything could happen. Anything. Remember, she just received a 1.21-gigawatt jolt of electricity. It would be a miracle if that fetus went to term."

Jack caressed Wendy's tummy. "Will the baby, if it goes to term, be okay?"

Dr. Vladik put the stethoscope in the pocket of his white lab coat. "It is hard to tell. When it comes to lightning, so many things come into play. Chemistry, DNA, even chirality."

"Ch—chirality? What the hell is chirality?"

"Chirality. How do I explain? It is what scientists refer to as right- and left-handed molecules. Some molecules have a mirror image. Their atoms have been assembled backwards, like a right- and a left-handed glove. It can cause an otherwise harmless molecules to fit into hormonal receptors in new ways and cause them to behave unpredictably.

"I can't say I've heard of that."

"Vicks is a common example."

"Vicks?"

"The medicine for colds. Some people inhale it when they are congested. Anyway, in the case of a developing fetus, a gene could get turned inside out, especially, if the mother was exposed to radiation, which I doubt most highly. But stranger things have happened. And other things may come into play, too. Even alcohol or drugs could play a role when it comes to the side effects of a lightning strike.

"Drugs? Wendy wasn't doing any drugs."

"Alcohol?"

"Well...she does occasionally drink the odd glass of wine. I kept a case of wine in the attic for six years. I had just broken it open."

"Six years?"

"I don't normally drink that stuff, unless I'm desperate."

"You do not like the taste?"

"Wine's for pussies."

"Hmm...."

"No offense."

"I prefer Vodka myself. What kind of wine?"

"Paul Masson, I think."

"Oh..."

"Is that bad?"

"It depends on the year."

Jack's eyes narrowed. "Are you trying to be funny?"

"No. I meant a specific year—and a specific batch of bottles. I do not know why I thought of it. Just a silly story I heard."

"What story?"

"Oh, it is nothing. I once had a patient, a postal worker with a herniated disc. He told me about a shipment of wine he had delivered to a nuclear laboratory. Apparently, the wine had been contaminated with some uranium byproducts. But the mistake was caught, and the wine was properly disposed of. The US Army buried it deep in a munitions dump in New Mexico, or so they say. It happened a number of years ago, I believe it was back in 1968. Nothing to worry about really. As I said, I do not know why I brought it up."

Jack tugged on his cap's bill and looked at the EKG.

Beep, beep, beep…

He turned from the machine and looked out the window. The sun had disappeared behind the mountains. The Denver skyline mirrored the sunset's golden colors. The city had changed since he'd last driven through it. He had been hauling a load of sugar beets to Salt Lake City. Back then Denver only had a few buildings higher than five stories.

But not now.

Cranes were everywhere. It was booming. The old brick buildings from the cowboy days were being demolished. New glass skyscrapers were taking their place. Big bland forgettable boxes built by people with college degrees.

He had a problem with people with college degrees.

Did Leonardo da Vinci have a college degree?

A new batch of well-thought-out trucker ruminations and conspiracy theories flooded his brain. He wondered if the people who built the Vatican held degrees in engineering. He wondered what those ancient architects would think of these tall glassy concrete piles of shit that blocked the view of the mountains.

Did Jesus go to college?

He thought about the employers who hassled him for not going to truck-driving school. They said he wasn't educated enough. And he did, secretly, feel a little lower on the totem pole than the drivers who went to truck-driving school. But where did it end? If he had got himself a trucker education, then he'd just feel inadequate that he didn't get a medical degree instead.

At least this way he felt sort of clever. He'd become a trucker without ever going to truck-driving school—or worse, medical school. Nothing like spending all that money in college and winding up driving a truck. Happened all the time. And besides, he made the same money as those truckers with all their trucker book-learning. What were truck-driving schools good for? Could they teach a man how to drive through a blinding snow storm, high on amphetamines and on one-hour of sleep while hauling tandem trailers of liquid nitrogen over an icy mountain pass?

Did they teach that in truck-driving school?

Did they teach that at Harvard?

And who delivered all their books to Harvard? Those thousands upon thousands of text books?

The book fairy?

No, truckers hauled them in. Hell, he was one who was educating those Ivy-League shits!

Jack's mind was spinning like a 9-lb test-lure taken by a great-white shark into the uncharted depths of his brain. He looked at Wendy, bandaged and burnt.

His wife!

In a coma!

He needed a drink. He needed a quadruple shot of Jim Beam. Then he remembered the wine. That damn wine! There *had* been something odd about that wine. Where it came from. How it wound up in his attic.

That seemed ordered up by the Big Bang as well.

"Well," said Dr. Vladik again. "Had she been drinking? That is important because alcohol could affect the fetus."

"Well, she did open up a bottle of wine."

"And how much did she have?"

"Not much. She threw it at my head. It got all over me."

"She threw a wine bottle at you?"

"It was for my own good."

"The same Paul Masson wine that you mentioned before?"

"Now that I think of it, it might have been a 1968."

"1968? How do you know?"

"My brother Elston gave it to me back in '68. I kept it on

hand for an emergency. You know, in case the liquor store exploded."

"I see."

Jack stared at the floor.

The doctor yawned.

"He got it for free," said Jack. "A whole case of it. He had this temp job as a cement mixer in some town in New Mexico, Los Aldalamosa, or something like that."

The doctor stopped yawning. "You do not mean Los Alamos do you?"

"Yeah, that's it. Los Alamos. How did you know?"

Dr. Vladik's eyes widened. His Dracula-pale skin turned whiter. "Los Alamos? The nuclear research lab in New Mexico?"

"Yeah, that was it. They had some kind of new plant being constructed there, and Elston told me that he found this crate of perfectly good wine in the dumpster. So he took it back and gave it to me. But I never drank it. I just stuck it in the attic."

"Mr. Hawks, those bottles could have been contaminated. That wine could have been radioactive!"

"Elston didn't say nothing about no radioactivity. He just said he found them for free."

"And you kept that same case for six years?"

"Yes."

"And your wife? She drank it?"

"She might have had a glass."

"Oh, my god! Are you sure?"

"Like I said, she threw the bottle at my head. I'm not sure how much she had."

"Oh, dear, God," said Dr. Vladik.

"What is it?"

The doctor stared at the floor.

"You're saying my wife might have drank radioactive wine?"

"That is exactly what I am saying!"

"No way. Elston said they kept the really bad stuff in lead boxes."

"You cannot be certain of that, Mr. Hawks. People make mistakes. That is what we doctors deal with. One mistake after the other. But this? This boggles my mind. It's bad enough when alcohol is combined with a lightning strike. That O-H molecular configuration is most curious. I could go on for days about that, weeks even—especially if they are supercharged with a gigawatt of electricity. But when radioactivity is added, who knows what could happen."

Jack took off his cap and faced the doctor. "All I'm asking is, will the child be normal?"

"I do not know," said Dr. Vladik. "Radioactive alcohol, a fetus...a gigawatt of electricity. Anything could happen."

The doctor walked to the door and fumbled for a switch on the wall and dimmed the lights. A faded golden sunset glowed through the room's windows. He looked at Jack's darkened profile. "Just promise me one thing, Mr. Hawks."

"What?"

"Should it be born, you must never allow the child, even when it grows up to consume any liquor. No beer, no wine, no whiskey, no gin, or any substance that contains the ethyl-alcohol molecule."

"No booze? Really?"

"No alcohol of any kind."

Jack crushed his cap into a ball. "What the hell kind of life is that?"

CHAPTER TWO

Thirty-Four Years Later
Tomahawk, Colorado
July 3, 2008

The night air cracked with the sound of breaking glass.

A dark figure, more of a shadow, stood by an empty newspaper box. His ears twitched. God, he loved that sound.

Like Dvorak.

Breaking glass. The prelude to crime's symphony.

The Shadow whipped his arm straight. A can of Coors shot into his hand, ejected from a spring-loaded runner attached to his forearm. Quite the gadget. And he had quite the costume to go with it: black jumpsuit, helmet, goggles, cape.

The Shadow drank the beer and smacked his lips. He sniffed the air. Crime not only had a sound, but it had a smell. A smoldering, electrical smell.

Reminded him of an old TV set.

The Shadow rolled his shoulders. Stretched his neck. Loosened his legs. Popped his back. He took another sniff of Tomahawk's air and slinked across the street. Toward the symphony.

He peaked into the dark alley behind JD Stevenson's Pharmacy.

And there it was.

Crime.

Two men. One wore a cowboy hat and wielded a baseball bat. Louisville Slugger, prime maple. The cowboy's cohort wore a blue bandana around his forehead. He carried a rifle, a Remington 572 with a rimfire pump.

Then the Shadow saw a cardboard box lying amongst the glass shards from the broken window on the backdoor. Whatever it contained was probably equivalent of ancient treasure. The kind of pirate booty that caused men like Blackbeard to risk unknown seas and battle fifty-foot ocean swells, curtains of rain, and monstrous hurricanes without a second thought.

"Strange thing, greed," thought the Shadow. "How much courage it instills in otherwise cowardly souls. But why choose such a path? Is it so terrible to be poor? Don't the great mystics embrace it? I don't care how bad it gets. Just leave me with a studio apartment, a clear conscience, and a bottle of Merlot. Some Leo Tolstoy. Some Jane Austen. Or a baseball game on the radio...ugh, you're talking too much...there's work to be done...crime to be thwarted!"

The Shadow finished the beer and dropped the empty can. He stomped on it. This was a big job. Not only did these burglars have rifles and bats, but they were fueled by insatiable greed. It had turned them into monsters.

Maybe even killers.

Bah! A single can of Coors would not do.

The Shadow needed more.

"Fine time for a robbery," he thought.

Across the street, the Raccoon Bar and Grill's neon sign blinked and went off. Closing time. Schulz's Liquor store had also closed. So was JD's old appliance store. But that had been closed for twenty-five years.

Everything was closed, and everyone in town had gone to bed.

Of course, this was when crime happened: while the shops were closed, while children slept, while drummers snored next to empty whiskey bottles and wayward women, while cats stared out the window and yowled at meandering raccoons, while dogs whined at strange noises in the dark.

Only the moon bore witness to these criminal actions. And the things it had seen! For it was at this time of night that society's vermin crawled out of cheap motel rooms, slithered from dilapidated vans, surfaced like crocodiles from half-way houses to do what they did best.

This is why the Shadow ventured out.

Somebody had to.

Although it was late, the Shadow was not sleepy. In fact, he was more than awake. Every nerve in his body quivered, ready to explode—a hair-trigger on red alert.

But, still, he was in trouble.

Dammit. I must THINK!

Across the street, he found his answer

An old hobo slumped on a bench, his dreams flapping madly in the winds of Fairyland.

The Shadow peered through the mist and honed in on the bottle on the hobo's lap. Wild Irish Rose. Fortified. Just what the doctor ordered. He crossed the street and approached the old vagabond and nudged him on the shoulder.

"*Injuns*," muttered the old man, "time to circle up the wagons...argh, you'll never get me alive ye feathered malcontent!"

"Wake up, ol' timer."

The old man stirred.

"I need a swig of your hooch."

The hobo's watery eyes opened. He scratched his gin-ravaged nose and yawned, revealing a gummy maw decorated with rotten teeth and wondrous bleeding canker sores.

"Huh? Am I dreaming?"

"This is no dream, old man."

"What's up with the costume?"

"Costume?"

"That motorcycle helmet? That cape..."

"Oh, this?"

"Halloween come early, young feller?"

"The bottle. I'm desperate."

The hobo held the bottle up to the street lamp. He swished the wine back and forth.

"I suppose I can relate," he said.

"I'm sure you can."

"Sometimes you just really need a drink—as badly as any Wall Street stockbroker or trauma surgeon does when they get off the job. They'll just casually reach over for a glass of single-malt whiskey like it was an iced tea, something they could take or leave. But they're fooling themselves. If they didn't get their lips on that glass, they'd go just as nuts as me! They just dress a little nicer."

"Sir, the bottle!"

"Hey, now—"

"There's a crime in progress!"

"Crime?"

The hobo looked around the shadowy figure. "And you need some of the ol' liquid courage?"

"Desperately."

"Take all you want," said the old man. "I got me another bottle waiting down by the tracks."

The Shadow accepted the bottle and unscrewed the cap. "I owe you."

"Don't worry about it."

"No, really. I'll get you a nice single-malt."

"Sure you will."

The Shadow chugged two quick swallows. Nothing. He choked down some more and waited a few more seconds. He stared down the street, to the darkened outskirts and then out to the highway. He watched the lights from the steady-rolling 18-wheelers in the distance. A flash of heat lightning illuminated the empty horizon. His skin tingled. Lightning always did that to him, kicked his senses up a notch.

And then the magic happened.

Always with the lightning. Even with just one look.

As the booze entered his blood stream and seeped into his DNA, the molecules in his body altered, like the crystal structure of carbon atoms configuring into those of a diamond. Same atoms...but a totally different beast.

His muscles turned to iron.

His mind launched into space.

He finished the bottle and his brain revved so fast that world around him seemed to stop.

A fly buzzed by the Shadow's head.

But to the Shadow's overdriven sight, the fly appeared to move in slow-motion. The Shadow reached out, plucked the unwitting insect out of mid-flight. It flinched and jerked between his fingers.

The Shadow smiled. "Fear not, timorous beastie. I shan't hurt you."

The fly relaxed. The Shadow opened his fingers and it buzzed into the night.

The Shadow had entered another dimension. He felt like he could lift a freight train and outrun one too. But it was more than just a feeling. Booze can make many people feel that way. But in the Shadow's case, it really gave him those abilities.

A battered brown Honda Accord swerved into the alley. The Shadow adjusted his goggles and thought, "It can't be...impossible."

The hobo looked around the Shadow's cape. "What's going on?"

The Shadow clenched the bottle. "Crime..."

"Shouldn't somebody call the cops?"

The Shadow squeezed the empty bottle. It shattered in his hand. "I'll take care of it."

The Shadow crossed the street and kicked the flattened Coors can into the alley.

"Who's that?" said the Cowboy. He was a big man. Could have been a real baseball player, a first-rate homerun slugger. But instead of mashing fastballs, he was using his bat to break into pharmacies. Besides the cowboy hat, the man also sported a handlebar mustache and green boots. Red Gila monsters embroidered on the side of them. They glinted in the Accord's headlights.

"Love the boots," said the Shadow.

The Cowboy stopped and stared.

"Larry Mahans?"

"What the hell you talking about?"

"Your boots. Those Larry Mahans?"

The Cowboy tapped the bat on the palm of his hand. "Run along, pal."

"Maybe I don't want to."

"Have it your way, asshole!"

The Cowboy marched toward the Shadow and swung the bat. To the Shadow's lightning-fast eyes, the bat's acceleration slowed as though it were a helicopter blade grinding through wet cement. The Shadow's forearm snapped up and busted the bat in two. Shards of prime maple flew into the night.

The Cowboy stumbled back and stared at the bat's splintered end.

A shot rang out.

Hot lead struck the Shadow's leg. He spun around and saw the Blue Bandana Man and his Remington, smoke rising out the barrel.

The battered Honda suddenly reversed and squealed out the alley.

The Shadow rubbed the hole in his jumpsuit. He had no idea where the bullet had gone. But although it had caused a stinging welt on his thigh, it had not penetrated his fortified, iron-tough skin.

The Shadow's eyes locked in on the Blue Bandana Man. A young, dark-haired hoodlum with a wiry build. He wore a muscle shirt. A wife-beater. His left shoulder had a tattoo: *86th STREET*.

The man fired again.

The bullet blew out of the Remington's barrel and zipped toward the Shadow's head. It would have spelled doom for an ordinary man.

But the Shadow was no ordinary man.

He plucked the hot slug from midair as if it were a grape. He bounced the bullet in his palm and walked toward the gunman, a confident walk. Full of swagger. The kind of walk that Evel Knievel must have had when he walked into a shithole bar after jumping seventeen school busses.

The man's finger slipped from the trigger.

"Out of bullets?" said the Shadow. "Or out of nerve?"

The man, slack-jawed and bug-eyed, dropped the Remington. He smiled nervously, revealing a gold tooth.

"Nice," said the Shadow. He thumped his index finger on

the man's tattoo. "86th Street. Is this so you can remember your way home?"

The Blue Bandana Man did not answer. The Shadow waved his hand across the man's frozen face. No response.

"You all right?"

"Yes..."

"What's your name?"

"...Lupe."

"Nice."

He judo-flipped Lupe and tossed him into a dumpster in the alley, and then a two-by-four smashed down on the Shadow's helmet. He spun around and yanked the board from the Cowboy's grip. He smiled.

The Cowboy ran. The Shadow hurled the board—struck him dead on the melon, dropped the Cowboy like a brick. But the Cowboy, maybe out of fear or adrenaline, staggered to his feet and scampered away.

A horn beeped.

The Shadow turned just as the Honda reared back into the alley. Lupe had snapped out of his trance, and now he was lifting the cardboard box into the car's trunk. He closed the trunk and battened it down with a red bungee cord. The passenger door swung open and he jumped in.

The Honda peeled out the alley, fishtailed down the street. But it was the back of the car that stunned the Shadow. That red bungee cord. He knew of only one man in Tomahawk who drove a brown Honda Accord and who used a red bungee cord to lash the trunk down. Most of Tomahawk's residents just used pieces of rope or even duct tape to hold their broken trunks. But that red bungee cord was unmistakable. And that meant the driver—if it was who the Shadow thought it was—was even more reckless than he had previously thought.

Somebody that high on the social ladder? An accomplice to a burglary?

The Shadow looked across the street at the newspaper box. The Honda's tires squealed through the night. Then it was silent, except for a breeze and a distant rumble of thunder.

He heard footsteps.

A man walked up to the box. He opened it, and its old rusty hinges made a grating squeak. The man restocked the box with the latest edition of the *Tomahawk Sentinel*.

The box slammed shut.

From across the street, the Shadow's powerful eyes read the headline displayed behind the Plexiglass front.

"Now that's interesting," he muttered.

CHAPTER THREE

Dalton Hawks woke up in his underwear. He rolled off the couch and fell to the floor. Something was not right. His head hurt like hell and his normally dark, ramshackle studio apartment was brighter than normal.

Really bright.

He figured it was the hangover, the kind screws up your eyes.

He climbed on the couch, the same ratty couch he had just used as a bed, and stared at the immense blue sky through the room's window. He contemplated the vastness. So big. So blue.

A sparrow flew by the window and made a confused loop de loop and landed on the window sill. It chirped and looked at Dalton. If it'd had shoulders, the bird would have shrugged. Dalton rubbed his swollen head and looked back at the sparrow. It chirped again, as if to say: "What the hell happened?"

Dalton shrugged.

The sparrow leapt from the sill and flew upward.

What impossible freedom that bird has, thought Dalton. *The big blue sky, all to itself. What freedom...*

"Ugh...fuck freedom," he moaned.

He had to visit his uncle in the county jail.

He rubbed his throbbing head.

"God, did I drink that much?"

He tried to remember the night before, any part of it. He had gone to the bar with his buddy Darnell for the open mic night. He'd ordered a bottle of Budweiser and waited his turn while a hippy couple from the nearby town of Battlesmoke strummed and sang Kenny and Dolly shit. He'd watched them stare into each other's eyes while they sang. He'd wanted to puke.

"And then what?" he wondered. "I must have drunk more than that!"

But he couldn't recall.

"I had one fucking beer! Was I on drugs? Did Darnell dose me?"

He looked at the floor and saw a newspaper by his feet.

When did I buy a newspaper?

He picked it up and stared at the front page.

TOMAHAWK SENTINEL

Friday July 3, 2008

SHERIFF KOVALESKI ANNOUNCES CANDIDACY

Tomahawk, CO – Jim Bridger County Sheriff Dale Kovaleski announced his candidacy for mayor on KJBC-AM radio this Thursday afternoon.

"It's my sworn duty," said the sheriff, "to maintain the utmost standards of decency, honesty, and hard work in the fine community of Tomahawk and the rest of Jim Bridger County. Our current mayor has undermined the office with the kind of behavior that is simply unbecoming of any public servant in these great United States of America."

His remarks referred to Mayor Starr's recent photo-shoot for a national men's magazine.

Sheriff Kovaleski also pledged to attack Jim Bridger Country's outbreak of meth-amphetamine addiction. He said he would restore Tomahawk's youth to "a higher standard of decency."

This comes in the wake of syphilis outbreaks at both Tomahawk High School and Battlesmoke High School.

"Our children are the future of the great state of Colorado," said the sheriff. "This recent wave adolescent promiscuity is a social blight that must be rectified."

Sheriff Kovaleski declined the Sentinel's questions regarding rumors of his own history with the sexually transmitted virus.

Dalton folded the newspaper and closed his eyes. A nail was being driven into his skull.

His stomach lurched.

He leapt from the couch and ran to the bathroom. The remnants of a hot dog and a handful of Cheetos spewed into the toilet.

He flushed, closed the lid, and sat down on it. He noticed a welt on his right thigh. He poked the wound and grimaced.

Tender, real fresh.

"Did I fall down on a piece of rebar or something?"

One fucking beer!

He noticed a bruise on his wrist.

This wasn't the first time he had woken up in his underwear, feeling horrible, suffering from amnesia, and finding himself marked with strange welts and bruises. It had happened a couple of weeks ago, around the time of a prison break at Jim Bridger County.

"What the hell was I drinking? Paint? Gasoline?"

He stared at the ceiling.

"That's it," he vowed. "No more booze. I'm done!"

Other people had changed their stars. Why not him?

It was time to re-invent himself. Maybe he could go to college. Maybe he could move out of Tomahawk, get a proper job, meet new people.

Normal people.

People not from Tomahawk, Colorado.

He got up from the toilet and looked into the mirror.

"It can only get better."

He leaned into the shower and turned on the faucet. The water came out brown and cold. It cleared quickly and then the water was just cold. He held his breath and hopped in, lathering and rinsing himself quickly as possible.

He jumped out and dried himself. He put on a white T-shirt and a pair of jeans. He found his boots under the couch and put them on.

T-shirt. Jeans. Boots.

Back to normal.

His right boot felt uncomfortable, had a stone in it or something. He tugged it off. He turned it upside down and shook it.

A spent .22 caliber bullet clanked to the floor.

He picked it up and examined it. He rubbed his finger over the welt on his leg.

Pieces of the previous day materialized like jigsaw pieces out of a mist. Prior to the bar, he had gone to work with Darnell. They'd wrestled with a cracked sewer line for eight hours. A temp job. A trench. A blue wheel barrel above them. Shovels. Dirt. All kinds of things in that dirt. A rusty Pepsi bottle cap. A little green plastic army man. An old yellow Matchbox car. Fossilized childhood. Other things could have been in that dirt, too. Why not? A spent bullet could have got into his boot. Stuff was always sneaking into his boots.

A perfectly reasonable explanation.
Phew!
He pulled the boot back on and walked to the door. The corner of an envelope stuck out from underneath the door. He slid the envelope toward him. He sat on the couch and rubbed his eyes. His room still seemed too bright. Again, he looked out his window.

Big blue sky.

So odd.

So much bigger than normal.

Something was missing. Something obvious.

Huh...

Dalton shrugged and looked at the envelope. He was hoping it was a check from Darnell. He opened the envelope. No check, just a note:

> *Dalton, pay your rent or you will be evicted.*
> *– Sheriff Dale Kovaleski.*

"God, if this day isn't already bad enough," he thought. "Now I've got to find steady work."

But only one place in Tomahawk was hiring.

The liquor store.

CHAPTER FOUR

Dalton stepped into the darkened hallway outside his room. He liked that it was so dark. It soothed his aching eyeballs.

A dim bulb in the hallway fizzled and then went out.

It reminded him of his brain.

He looked down the hall, toward Maureen O'Leary's apartment. A blue light flickered from her TV and seeped under the door.

Dalton, in no mood for conversation, crept down the hall and rounded the staircase.

Maureen's door swung open.

"Dalton, where are you going?"

He looked up and saw her silhouette, haloed in TV light. Maureen was in her mid-sixties. She wore a pink bathrobe and carried a worry-eyed Chihuahua-Dachshund mutt in her arms.

"Morning, Maureen."

Maureen flapped her little dog's paw up and down. "Say, hello to Dalton, Sparky."

"Hi, Sparky," said Dalton.

"You avoiding me?"

"I'm not. I'm—"

The little dog licked her nose. "It's okay, my little snookie-wookie. That's just Dalton. He's trying to sneak by without saying, hello."

"Sorry, I'm just late. I have to visit my uncle."

"Elston?"

"Yes."

"He's still in the pokey?"

"Twenty-five years."

"It's so unfair."

"I know. He still claims Sheriff Kovaleski framed him."

"Our esteemed sheriff?" she said sarcastically. "And our landlord and the owner of this fine building? He would do such a thing? Never!"

The original owner of the apartment building had been Sheriff Kovaleski's ex-wife. But Mrs. Kovaleski had left him for a Greyhound bus driver from Ogallala. She claimed infidelity, and spread the rumor that Kovaleski ran around on her and contracted VD. As part of the divorce settlement, the sheriff had inherited the apartment building.

Sheriff Kovaleski never cared about the apartment. It was distraction from his law enforcement duties, and he probably saw the building as just cheap housing for Tomahawk's losers and outcasts. The people who made his job difficult.

And Kovaleski did little for upkeep. The broken washer and dryer in the basement stayed broken. Burnt out light bulbs did not get replaced. Litter surrounding the apartment never got picked up. Snow was never shoveled. The brown grass stayed brown.

Maureen kissed Sparky's head. "Poor Elston. He was such a nice man. Such a good soul. Much wiser than he lets on. Don't you think?"

"Sure," said Dalton. "Uncle Elston definitely has his moments."

"Then why are you in such a rush? It's not like he's going anywhere."

Dalton squeezed the banister's old handrail. He really wasn't in that big of a rush. And if his car started right away, which occasionally happened, he could make it to the prison easily by one o'clock. He was really just in a rush to get away from Maureen.

"You're right," he confessed. "I'm being a dummy."

"I'll say."

"What was your question?"

"Well, Dalton, last night at about 3:00AM, a big loud crashing noise woke me up. At first, I thought it was kids setting off fireworks or something."

"Fireworks?"

"People set them off this time of year. Anyway, when I got out of bed—and yes, I'm still sleeping on that crappy Futon, and I don't know why I don't get rid of it. It's killing my back—and, anyway, where was I? Oh, yes, I looked out the window, and, Dalton, I saw something very strange."

"What?" said Dalton, trying to hurry Maureen along. Her stories usually took the scenic route and if Dalton didn't cut her off, he could wind up listening for hours.

"I saw a shadow."

"A shadow. And?"

"The shadow of a man. And he had an axe."

"An axe?"

"Yes, an axe—that tool people use to chop up firewood. And you know what else?"

"What?"

I think that shadowy man chopped down that tree outside of your window. Did you notice it was gone? That big tree?"

Holy fuck!

He rubbed his bleary eyes.

"Of course I noticed," said Dalton. "I noticed it soon as I got up. No one could miss something as big and obvious as a missing tree."

"Just making sure."

"But who cuts down a tree in the middle of the night?"

"That man with the axe, he was dressed in some kind of black jumpsuit. He had a cape, and he wore a helmet—"

There must be a gas leak in this building, thought Dalton. *It's poisoning everybody's minds.*

"—and ski goggles," continued Maureen. "Anyway, after the tree crashed down, the man started chopping it into smaller and smaller pieces. And when he was done, he took off his helmet and goggles."

"What did he look like?"

"Well..."

"Well what?"

"He kind of looked like you."

The hairs Dalton's neck stood straight up. "Me? Are you sure?"

"It's possible that my mind's playing tricks on me. That happens to people my age. That's what Dr. Shotz told me: the mind eventually wears out like an old clutch. Doesn't even matter how smart you were to begin with."

Dalton rubbed his swirling belly. He was still nauseous, and his head felt like it was going to erupt.

"If I chopped down an entire tree by myself, I would remember it. Don't you think?"

Suddenly an axe flashed into Dalton's head.

He blinked, and the axe disappeared.

Maybe Darnell slipped some peyote buttons into my beer last night. Bastard!

Dalton held onto the banister and regained his composure. "And if I did cut it down, I'd be the first to tell you. I mean, I've got an axe in my car's trunk. But I don't use it much, except as a can opener from time to time."

"Dalton, I didn't think it was you. That shadowy man did something I rarely see you do."

"What was he doing?"

"He was drinking." She set Sparky on the carpet and scratched the little mutt's head. "You are such a good little boy, Sparky. Yes you are!" The poodle sniffed her hand and tinkled on the carpet.

Dalton said, "Well, I do drink an occasional beer now and then."

"No, Dalton. There's drinking and then there's *drinking*. And this guy was *drinking*, like my late husband did before he turned his liver into cardboard."

"I remember," said Dalton. "Danny was a good man, and a great bass player."

"He sure was. But it was me who taught him how to play it."

"You can play bass?"

"I played tuba in high school marching band. Same principle." She cleared her throat. "Anyway, that man with the axe and the cape was guzzling a bottle of hooch like it was lemonade on a hot summer day. But then again, I couldn't see clearly. Maybe it *was* lemonade. I mean, there's no way somebody could chop down a tree all boozed up, could they?"

Dalton rubbed his throbbing temple. The hangover roiled like a sick thundercloud. His stomach turned upside down. He wanted to wretch.

Easy, Dalton. Deep breaths. Deep, deep breaths.

"Anyway, I'm glad that it's gone. Kovaleski should have cut that thing down years ago. He's lucky that old rotten cottonwood didn't fall on somebody and kill them."

Dalton agreed.

He had wanted to get rid of that tree forever—to just lop

the damn thing down and hack it into neat little bundles of firewood and then sell those bundles for five bucks apiece outside a gas station.

But he'd never pursued the idea. He didn't know a thing about lumberjacking or chainsaws or running a firewood business, or any kind of business. And, mainly, he didn't want to get in trouble with the town's so-called law.

Maureen reached into her dressing gown and pulled out six crumpled dollar bills. "Dalton, I have a favor to ask."

"Favor?" He looked at Sparky. The little pup was chewing on Maureen's pink slippers. "You need more Puppy Chow?"

She smoothed out the bills and evened out the corners. "That little pisser's got plenty of food. I was hoping you could run down to Schulz's and get me some smokes. I'd do it myself, but my hip's sore."

"Pall Malls?"

"Sorry to trouble you."

"I've got to run down there anyway. I need to apply for—"

"Filterless." Maureen handed him the money.

––––––––

Dalton trudged down the stairs. He stepped out of the foyer and into Tomahawk's hot, tinder-dry air. The burst of sunlight forced his eyes shut. When he opened them, the sight of a battered brown Honda Civic greeted him. It was parked by the curb in front of the apartment building.

Only one man in Tomahawk drove a brown Honda Civic.

"Hawks!" said a gruff voice.

Dalton turned to his right.

Sheriff Dale Kovaleski stood, in full uniform, beside a tree stump. About twenty bundles of firewood were neatly stacked around the stump.

"Howdy, Sheriff. How come you're not driving the squad car?"

A distant train whistle cut through the air.

Kovaleski marched up to Dalton. "None of your business, Hawks!"

He pushed his aviators up on his forehead, revealing his bulgy gray-blue eyes. He was a barrel-chested man in his mid-fifties with a beefy build. His mealy arms still looked strong enough to break a bull's neck. His left hand was tucked suspiciously behind his back.

"You must think you're something, Dalton Hawks."

"What do you mean?"

"Do you think I'm stupid?"

"No."

"Dalton?"

"Sir?"

"I want you out of here."

"What? I didn't do anything!"

"Oh, is that right?" Kovaleski produced an axe from behind his back. "Then explain this. I found this axe stuck in that stump that used to be attached to a perfectly fine tree. Go ahead, moron, read what the handle says!"

Dalton grabbed the axe and looked the handle. He shuddered. A familiar name was carved into it:

J. HAWKS

That was his axe, all right. The very same one that had belonged to his long, lost daddy.

CHAPTER FIVE

Kovaleski snatched the axe from Dalton.

He was not happy. But Kovaleski was never happy. Not with himself. Not with his ex-wife. Not with the town of Tomahawk. And certainly not with its citizens, whom he considered dimwitted enough to be put in zoos for public display. In mayoral campaign speeches he had said Tomahawk and its citizens deserved better and that the town was sick of being duped. But in reality, he hated the town and looked down on its people.

But they still voted for him.

In some minds anything was better than Mayor Starr, who had disgraced the office by posing for a nudie magazine even though she used the proceeds to build an addiction rehab center for meth addicts. "You do what you gotta do," she had said. "And if it means I've got to disgrace myself, then so be it!"

The sheriff stared at Dalton and pointed the axe blade between his eyes. "Listen, you jobless lout. You're late on rent. Find yourself another place to live. I don't care if it's in Tomahawk or if it's in Battlesmoke or if it's in Ogallala or if it's under a bridge in Denver or in a cornfield in Nebraska. But you're getting the hell out of my building!"

"Come on," said Dalton. "It's been slow. You know I'm always good for it."

"Dalton?"

"What?"

"You're a menace."

"A menace?"

Dalton wasn't arguing with a reasonable person, a person who understood or cared about people on low incomes. Kovaleski was missing something. But it was hard to pin down exactly what. He had two good arms, two good legs, a good head on his shoulders. But he lacked something harder to see. A moral compass, maybe. Nothing kept the man awake at night. Dalton had heard a story about how a local gas station attendant—new at the job—accidentally handed Kovaleski an extra twenty-dollar bill with his change. Kovaleski had bragged about the mistake and how he spent the money on a twelve-pack of Heineken to teach the clerk a lesson. "They'll take it out of his paycheck for sure," he'd laughed.

A man can aspire to anything.

Especially when nothing bothers him.

It was like birth defect.

It was easy for Kovaleski to kick people out of apartments, arrest them, bilk them, and take advantage of them. He wasn't hampered by a conscious. That same thing that dictators and many captains of industry were missing. That thing that often masked itself as "financial success."

It really wasn't something to brag about.

It was more like a condition, a scurvy of the soul. Its visible symptoms included: thrones, big cars, heavy watches, silicone implants, and gated communities.

"You can't evict me," cried Dalton. "Not without proper notice!"

Kovaleski patted the axe's handle against his palm. "This isn't *proper* enough for you?"

Dalton's throbbing head whirled. *I wake up covered in bumps and bruises, and now I'm being evicted.* His mind reeled back to the previous evening.

He remembered a few more things: digging the ditch, sweating, not getting paid, going to the Raccoon Bar and Grill, drinking a beer, and then going to Darnell's trailer home. They watched *Earthquake*, Richard Roundtree as the motorcycle stuntman. The Black Evel Knievel. But that was all he remembered. He had no recollection of even walking home, much less chopping down a tree. Surely, he'd remember that.

Dalton looked at the large stump. The sparrow that had been on his window sill earlier flew down and landed on the stump. Again, it shrugged its wings.

"Honest, sheriff, I don't remember cutting down any trees last night. And there's no way to prove that I did."

"Dalton, I can prove anything. I'm the sheriff, the judge, the jury—and, as of late, your landlord!"

"Anybody could have stolen that axe from my car and chopped that tree down."

Kovaleski dropped the axe to the ground and leaned on the handle's end-knob as if it were a cane.

"Dalton, Dalton, Dalton. I highly doubt somebody broke into your piece-of-shit Buick and stole your old man's axe for the sole purpose of chopping down a tree. That's just not how the criminal mind works."

"Then how does it work?"

"It doesn't work. The criminal mind avoids work at all costs."

"How would you know?"

"It doesn't matter. Your rent was due two days ago, and I can still nail you for that."

Nail me?

Something didn't fit. Kovaleski's tenants, especially the ones in the low-rent studios, were late all the time. And like many landlords in small towns like Tomahawk with lousy economies, he wheeled-and-dealed for rent. Kovaleski's ex-wife would take money in any form she could, in favors ranging from free dentistry to free drinks. Dalton suspected that Kovaleski was looking for an excuse to run him out.

"Listen," said Dalton, "Darnell owes me money for an excavation job I helped him with yesterday. He's just waiting for a check to clear. I'll have the money real soon."

"You worked?"

"It was a temporary job."

Dalton recalled being knee-deep in mud and sewage, filling the wheel barrow and Darnell pushing the wheel barrow up a wooden ramp and into the back of a dump truck. Back breaking work on a one-hundred-and-two-degree day without a cloud in the sky. But he ate it up like a bowl of chili.

Dalton enjoyed that kind of work. Simple and hard. The best life a man could lead, he thought. It kept his sanity. A man was too tired and worn out after a day of digging ditches to let his mind go too crazy.

He wondered about an old expression: it beats digging ditches. Dalton loved digging ditches. He felt great at the end of a hard, physical day. He loved being covered in dirt. It meant he had done something. And ditch digging wasn't something just anyone could do. It separated him from the pack. It was hard, but it was also kind of meditative. It kept him strong. Why did his teachers believe that digging ditches was a just punishment for those who did not do homework? To punish those for not paying attention in school. A blue-collar damnation.

"See that man flipping burgers? You'll wind up like him. That's what happens when you don't study." The reward of graduating college was a "good" job, a desk, tight pants, tight shoes, and a tight tie.

What was wrong with dumb physical labor?

Did Jesus have a "good" job?

Ditch digging was a good job.

So was flipping burgers.

And so was being a cop.

But Dalton knew Kovaleski's problem. Kovaleski felt that police work was beneath him. The old sheriff would never be happy. No amount of money could fill his humorless, hollow heart.

Kovaleski shook his head. "So you're getting a check from that job?"

"I'll probably have it tomorrow."

"That sewer line you just dug out?"

"Yes, that sewer. We even got it done ahead of schedule."

"Shit, Dalton, is that only kind of work you can find? Didn't ever occur to you to go to college? See the financial hole you're in now?"

"I like holes."

"You know it could take the county weeks to process that check."

"Give me a break," pleaded Dalton. "Maureen was late on rent three months in a row, and you let her off the hook."

Kovaleski smiled. "We'll just say Mrs. O'Leary and I worked something out."

"What do you mean?"

Kovaleski shot Dalton a sly smirk. Dalton's fists tightened. He forgot all about the hangover, and he glared at Kovaleski with a murderous stare.

"Are you kidding me?" said Dalton. "She's sixty-four years old!"

"So?"

Dalton raised his voice. "Her husband just died!"

Kovaleski's posture stiffened. A wave of fear passed through his eyes. The color drained from his face. He rolled his meaty shoulders and the wave subsided. His pupils narrowed into snake slits, and he scrutinized Dalton from head to toe.

"What?" said Dalton.

"Were you hanging around Stevenson's last night?"

"The pharmacy? Last night...geeze, I don't know."

Dalton could only remember as far back as watching *Earthquake* inside Darnell's trailer home. He thought about the movie, and then he remembered some more. He remembered Charlton Heston and Richard Roundtree were in it. He remembered that George Kennedy was also featured, playing jaded cop Lou Slade. He wondered why Kovaleski couldn't be more like Officer Slade. A solid, hard-working police officer. A good guy. But no. Kovaleski always had to have more than the next guy. Never wanted to be amongst the people, just above them. Dalton thought some more. He remembered opening a second can of PBR at Darnell's trailer home. And Darnell pouring a shot of whiskey. And then it was all a blank.

No, not a blank—a black hole.

"What do you mean, *you don't know?* It's a simple question: were you or were you not hanging around Stevenson's Pharmacy last night?"

"What difference does it make?"

"It got robbed."

"Robbed?"

"Early this morning, about 2:00AM."

"What got stolen?"

"Doesn't matter. I was just wondering—"

"You think *I* robbed it?"

Sheriff Kovaleski wiped his pink forehead and then straightened his belt. Dalton turned around and looked at Kovaleski's brown Honda. He wondered why the sheriff wasn't driving his police cruiser. *Maybe it's in the shop,* he thought. *Or he maybe he's taking the day off. Maybe Deputy Harden is on patrol.*

"No," said Kovaleski. "I don't think you robbed it. I was just wondering if you saw any suspicious activity."

"Why you so interested in me?"

Kovaleski dropped his sunglasses back over his eyes. "Just checking for leads, Dalton. That's what I do. Anyway, skedaddle before I haul you and your Buick out of the county for good."

"I'll get you the rent money tomorrow," said Dalton. "I promise."

Kovaleski thought for a moment. He slapped his belly and smiled. "Let's make a deal. Since I could use your vote, I'll give you until two o'clock this afternoon."

"My vote?"

"I'm running for mayor. Didn't you read the paper?"

Dalton rubbed his aching head, which suddenly hurt even more. "Mayor?"

"I trust I have your vote."

"Two o'clock might be a little early," said Dalton. "Can't you give me more time?"

"Sorry, Dalton. No can do."

"Like I said, Darnell has a check coming to me *tomorrow*."

Kovaleski picked up the axe. He bounced its handle along his fingers, feeling for the center of gravity. He aimed the axe at the sparrow standing on the tree stump. The bird looked at the axe and chirped. Kovaleski launched it. The axe windmilled twenty feet through the air toward the sparrow. The sparrow darted into the air, and the axe impaled the stump with a solid *thwuck.*

"Still got it," Kovaleski muttered with a satisfied grin. "I'll see you at two o'clock."

"Can't you wait just one more day?"

"No. I'll be in Denver tomorrow."

Dalton didn't buy it. "Denver?"

"The capital of this glorious Centennial State. I'm finalizing the paperwork for my candidacy at the State Capitol. Ever been there?"

"Denver?"

"Heaven on earth, Dalton."

"You can see the mountains real nice there. And I hear there's a lot of jobs and parks and resources for poor people."

"Lots of pussy, too."

Dalton rubbed his sore head.

"Have you seen my banners?"

"No."

"'Vote Dale Kovaleski for Mayor, Change You Can Count On!' Highly original, isn't it?" He walked toward his car. He opened the door, plopped himself behind the wheel, and rolled the window down. "Remember, Dalton, two o'clock today—or I'm tossing your shit all over the sidewalk." He revved the engine and drove away. Dalton stared at the red bungee cord.

With all his money, he could at least get his trunk fixed properly.

He pried the axe from the stump and scraped his thumb over the blade. Dull as a butter knife. He looked at the bundles of firewood stacked around the stump. Something glinted by his boots. An empty bottle. He picked it up and examined the label. THUNDERBIRD.

Who drinks this crap?

He set the bottle down and stared at the stump. An axe blade whipped through his mind. It sliced underneath a night sky in slow motion and cut deep into a tree trunk, shooting large wood splinters into the air like broken wheat stalks. He scrunched his eyelids closed and slowly opened them. The axe disappeared.

"Vicks," he muttered.

CHAPTER SIX

Dalton found his car in its usual place, under an elm tree rotting on 4th Street, parked between an old pickup truck with two flat tires and an El Camino with a smashed-out rear window.

The '73 Buick Apollo was one of the few items Dalton had inherited from his estranged father, besides a rusty axe, an old guitar, and a head full of anger.

The Apollo was a GSX edition. Dalton didn't know what GSX meant. But, in any case, the car had two doors, bucket seats, and a manual transmission. Simulated intake ports were mounted on the quarter panels. They gave the car a shark-like appearance. The dent on the rear bumper was not part of the original GSX package, and neither was the disconnected CB-radio under the dashboard.

Dalton climbed in, rolled the window down and let the heat escape. He turned the ignition switch. Nothing happened. Just a clicking noise. He turned it again.

He wished he had a Honda or a Subaru. Those cars always started. They were never in the shop. And some of them even had four-wheel drive. A person really had to be a mechanic to put up with a relic like a Buick Apollo. But crappy cars like those had a way of turning anybody into a mechanic. Anybody, except him.

After nine more attempts and several curses to the Lord above, the Apollo's arthritic V8 creaked and groaned to life. He geared into first and rolled onto 4th Street and then gunned the gas and ascended 4th's slight climb until he reached a traffic light at the top of Enfield Avenue, Tomahawk's business center.

The light turned red.

Dalton braked and peered out the driver-side window. The dusty town of Tomahawk, Colorado spread out before him: a population of 1,280 souls—a town topped with a high school, two liquor stores, a tattoo parlor, a Waffle House, a pharmacy, a little grocery store (where he worked during high school), a small newspaper and radio station, a burned-down hardware store, a burned-down fire station, two bars—The Raccoon Bar and Grill (where he and Darnell had once worked as cooks) and The Last Straw (where his country band once played)—an unscrupulous police force (that persecuted him), a fraudulent insurance agency (that had fired him) and an old gray-stone chapel that barely kept its doors open. Its congregation had diminished by a quarter after his uncle had got sent to the hoosegow.

A trailer park and a prison lay on the town's outskirts. Most of Tomahawk's citizens, those who weren't collecting SSI checks or living in the penitentiary, worked for the penitentiary.

From what Dalton had read of the town's history, he knew that in its heyday, back in the late 1860s, Tomahawk was one of the original hell-on-wheels towns, which were townships built along the railroad tracks during the construction of the Union-Pacific Railway. In those days there was a town built along the tracks every twenty miles or so because those old steam engines needed a place to stop and refill with water. And that's how those dusty forsaken towns in the middle of nowhere came to be. They were stopping points for people going someplace else.

And like many of those rowdy frontier towns, Tomahawk had hosted gambling, prostitution, alcoholism, and at least a murder a day until the rails moved westward, spreading more sin and more vice to places like Julesburg and Cheyenne.

Then an Arapaho tribe was starved, subdued, and shipped to a reservation. After that, the homesteaders came, usually European immigrants who managed to toil and turn the dried wasteland into fertile ground for wheat and then more wheat.

Farming on those dry plains was never easy, which is why the land was so cheap. Many quit and left or went crazy from the ceaseless winds and barren landscape. Some got jobs in factories out east. Some returned to Europe.

But the really desperate ones stayed.

Later, during World War II, a POW camp was built outside of Tomahawk. It held German soldiers, the lucky ones who got captured and escaped the horrors of combat for the rest of the war.

The prison guards, who were equally lucky not to be overseas dodging machine gun spray, tank shells, land mines, torpedoes, kamikazes, and anti-aircraft fire—or being captured themselves—didn't have to try too hard to stop the POWs from escaping.

Escape was pointless.

Jim Bridger County, in the middle of the dry wasteland of the immense USA, may has well been the moon. Where would those prisoners go? So they, prisoners and guards alike, just waited until it was all over.

And one of the former POWs even came back. A tank commander, aghast at what the Fatherland had become after the war, returned to Jim Bridger County and opened a liquor store. He married a nurse from nearby Battlesmoke and had two sons, one who had moved to the East Coast and worked as a mail handler for the United States Postal Service.

The other son got into law enforcement.

The POW's name was Ernst Schulz. But, strangely, he adopted his wife's family name after he got married. She was of Polish descent, and her last name was Kovaleski.

By the time Dalton was born, most of the prison camp's remains had vanished—just a few concrete slabs sticking out from the prairie grass, which served as the town's only link to a war fought so far away and so long ago.

But it wasn't Tomahawk's last prison.

The town's experience with the POW camp led to its appointment for Jim Bridger County's correctional facility. And soon after the aquifer that fed Tomahawk's surrounding farms dried up, the new jail became the main employer.

Dalton was one of the few in Tomahawk who had never worked, or even spent time, in that penitentiary.

The light turned green.

Dalton tapped the gas, and the Buick sputtered through the intersection and bounced over a set of railroad tracks. The remains of a burnt and mangled van sat near the tracks. He drove by the van and stopped before an east-west frontage road.

Heading east would take him to Darnell's place, where Dalton could hopefully get an advance for his rent. And to the west was the Jim Bridger County Correctional Facility, where Dalton could visit his uncle.

Dalton needed rent money. So he turned east and drove down the dirt road until he reached the entrance to the Sunny Acre's Mobile Home Community. *A PLACE FOR FAMILIES*, the sign said.

"Geeze, what kind of families?" thought Dalton.

He turned down the community's main street, a bumpy

road aligned with beer cans and chain-link fences that served as cages for snarling, wild-eye pit bulls on short, frayed leases.

He bumped and bounced down the dirt road and coasted to a stop in front of Darnell's trailer home, a twelve-foot by sixty-foot singlewide. It wasn't the biggest trailer in the park, but it was the nicest, featuring a yard smartly xeriscaped with prairie grass and cactus plants. A six-foot statue of a rooster stood by Darnell's pickup truck. The man had created the rooster from rusted nuts, bolts, screws, and an assortment of old tractor parts.

Dalton climbed out the car and knocked on the trailer's door. Darnell took off his oven mitts and unlatched the screen. He was a lanky African-American. His parents were from Pittsburgh, and they had immigrated to Tomahawk and become truck drivers. But then they got tired of it and moved out to Baker City, Oregon. But in Tomahawk, Darnell stayed.

"Dalton, what's up? Did you leave something here?"

"Yes," said Dalton, "my mind."

Darnell pushed on the door.

"Come on in," said Darnell, "let's have a look."

"Actually, I was just hoping you could help me out."

"Help you out?" Darnell pretended to re-latch the screen door.

"Funny. You wouldn't happen to have that money for the sewer job, would you? I'm late on rent."

"Oh, geeze," sighed Darnell.

Inside the trailer, Dalton was greeted by the smell of burnt cookies. Bowls of batter and several spice containers were laid out neatly on a handmade kitchen table.

The table impressed Dalton almost as much as the iron rooster did. It was made from an old door, sanded smooth and varnished with a patina coating. The rest of the trailer's interior was just as creatively decorated. A clock, cleverly made from a large cable spool, hung on the wall. A wine rack made out of an antique mail-slot box sat in the corner. Arty black-and-whites of found objects like doorknobs and beer cans were displayed inside attractive homemade frames.

"You baking?"

"Cookies, Dalton." Darnell sampled some raw batter with his finger. "Mm-mmm. I'm thinking of selling them over the computer."

"Online? I didn't know you could do that with baked goods."

"They sell everything on computers these days. Clothes, books, records, lawnmowers...kidneys. Where have you been?"

"In my apartment. Anyway, I was stopping by because—"

"You need rent money." Darnell stared at the floor and scratched his head. "Do you know how long it takes Jim Bridger County to process a check?"

"Weeks?"

"Not that long. Actually, if we're lucky, I think they can process it by noon tomorrow."

"I need it by two o'clock today."

"Can't your landlord wait?"

"Kovaleski? He's threatening to evict me if I don't get him the rent by two."

Darnell looked at the wooden clock. 12:45PM. "Sounds rash. It's only the third day of the month. You must have made him real angry this time. What did you do?"

"I have no idea."

"Take a seat, relax," said Darnell. He reached into the oven and pulled out a tray of burnt cookies. "Have a snickerdoodle."

"I just ate."

"Please, I need a guinea pig."

Dalton selected the least-burnt snickerdoodle.

"Let me see if I've got some money."

"If you can't do it, then you can't do it. It's okay. Really."

Dalton sat down on the couch. He choked down the cookie and stared at the blank TV set. There was a bottle of Wild Turkey sitting on top of it. Empty. It was the only evidence left of the previous evening's debacle. Otherwise, not one beer can in sight. *Or were there ever any beer cans?* He wondered if he had just imagined the whole episode.

Darnell walked into the living room and sat down on a ten-gallon tub of paint. He opened up a checkbook. "How much is your rent?"

"Three-fifty."

"For that dump?"

Dalton nodded. He looked back at the whiskey bottle. "I *was* here last night, wasn't I?"

"Just as much as I was."

"Huh—"

"What are you thinking about?"

"Nothing. I can't remember anything about last night."

"Let's see, yesterday we dug out that sewer, I bought a twelve-pack of beer, I drove you down here in my truck, I turned on the TV and we watched a movie. That's what happened."

"*Earthquake,* right?"

"Richard Roundtree as Miles Quaid—which reminds me, I've got to get that Halloween costume back from you."

"What Halloween costume?"

"My Miles Quaid costume. I made it a year ago for that show at the Last Straw. Only a truck driver from North Platte threw-up on me, and I had to take it off. You said you'd wash it. You still have it, don't you?"

"I..."

Darnell clicked a ballpoint pen and stated writing. "I put a lot of time into that costume. Jumpsuit, cape, helmet, lightning bolts—sewed it up all by myself."

Cape? Helmet? Dalton was stunned. He gazed at the whiskey bottle. *Maybe Maureen isn't going out of her mind.*

Darnell stopped writing. "You look like you got hit by a bowling ball."

"Huh..."

"Are you all right?"

"I'm fine." Dalton was going to ask Darnell if he'd felled any trees the night before. But he decided to keep it to himself. He figured that maybe somebody, somehow, got hold of the Halloween suit, maybe to pull some kind of prank on Kovaleski. And, who knows, maybe they *did* break into his piece-of-shit Buick and steal that axe.

But who?

Dalton looked around the room. He noticed strips of masking tape lining the ceiling above the TV. He looked at the tub of paint and figured Darnell was intending on painting the wall. Probably some interesting accent color. Black-bean violet or atomic tangerine. If he didn't know any better, he would have thought he was lounging in a New York City penthouse or something—certainly not a trailer home. Geeze, he thought, Darnell should be selling his giant rooster or his table or his clock or his wine rack on the Internet. Not cookies. Especially, those cookies.

"What happened after the movie?" asked Dalton.

Darnell ripped a check from the book and looked it over. "I think I fell asleep about the time Charlton Heston got sucked down into the sewer. All I know is that when I got up this morning that Wild Turkey bottle was empty, and you were gone. And I know that *I* didn't drink all of it."

"Don't look at me. I don't drink whiskey."

"Apparently you do, especially when you're heartbroken."

"Me? Heartbroken?"

"Yes, you. Two beers and you started moaning about Helen

and how you're through with women. And then suddenly you were begging for a shot of whiskey."

"*Begging?*"

"You know what I think?"

"What?"

"I think you miss Helen."

"Whatever."

"Ah, *whatever.*" Darnell handed Dalton the check. "Here, just give Kovaleski this. I made it out to him. He probably won't cash it until Monday—and by that time, I'll be able to cover it with the county's check. Easy!"

"I really don't know what else to say."

"Don't say anything, Dalton. Just get your band back together." Darnell tapped his fingers on his stomach. "See these hands? They are just dying to play again. You know, I've got that train-beat nailed down good. And Jac Lu, apparently, when he's not at the liquor store or squabbling with his wife, has been taking guitar lessons."

"So he says, on YouTube. Anyway, thanks again."

"Don't mention it. Just get the band back together."

"I'll think about it. But I need to get going. I have to visit my uncle."

He walked outside, stepped into his car, and turned the key. It didn't start. After ten more tries, he quit and knocked on Darnell's door again. Darnell came out with a hammer and popped the hood and gave the starter a solid whack. The Buick started right away. Before his stint at the Raccoon Bar and Grill, Darnell had learned a lot about auto-mechanics at his father's garage back in Pittsburgh. He was handy with old beaters. A genius, in fact.

Dalton revved the engine, and Darnell motioned him to roll down the window. "I forgot to ask you, how was that snickerdoodle?"

"Great," said Dalton. "I *loved* it!"

Darnell smiled and tapped the Buick's roof.

Dalton reached over and found *Anna Karenina*, a book he'd bought for his suddenly literate uncle, in the glove box. It had been a long while since Dalton's last visit, and his uncle Elston would have an earful for him. But Dalton barely had an hour for the visit, and then he had to meet Kovaleski with the rent check.

"And cigarettes," he muttered, suddenly remembering Mrs. O'Leary and that he still had to get a job.

CHAPTER SEVEN

A pane of bulletproof glass separated Dalton from his Uncle Elston. The two talked through telephones while a heavy-set guard leaned against the wall and under a clock. The guard peeled the wrapper from an ice-cream bar and took a nibble.

To Dalton's left, sat a man who was also on a phone. He wore a blue bandana around his head. He also wore a muscle shirt that showed off a tattoo on his sinewy right-shoulder. 86th *STREET* was crudely etched in a faded blue-ish ink, gangster-tag lettering. He was sure he had seen it before. *But where?*

Dalton had thought about getting a tattoo, but he never worked up the nerve. At first, he couldn't settle on a design. But then one day he did. A spark plug, the word *CHAMPION* inscribed across the top. But although there was a tattoo artist in Tomahawk, Dalton never went through with it.

He would walk toward the storefront. Stop. Turn away. Go around the block. Talk to himself. Walk back to the shop. But he just couldn't do it. It wasn't the pain of the needle, and it wasn't having something etched on his body forever that stopped him.

CHAMPION.

It did not feel honest.

He never felt like a champion.

He looked at the *86th STREET* tattoo again. Maybe that man was at the Raccoon Bar and Grill. No, it was always the same six people who came in there every night. Same lonely group night after night, hoping things might be different, hoping the girl of their dreams would walk in and sit down beside them. It generally didn't happen.

But it once happened to Dalton.

He was playing guitar during an open mic night, and a girl walked in. He had known her since high school. She was his everything. She was the girl who kept him up at night, thinking about how wonderful his life could be if she were in it. And when she entered that shitty bar nothing else mattered. Not his lousy day job. Not his missing parents. Not his bad guitar playing or his lousy voice. There was only her.

Helen.

Dalton grit his teeth and snapped out of dreamland. He turned his attention to Elston, who sat behind the window.

Elston yelled into the phone. "Kovaleski's nothing but a drug-dealing sumbitch!" He collapsed back onto a wooden stool and banged his fist on the counter. The guard turned his head toward Dalton. Elston calmed down and wiped the spittle from his beard and straightened his orange jumpsuit.

Dalton leaned toward the glass and saw that prison life was taking a toll on his fifty-eight-year-old uncle. His eyes had sunk, his hair had thinned. But, still, the old man was tough. He had a light frame, but broad shoulders. And he had a strong and chiseled jaw, and big hands that had been on the winning and losing side of many bar fights, not that he was violent.

He just never backed down.

Elston was a difficult man to figure out.

But mostly he was honest. Just not smart. Or he was smart,

but in a dumb kind of way. Or maybe he was so smart that he was stupid.

No one, least of all Elston, could figure it out.

But most thought Elston was kind of dumb, which was fine with Dalton. Dalton liked so-called dumb people. They were usually honest. Smart people tended to be dishonest. But dumb people had to be honest. They weren't smart enough to snake their way out of sticky situations, extracting truths from lies, conjecture with silver-tongued eloquence. And dumb people were also clumsy at rationalizing bad behavior. So they just told the truth and took the consequences.

That was Elston.

That was stupidity, but that was also honesty. And that was greatness. Greatness did not lie in perfection. Greatness lay in being truthful, manning up and admitting to mistakes.

Elston was great.

"Christ Almighty," lamented Elston. "Are you kidding me? Why the hell does he need to add *mayor* to his resume? He owns half the goddamn town, half the apartments, the hardware store, and the gas station. And now he wants to be mayor?"

"He'll probably win." said Dalton, "especially with how things are going with our Mayor Starr."

Elston stroked his beard. "Mayor Jessica Starr. She's cute. And smart. A real pillar of the community, wouldn't you say?"

"Not really," said Dalton.

"How come?"

"Come on, Elston. She posed for *Hustler*."

Elston scratched his chin. "Have you seen that issue? Oh, man. *Grandes Melones* she has!"

"How did you get hold of a *Hustler* behind these walls?"

"We can get those kinds of things back here. This is Jim Bridger County, remember? Hoo-wee! She should be in Hollywood or on the cover of *Sports Illustrated*."

Dalton shook his head.

Elston frowned.

"Dammit! He's running for mayor? You sure? If Kovaleski gets in, I'm never getting out. Never! Mayor Starr is my only hope. With Kovaleski, the innocent get jailed and the guilty go free!"

Dalton nodded.

Elston sighed. "I did owe him some gambling debts, but that happened way before he became sheriff. And then that bastard planted cocaine in my truck—years and years later, just to get back at me! Talk about holding a grudge. And I swear to you, Dalton, on all that is holy, that I never sold or touched that shit in my whole stinking life. Not once!"

"Never?"

"Not since I got run out of New Mexico with that go-go dancer back in '68."

Dalton rubbed his eyes and looked at the clock ticking above the guard. 1:22. The guard had finished his ice-cream and was licking the inside of the wrapper. Dalton only had a few more minutes left to talk to Elston and another half-hour to get the rent check to Kovaleski. He wondered why Kovaleski was so bent on evicting him. But as Darnell said, he must have really made him angry. He thought about the wave of fear that had passed through Kovaleski's eyes earlier.

Maybe I scared him, he wondered.

But how?

"What's the use," sulked Elston. He gently touched the glass as if his hand would magically pass through it like it was made of mist. "No one's going to believe me, anyway. I've led a wicked life, and it's finally caught up to me. You know, you get away with so much in life, and then one fine day you get busted for something you didn't even do."

Elston's voice had a resigned tone, as if being a prisoner

had been his destiny since he crawled from crib. And he had done little to change his stars, never hired a lawyer, never appealed. It was as if he just assumed he belonged behind bars.

"Oh, well," he continued. "Somebody's got to fix the plumbing. Somebody's got to pick up the trash. Somebody's got to stock the grocery shelves. Are you going hire a brain surgeon to do that? You know, half this town would be unemployed if it weren't for the likes of me. So in a way, I actually do contribute to society."

Dalton sighed and changed the subject. "I handed in that book you wanted to the check-in station. The guard said you'd get it tonight."

"*The Idiot?*"

"That guy with ice cream bar? He doesn't seem that stupid."

"You walked right into that one," laughed Elston. "Not the guard, silly. I mean, *The Idiot*. It's a book, by Dostoevsky. He's another Russian. Is that what you got me?"

"No. *Anna Karenina*. It's by Tolstoy. He's Russian, isn't he? Heard of it?"

"I can't wait. I hope it's big."

"Looked like about six-hundred pages or so, tiny print."

"Good, I've got lots of time to kill. I figure that's why them Ruskies got so good and reading and writing. Time. Nothing but time in that Siberian wasteland...just like me. The weather's better here. This place is probably a day at the beach compared to busting rocks in a salt mine in the 1850s. What am I even complaining about? It can always get worse."

"It can?"

"I've come to believe that there's a ceiling on happiness. You can only be so happy. But misery? That's something altogether different. It has no bottom."

Dalton decided to keep his uncle engaged and to continue

with the book topic. "So what else have you been reading, besides Russian books?"

"American books," said Elston. His eyes widened. "*Moby Dick*, for one."

"I tried reading that in high school...tried."

"Why do teachers insist on handing them big-ass tomes to high-school kids? It bores the crap out them. You've got to go around the block a couple of times to feel the kind of insanity Melville was talking about. *Moby Dick* really has nothing to do with big whale, does it?"

Dalton shrugged.

"Some kids might follow the plot okay. But can they really understand it? Can they really *feel* it? You've got to lose your marbles in a major way to fully comprehend that novel. Those kids should be reading *Jaws* instead."

It sounded like a good idea to Dalton.

"Anyway," said Elston. "*Moby Dick*. Now that's a good read. And, you know, this prison has become kind of like a ship in a metaphorical sense. Remember that word? Metaphorical?"

Dalton nodded, recalling Elston's old story about a broken bike-chain. The bike chain was supposed to be a metaphor for his mother's mental state. But Dalton had only been eight at the time. Too young to understand. And Elston had been too drunk and distracted by a football game to explain it properly.

"And guess who my White Whale is?"

"Kovaleski?"

Elston affected his best pirate accent. "Arr, unhand me, ye gray beard loon!"

Dalton looked at the clock.

Elston flashed Dalton a sneaky grin and whispered into the phone. "You know what else they got in this joint?" His eyes shifted from left to right. "Besides books?"

"What?" sighed Dalton.

"Ever heard of the Internet?"

It occurred to Dalton that a lot of computer technology hadn't been around when Elston got sentenced. But he was surprised that a county jail would give its prisoners Internet access. But then again, Elston wasn't doing time in just *any* county jail.

"Everybody's on it these days," said Dalton. "That's how I ordered your book."

"Can you get on them sexy pages?"

"Probably."

"Type in the word like BOOBS, and you know what comes up?"

"I can only imagine."

Elston cackled like a crazed mountain man. "Hoo-wee! I'll tell you what!" He stood up and started dancing. "It's a crazy world out there nowadays, ain't it? Crazy, crazy, CRAZY!" He sat back down and gazed at Dalton with an all-knowing smile. Dalton shot Elston a quizzical stare and Elston exploded into another fit of laughter.

"What? Do I have snot hanging out my nose?"

Elston tried to contain himself. "It's nothing." But his jiggling sides betrayed him.

"Elston!"

Elston gathered his thoughts, and he pressed the phone to his lips and looked both ways. "You still seeing that lady friend of yours?"

"Helen?"

Elston's eyes shifted back to the inmate on his right. "That's right, Helen. You two still dating?"

Dalton stared at the floor. "No, she dumped me. I thought I told you that."

"Come on. When?"

"About six months ago, and I'd really rather not talk

about it."

"She cheat on you?"

"No."

"You cheated on her?"

"No."

"Then what?"

"Personal stuff."

Elston smiled. "At your age? What are you? Thirty?"

"Thirty-three."

"Thirty-three? Don't worry about it. They got Viagra for that. And they advertise *that* all over the Internet, too. But let me tell you something before you rush out and stock up."

"What?"

"You're better off."

"How?"

"She's all over that Internet."

"Helen?"

"Yes—your ex-girlfriend." Elston clenched his teeth and spoke quietly. "I can't say her name right now." He pointed to his right and then shielded his lips with his hand, like a struggling pitcher during a mound visit. "That guy next to me. I think that's her brother."

Dalton looked at the inmate. He was the one communicating with the man with the blue bandana on Dalton's left. He looked at the tattoo again.

Elston's voice returned to a normal speaking level. "But, anyway, she now goes by Randi Larue now. That's her new stage handle."

"Stage handle?"

"Apparently, nobody uses their real names in that racket. It's like being a rock star these days. They make up a stage name."

The guard tapped on Dalton's shoulder. "Time's up, sir."

Dalton stayed seated. "Elston, what are you talking about? What do you mean, she's all over the Internet?"

"Sir, it is time to go." The guard pointed at the clock and scrunched the ice-cream sandwich's empty wrapper.

"Hang on a sec," said Dalton.

"It's time to leave, sir."

"Forget it," said Elston. "It's not important. Just let me know what happens with that election. You hear me? Kovaleski cannot get elected. Or I'm doomed, Dalton. Doomed!"

CHAPTER EIGHT

Dalton leaned out the Buick's driver-side window and handed his license to the guard.

"What time is it?" asked Dalton.

The guard groaned, and Dalton felt like hell for asking that question.

He once held a job holding an orange diamond-shaped 'slow' sign on a highway crew. Hard, boring job. Painful. The heat and the asphalt that filled his nose was nothing compared to pain of the boredom. He had made up a game where he would not look at his watch until he was sure an hour had gone by. And when he finally checked, convinced that more than an hour had elapsed, he'd find it was only three minutes.

Sticking out that kind of highway job required economic desperation. Either Dalton held the sign or he became homeless. So he held the sign and suffered in silence and in amazement, born onto a unique and beautiful blue planet on the outskirts of the Milky Way, awarded with the unfathomable gift of life: his miraculous consciousness and inclusion into the Great Cosmic Mystery.

He wound up holding a sign under a 102-degree sun for minimum wage.

Tick...tock....

The guard handed the license back. "It's 1:47."

Dalton tossed the license on the dashboard. The gate lifted, and he turned east down the frontage road and sped toward his apartment. He crossed the railroad tracks and scratched his head. He'd forgotten something. He stopped at Enfield's sole traffic light. His mind went back to the chopped-down cottonwood. The axe. The bullet. Maureen...Maureen.

"Cigarettes," he groaned. "And that job application."

He hooked an illegal U-turn, a dumb thing to do in any small town with a bored police force. He checked the mirror. No flashing lights. *Strange,* he thought. *Where are they? Huh...maybe it's just my lucky day.*

Dalton passed the Tomahawk Pawnshop and Music Emporium, KJBC-AM's small radio station, Skylark Tattoos, the Waffle House, and then he finally rolled to a stop in front of Schulz's Liquors. He hopped out the car and stepped inside the store. A bell attached to the door tinkled. The red-and-white *HELP WANTED* sign was still taped to the window.

Jac Lu, the newest of several new store owners, stepped out from the back room, carrying three cases of Mad Dog 20/20.

Mr. Lu was a thirty-five-year-old South Korean immigrant who struggled admirably with his English. He had only lived in the country for three years. But, despite that, Korea was a distant memory to him. He embraced the USA with both arms. He was dressed casually in blue jeans, T-shirt, and black boots. He also sported large sideburns and a rockabilly pompadour. His shirt was silk-screened with a Fender guitar logo.

Jac Lu set the cases of Mad Dog 20/20 on the counter. "Special sale on Mogan David, Dalton."

"Mogan David?" said Dalton. "Who drinks that shit?"

"You do." Jac Lu sat on a stool behind the cash register. "You buy case of Mad Dog two weeks ago," he said in his broken but rapidly improving English. "Blue Raspberry, Red Banana, all kinds of flavors."

"Me?"

"And bottle of Thunderbird," continued Jac Lu. "And two bottles of Old Grand-Dad, and a bottle of—"

"All right, already. Geeze!"

Dalton scratched his head. He had no recollection of that transaction. He scanned the cigarette rack for Mrs. O'Leary's Pall Malls. Above the rack was a poster of an alluring woman pressing a cold bottle of Miller Light to her bee-stung lips. Beer frothed out of the bottle's neck and spilled over her sweaty cleavage. A construction worker's hard hat and tool belt complimented her yellow bikini.

Maybe she was digging out a sewer line, he thought. Maybe in Miami Beach or Honolulu. And maybe she was operating a backhoe and then she got thirsty.

Dalton steered his eyes back to Jac Lu. "Mad Dog? You kidding me, Jac? I really bought a whole case of Mad Dog 20/20?"

"Yes."

"When?"

"Two weeks ago. It was same night that prisoner escaped. He captured hostage inside Raccoon Bar and Grill, remember?"

Dalton did remember the headline regarding that episode in the *Sentinel*. Apparently, some masked vigilante had intervened and the bartender was saved. He also remembered being laid up in bed the day after it happened, suffering from the worst hangover of his life.

"You sure it was me, and not Darnell that bought it?"

Jac Lu stuck a cigarette behind his ear and patted his pompadour into shape. "No, it was you."

"I hope I didn't drive."

"You carried that stuff home by yourself. One box in each arm. You lift weights now? You some kind of Arnold Schwarzenegger?"

"You kidding?"

"You go through hard times, Dalton. You quit band and you not used of being single." He pointed at his temple. "No good. You let wifey-wife go to head. Very, very bad."

Wifey-wife?

"No matter. Many eels in ocean, Dalton. Anyway, maybe we can work out deal. You buy six-pack from me, and I give you free half-pint of tequila. You just stay away from wifey-wife's store."

Helen has a store?

He looked back at the poster. The bikini girl reminded him of Helen. Especially with her unkempt hair and magnetic eyes. But he knew it wasn't her. Helen was better looking. And she had too much class, in his opinion, to pose so suggestively for a beer ad. *But who knows*, he thought.

He studied the poster some more. It was hard to tell if the woman was really on a beach because the background was blurry. She could be in somebody's room and the beach in the background could just be a backdrop. And maybe the hard hat belonged to someone else, too. Another construction worker? Made more sense. She was probably into guys who drank Miller Light and wore hard-hats. And then she liked to put on their hats and drizzle cheap beer over her cleavage.

Jesus, he thought. *Darnell's right. I can't get her out of my mind. Everywhere I look, I see Helen.*

"You hear me, Dalton?"

"Huh?"

"Listen, wifey-wife say things like this." Jac Lu placed his hand girlishly on his hip and pitched up his voice. "'Oh, I have big, big discount.'" His voiced dropped back down. "But no discount, Dalton. Lies. All lies! She just put price higher to begin with!"

It occurred to Dalton that Jac Lu was not talking about Helen anymore. He was talking about his own *wifey-wife*, Su Lu. Su Lu and Jac Lu were recently separated, and she had opened a liquor store next to the old hardware store—part of a concerted effort to drive Jac Lu out of business and back to his homeland in ragged disgrace.

Jac Lu raised a stern index finger. "Dalton, wifey-wife no-good vicious snake."

"But I thought you two were a great couple."

"Evil fire-breathing sea dragon!"

Dalton rubbed his throbbing head and looked at the Mad Dog cases on the counter. It was strange. Outside of occasional beer runs for Darnell, Dalton seldom bought alcohol.

I wonder if Jac confused me for Darnell.

After all, things like that do happen, he decided. People mix things up all the time. They pick up somebody else's keys by mistake. They knock on the wrong door. They put on the wrong coat. They grab the wrong suitcase at the train station. Happens all the time. But Darnell didn't *drink* Mad Dog 20/20. And he'd definitely bought a case of Pabst Blue Ribbon the night before. And besides, Dalton was white and Darnell was black. How could Jac mix that up? Now if they were both black or both white and dressed the same, maybe.

Dalton looked at the clock beside the Miller Light girl. 1:55. It was just enough time to make it back by 2:00, assuming the clock was correct.

"So, what can I get you? More tequila?"

"No. No booze. I need cigarettes, Pall Malls. Filterless."

"You smoking now, too?"

"They're for Maureen."

"Ah, Mrs. O'Leary. That old woman smoke like Weber grill." Jac Lu handed over the cigarettes. "Three-fifty."

Dalton handed Jac Lu four crumbled one-dollar bills and took his change.

"And one more thing."

"Yes, Dalton."

"A job application?"

"You want job? You need to cut down on your drinking first, Dalton Hawks."

"I swear, I've quit for good. No more booze for me—ever!"

"That's what everyone say," said Jac as he reached under the counter. "And one day later they come right back here and buy two more bottles of whiskey and twelve-pack of PBR!"

"They must be alcoholics."

"I feel bad and I tell them, 'No, you go to the church! Nice old gray church at end of street. You go there, not here! And you get help from preacher man!' Anyway, take this application home and fill this out and bring it back to me. I've got long line of good applicants. Times are hard. You must work weekends and nights."

"No problem."

"I'll put your application at the top of list. Everybody knows what good worker you are. Much better than digging ditches."

"I like digging ditches."

"Much more stable. Guaranteed thirty-two hours a week. And you have more time to play in band."

"I'm sorry about the band, Jac."

"I watch YouTube guitar lessons every day. I can play like Glen Campbell."

"Nobody plays like Glen Campbell."

"I can!"

Dalton left the store with the job application and the cigarettes.

He hopped in the car and turned the key. Nothing. After three more attempts, he opened the hood and tightened the battery cable. Started right up after that. He checked the mirror for Tomahawk's finest and flipped a U-turn and rumbled back up Enfield. Not a cop in sight.

Amazing.

He parked in front of his apartment building and climbed out the car. A portable record player was sitting upside-down on the lawn. An album sat on the curb next to it. Glen Campbell, *By the Time I get to Phoenix.* Dalton sighed and saw a garbage bag sitting on the front steps. He opened it and inspected the contents. Mostly clothes and kitchen utensils. He reached inside the bag and blindly pulled out a shirt, *his* Mount Rushmore shirt.

"Bastard," he mumbled.

He tossed the bag onto the Buick's back seat, along with the record player and the Glen Campbell album. He looked around the lawn for more items. He was sure there was something important missing. Something of value. *But what?* And then it dawned on him.

He darted inside the building, raced up the stairs, and charged down the hall. He barged into his room. Except for the unplugged refrigerator, the place was bare. Even the couch was gone. He searched the closet. Empty. He collapsed onto the floor and slumped against the wall.

Where could it be? He grit his teeth, wondering what Kovaleski could have done with it. *That bastard better not have sold it!*

The item in question was a 1966 Martin guitar, and he realized that he was being paranoid. Kovaleski hadn't done anything with it. The guitar was never in his apartment to begin with.

Helen had it.

He got back up and noticed an envelope taped to the inside

of the door. Surprise, surprise—his official eviction notice, signed by the man himself: Jim Bridger County Sheriff Dale Kovaleski. He wadded up the note, sat on the floor, and did the math. He needed a new apartment, which meant six-hundred bucks to pay for the first month's rent and the deposit for another single-room dump.

Six hundred? How am I going to come up with that kind of loot? Well, there's always that old Martin...

But the thought sickened him.

He got back up and left his room and trudged down the hallway. He needed to clear his head. He needed air. He reached the staircase and stopped. He weighed his options. He examined the staircase's old banister. He felt its wooden surface and thought about Helen. Jac Lu's conversation came back to him. Evil fire-breathing sea dragon. Was he talking about his wife or about Helen?

Dalton rubbed the railing with his thumb. The etchings and filigrees were long worn down on balusters. The wooden ball cap on the newel post was missing—and had been for at least fifty years. Probably shaped like an acorn, he mused. The banister must have once been beautiful, back in the 1920's. In fact, the whole building had probably been beautiful. He imagined railroad tycoons wielding deep martini glasses and fat cigars, and curvy mistresses who once paraded down the staircase he was now standing on. *Probably had a red velvet carpet back then and a harp player in the foyer.*

Miss O'Leary's poodle barked, and her door swung open. "Did you forget about me?"

Dalton turned around.

"Cigarettes."

He handed her the Pall Malls and the change.

"Just fifty cents?" She flipped the pack upside down and smacked it on her palm. "The prices these days."

"Nothing stays the same."

Miss O'Leary peeled off the cellophane and pulled a lighter from her dressing gown pocket. "Dalton?"

"Yes…"

"The sheriff was here a little while ago with, uh, Deputy…what's that dumb bastard's name?"

"Deputy Harden?"

"That was him, Deputy Rhett Harden. While you were away, those two were messing around in your room. I just thought I'd let you know. Is everything okay?"

"Kovaleski evicted me."

"I'm sorry."

Dalton shrugged.

"What are you doing to do?"

"Pawn my guitar, find a new place, move to a new city…who knows…" He glumly scratched the railing and tried to dig out a single atom from its happy, rollicking past.

…*Helen*.

A wave of dread crashed through him. He was in no mood. But the more he thought about it, there was no way around it: paying for a new apartment required pawning the guitar. And, like it or not, Dalton needed to pay his own Evil Sea Dragon a visit.

CHAPTER NINE

The noonday sun grilled the eastern plains like a two-dollar steak. Truck drivers turned their AC's on high as they rolled through the endless ribbon of molten highway before them.

Dalton rolled the Buick's window down, wiped the sweat from his forehead, and slipped the key in the ignition. He turned it. Just a *click*. He turned it six more times and gave up.

He rested his aching head on the steering wheel and finally reached into the glove box and pulled out a large flathead screwdriver. It had a sturdy yellow handle, which he figured could double as a hammer. He bounced it up and down in his hand. It was a serious screwdriver, looked like it could fix anything: a bicycle, a rocket engine, a dump truck, a broken heart.

Anything.

Except *his* broken heart.

"Damn starter," he mumbled. "Or maybe it's vapor locked."

Dalton really didn't know what vapor lock was, just a term he once heard at a garage while getting a tire fixed. It had been a hot day, and he'd overhead a mechanic on the phone saying, "It's vapor locked...just let the sun go down and then see if it starts."

Dalton's brain felt vapor locked.

And although Dalton looked like a man who was good with a wrench, the kind of guy who regularly spent his afternoons listening to baseball games while changing oil or replacing brakes, he wasn't that mechanically inclined. But he had no choice. He couldn't afford a mechanic on his lousy income.

He popped the hood, stepped out the car, and leaned into the Buick's grimy V8. A simple engine: carburetor, fuel pump, distributer, starter, battery, radiator, some hoses. Basic gearhead stuff. Something the average red-blooded American was supposed to be able to fix with a good screwdriver, an adjustable wrench, and some of that good ol' fashioned know-how.

Dalton stared at the engine, hoping there would be a nice orange tag over the faulty part saying: FIX ME—I'M THE DOOHICKEY THAT'S BROKEN!

But no such luck.

He grunted. He scratched his head and tugged on a radiator hose. It seemed tight enough.

Maybe that's it. No, maybe it's that thing. What the hell is that? A fuel pump?

He banged it with the screwdriver handle and tried starting the Buick. Nothing. He looked up at the sky and cursed his life. Other people could have good jobs and cars that started.

Why not him?

He spent the next twenty minutes randomly pulling on wires, loosening screws and then retightening them, bruising and scrapping his knuckles, cursing and wondering how anybody could do this forty hours a week. Probably because they had the proper tools: hydraulic lifters and impact wrenches and stuff like that.

He reached to the bottom of the engine and jabbed a cylindrical starter-looking-thing with the screwdriver as hard as he could, and then he banged it three more times for good measure.

He loosened and re-tightened the battery cable and climbed back in the car and cranked the engine.

The Apollo wheezed to life.

His soul swelled with pride.

He stuck the screwdriver back in the glove compartment and contemplated a career change. He could work in a garage, restoring old muscle cars. Good money in that, he figured. A restored Shelby Mustang could fetch about two-hundred grand, or so he had heard.

He imagined himself spot-welding a broken muffler and wearing a blue work jacket with a patch that read: *DALTON HAWKS, CERTIFIED MECHANIC*. His mind drifted like a stray balloon. He thought about growing a bushy beard and wearing overalls. He thought about getting tattooed. Weren't most grease monkeys into tattoos? Of course, he knew what he would get, a spark plug with *CHAMPION* written across the top.

Maybe he would go the other direction, be one of those trustworthy, clean-cut, nerdy mechanics: a man who ran a clean shop and held an engineering degree, a brilliant car guy who had engines and brakes and cooling systems down to a science, a mechanic who washed his hands like a surgeon before and after rebuilding an engine.

The engine sputtered, and the balloon of his imagination popped and plummeted to earth.

Dalton pumped the accelerator and checked the indicators. Gas, near empty. Odometer, 292,517 miles. Temperature gauge, in the red. But that was always the case, no matter how hot or cold the engine. And the oil light was on—like always, no matter how much oil was in it.

He pumped the gas again and jammed the car in gear. He drove back to Enfield Avenue. He passed the radio station— KJBC, the five-thousand-watt voice of Jim Bridger County—

and Schulz's Liquors. He crossed 5th Street and passed the Tomahawk Casualty and Insurance Company. He had once worked there as a temporary data-entry clerk—a dull job, made worse because he was forced to wear a tie. But, mercifully, it didn't last long. He was fired because of a urine test.

Dalton had tested positive for methamphetamine.

"Sorry," said Wendel Boltman, his boss, the day after the test. "But it's company policy."

"Company policy?"

"Believe it or not, most employers frown upon a meth addict."

Dalton had never liked Wendel much. But that was mainly because Wendel had dated Helen back in high school. It still drove Dalton crazy that she had preferred Wendel to him. And it drove him crazier that Wendel, whom he considered to be an idiot, was so much more successful in life.

"Addict?" Dalton sneezed and reached for a Kleenex on Wendel's desk. "I've never taken meth in my life. That test screwed up."

"No," said Wendel, "you screwed up. I knew something was going on. You've been acting bat-shit crazy for over a week." He leaned back on his chair and patted his receding hairline. "Addiction's nothing to be ashamed of, Dalton. It can happen to anybody. Even I did a twelve-step stint at Betty Ford, took me forever to admit that I had a problem. I used to put down a half a bottle of Johnny Walker Black every day. Did that for nine years. Told myself that it was just a phase. Cost me my marriage, my home, my rig—"

"You drove a truck?"

"I had to. I tore my UCL while pitching at K State. I had a bright career ahead of me. But the Tommy John didn't work. Never got the arm back. So I wound up hauling liquid nitrogen from Spokane to Flagstaff for nine years."

"While you were drunk?"

"Baseball hadn't panned out. I hated my job. I hit the bottle. Only thing was, I started to *like* truck driving, even more than baseball. But by then I couldn't get off the sauce."

"Sorry to hear that."

"DUI ended that, and I deserved it. But it kills me to this day. I had a '77 Mack. You ever ride in one of them monsters?"

Dalton shook his head.

"Kris Kristofferson drove one in *Convoy*. Mine was just like it, except it was cherry-red with a white stripe down the side. I lost that too."

"That's too bad."

"I saw a lot of places: South Dakota, New Mexico, even Canada. Even Wyoming. Ever been to Wyoming?"

"No."

"Lots of nothing."

"Just like here."

"Miles and miles of empty highways, Dalton. You feel like you're on the moon. It never ends."

"I know..."

"At night, I'd pretend I was an astronaut. Helped the time go by."

"I get it."

"I was piloting a space capsule on a dangerous mission to Mars; it made the job more interesting. But enough about me. This is about you, Dalton. Just admit you have a problem, and do something about it. I mean it. Get some professional help before it's too late. You know, there's all kinds of places in Jim Bridger County that can put an addict back on track."

Dalton raised an eyebrow.

"Okay, maybe not in this county. But in any other county. I'm sure Kit Carson has got some place you can dry out."

"It does?"

"Ever been to Burlington?"

"Is that in Colorado?"

"It's in Kit Carson Country, just about ten minutes off the Kansas border. Beautiful. Got a nice new Love's truckstop there—and a Wendy's."

"There's a Wendy's in Burlington?"

"I think so. Or maybe it's in Limon. Or is it Limon that has the McDonald's. No, it's a Wendy's. Now I'm confused..."

"Battlesmoke has a Wendy's."

"I thought it was closed."

"I heard it's still open." Dalton covered his nose with his arm and sneezed.

"That's some cold. Seen a doctor?"

"Just Dr. Shotz—for that pee test I didn't pass."

Wendel tossed Dalton the Kleenex box. "How long you had it?"

"Two weeks."

"You should get some medicine."

Dalton pulled a tube of Vicks inhaler from his pocket. "See? Medicine. I've been huffing this all week. And I swear it's *this* that's making me crazy!"

"Vicks?" said Wendel. "Right..."

But, surprisingly, the very next day, Dr. Shotz had confirmed that the pee-test had confused the Vicks cold medicine for methamphetamine, which was understandable, in the doctor's words, because the active ingredient in a Vicks inhaler was the benign left-handed version of the methamphetamine molecule, L-(levo)-methamphetamine (not something anyone would take at a rave party because it only cleared the sinuses and did not fit the brain's right-handed dopamine receptors, triggering the side-effects associated with its nefarious right-handed twin, D-(dextra)-methamphetamine), but Dalton didn't believe Dr. Shotz because he'd been getting all of D-methamphetamine's notorious side effects—the Vicks inhaler *was* making him high as a Mt. Kilimanjaro and giving him tons of energy—and then Dr. Shotz told him that it was impossible, unless Dalton's right-handed dopamine receptors had somehow been turned inside-out—like gloves in a dryer—and then a spray of obscure chemical jargon spewed from the doctor's lips, including a curious word that Dalton had never heard of.

Chirality.

Dalton drove by Insurance and Casualty office and crossed 7th Street, passing the old hardware store, and another liquor store, Su Lu's Liquor's, and then The Last Straw. He licked his finger and rubbed the dust off the gas gauge. He tapped the glass. The needle didn't budge.

Dalton eased back into the Buick's hot vinyl seat and turned on the radio. He rolled the dial to 990-AM. The static cleared. The station's anchors, Molly Trexler and Don Torrino, recapped the day's headlines.

"...the Superman of Tomahawk, I'm calling him," said Molly.

"Amazing man," said Don.

"Now hold on a minute. Why does it always have to be a man?"

"You just called him a super MAN. I was just—"

"But we can't just assume this vigilante is a man, Don. It could be a woman. I'm not saying that it is, but—"

"Right you are, Molly. But, in any case, a burglary was thwarted, and the town of Tomahawk may owe him, or her, a big debt of gratitude. That's right, folks, another alleged spotting of the Tomahawk Vigilante—and this time right outside of Stevenson's Pharmacy."

"And what about that witness?" said Molly.

"A drifter, according the police report."

"A drifter? You mean like a hobo? A bum?"

"Hey," said Don, "maybe *he's* the mysterious vigilante."

"Could be. These are crazy times."

Crazy, crazy, crazy, thought Dalton.

"We'll be right back with the weather after these messages."

"Jim Bridger County could be under a tornado watch later this afternoon," said Molly. "So stay tuned. You're listening to *The Mid-day Report* on KJBC-990—the voice of Jim Bridger County, including Tomahawk, Comanche Hills, and Pawnee Ridge."

The station cut to an International Harvester commercial. "Big, big discounts," said the announcer. "Come on down to Battlesmoke Tractor and Combine for our annual Fourth-of-July sale. And tell 'em Marty sent you!"

Big, big discounts, thought Dalton. Probably just marked up the price to begin with.

He and slowed down as he passed Stevenson's Pharmacy. There was no yellow crime-scene tape. It looked normal. The same old tan and aqua-blue sign still hung over the front steps. Dalton figured Mr. Stevenson's son (now seventy-seven) was behind the counter, selling pills and prophylactics like always.

Like always.

That was Tomahawk.

It never changed.

If a traveling salesman were to come to Tomahawk and start knocking on doors, he'd wonder if the town had gotten frozen in time back in 1956. And, in many ways, he'd be right. A lot of the store signs still sported those 50s-style logos. What jobs were available in place like Tomahawk, people never quit. Nobody got rid of their cars. They just kept fixing them. The gas-station pumps still didn't take credit cards. Tomahawk may as well have been Cuba.

Dalton pulled over beside a park bench and wondered what exactly had gotten robbed. Drugs, obviously. Pain killers, especially. Vicodin. OxyContin. Percocet. But perhaps the robbers were more interested in money. And maybe the pharmacy had money in a safe, and the robbers put some nitroglycerin on the door and blew the lock off. He'd seen that in a bunch of old TV shows. Plastic TNT. Handy stuff.

Dalton looked down the alley between the pharmacy and grocery store. A strong sensation of *déjà vu* overcame him. A baseball bat swung through his head.

He turned to the right and looked out the passenger window. The bat vanished and was replaced by the image of a tramp sitting on the bench. The tramp smiled and tipped a bottle of Wild Irish Rose toward his rotted teeth.

Chirality...reversed molecules...Vicks...

"Geeze, maybe I do need professional help," he wondered.

He shivered in the sweltering heat. Everybody succumbed to some kind of problem sooner or later. Maybe he was going insane. Maybe he would have to be committed. It made sense. No career. Living like a teenager in a crappy apartment. But then again, maybe this *was* the pinnacle of his life. Having a beat-up car, a rundown apartment, and occasional work as a ditch digger. Maybe it was all downhill from this point on. Maybe he would look back on it and realize how great things were.

Dalton blinked and the vision of the tramp dissipated. He tapped the accelerator, turned left on 8th Street, drove four more blocks, and spotted Helen's second-story apartment on Deer Trail Drive. It was on the top floor of a two-story six-unit row house. He pulled into a dirt driveway and parked the Buick Apollo next to a white '72 Chevrolet Nova.

Dalton cut the engine. A wave of dread flooded his chest. He rubbed his stomach, gathered his thoughts. It had been six months since he last climbed those steps. And he had vowed, *never again.*

He remembered Helen's parting words. "Just go see a doctor," she said.

How could he forget that evening?

She'd been dressed in a sheer nightgown, and the porch light went right through it.

"Get some medicine," she ranted. "It happens to everyone. Football players, movie stars, everybody. We women have our needs too, you know! Don't be such a chicken shit. One damn blue pill, and everything's fixed!"

He stared through the windshield and watched two squirrels frolic on a tree beside the staircase.

"Young love," he thought. "Just give it a few months. It'll evaporate like the morning mist. And then you'll be throwing casserole dishes at each other—or crabapples, or whatever the hell it is you little bastards eat!"

Dalton took a deep breath and opened the car door.

Just relax. Nothing to worry about, Dalt. She might even be happy to see me. Hell, if I'm lucky, she might even let me stay until I get a new place.

CHAPTER TEN

"What now, you impotent bastard?"

Dalton braced himself on the staircase's hot metal railing. Helen was in a bad mood. It didn't matter why. He was going to take the brunt of it. Her temper popped out of nowhere, like a storm cloud over the plains. It rained and blew, and it vanished.

Dalton would have to ride it out for a few minutes. Then she would relent and move on to something else. She was predictable that way, just like the town she lived in.

Like Tomahawk, Helen had not changed: same short fuse, same hair-trigger temper, same dark eyes and mild overbite and slightly knocked-kneed pigeon-toed stance and bed-head hair. She wore a tank top and loose shorts that seemed on the verge of falling from her hips like an autumn leaf.

"Think you could say that a little louder?" said Dalton. "Some of the neighbors might not have heard."

"You want me to?" said Helen. "I will."

Dalton huffed.

"Make it quick."

"I—"

"Let me guess. You're getting evicted. It's written all over your goddamn face. You're late on rent, huh?"

If tongues were weapons, hers was an AK-47.

"Listen—"

"I'm listening."

He wiped the sweat from his head. Helen crossed her arms and looked into his eyes and sucked the truth of them.

"If you need money, get a proper job, Dalton. I hear they're hiring at the penitentiary. Pays $9.50 an hour, plus bennies. You've got a diploma. Go for it. Even a GED will get you in as long you can pass the pee test."

Dalton sighed. "I wasn't evicted. I just—"

"Bullshit," she said, somehow drawling a two-syllable word into four. "And, no, you can't stay the night."

"I wasn't planning to."

"Like hell."

"Who says?"

"Says your lying eyes."

"I just want to pick up some things."

"What things? What did you ever own besides a record player and a crapped-out Buick and a bunch of dumbass records. Glenn Campbell? Are you kidding me? Where's the Hank Snow, the Lefty Frizzell, the Merle Haggard?"

"Glenn Campbell's got some good tunes: Gentle on My Mind, Rhinestone Cow—"

"—so does Kenny Chesney, but you don't see me buying his whole catalogue."

"I didn't buy it. It belonged to my—"

"Never mind," said Helen. "Save the mamma-drama for the shrink."

Dalton stared at a crack on the staircase. He looked back up just as Helen stretched her tank top over her waist. It tightened against her breasts—just enough so Dalton could tell that she wasn't wearing her C-cup.

Holy smokes, he thought. She really was worth enduring, her and her relentless mouth.

And what a mouth.

He wanted to kiss it all over again. He took a breath and forgave her temper. She had plenty of reason to be mad at him. He had been a lame-ass boyfriend, and probably just one of many that she had endured since high school. It always seemed to happen to bright, attractive women like Helen. The ones who should have been marrying doctors or lawyers always wound up with ditch diggers.

He suddenly felt predictable: just another local loser doing the typical thing, standing broke before his ex-girlfriend, trying to get back with her because he had no money.

But who could blame him?

If she were a menu item, she'd be the kind of blue-plate special that sent truckers on five-hundred-mile detours just for a look. That was Helen: simple, but mouth-watering. Built and stacked like a five-star pastrami sandwich.

"So," she continued, "if you didn't get evicted, why are you here? What do I possibly have that you need?"

"You know…"

"I don't know."

"I…"

"My God, Dalton, out with it! I've got shit to do. Dishes to wash. Laundry to fold. Bills to pay. Pictures to take."

"Pictures?"

"Never mind."

"You into photography?"

"So what if I am?"

"What kind of photography? Nature?"

"Yes, *nature* photography. I like that. That's a real good word for it. Anyway, what the hell did you come here for?"

"My..."

"You know, that's always been your biggest problem. You got no guts. I mean, open your mouth. Why is it so damn difficult for you men?"

Dalton stared at the crack in the cement. "My guitar."

Helen slapped her forehead. "Your guitar? Really? You're not aiming to resurrect that music career of yours, are you? What the hell did you call that band? I can never remember. No, wait. I got it. Dalton Hawks and the...Tomahawk Tornados, right?"

"Twisters."

"That's right. The Tomahawk Twisters. Boy, did you guys ever suck."

Dalton stared deeper into the crack. He bit his tongue and decided to hop the next Greyhound to Laredo or Casper or Ogallala. Or anywhere. Maybe Hades was nice this time of year. He wondered if he could get a job at the bus station down there, mopping bathrooms and plunging its fiery toilets. It was the second optimistic thought he had all day, and he decided to act on it.

"Forget it."

"I'm sorry," said Helen. She put her verbal assault rifle away. "That was a shitty thing to say. I mean, your band didn't suck that bad."

"Thanks."

"Come on in," she sighed. "Let's take a look."

Dalton followed Helen into the living room. He saw a pair of cowboy boots sitting on the floor by the couch. Cactus green. They had pistols embroidered on them. A two-by-four ripped through his skull. He rubbed the bump on the back of his head, and the plank of wood vanished.

"Those boots yours?" asked Dalton.

"No."

"Somebody else living here?"

Dalton sensed a disturbance in the Force. "You still got that waitress job at the Last Straw?"

Helen sighed. "No."

"No?"

"I got fired."

"I'm sorry."

"Why are you being so nosey?"

"What'd you do?" said Dalton. "Punch your boss on the nose?"

"Uh-uh," she said.

"You didn't?"

"Clocked that asshole square on the mouth."

The apartment was laid out the same as the day she'd dumped him. Same Van Gogh sunflower hanging on the wall. Same dinner table in the same spot, under a red chandelier beside the kitchen. Same cat calendar on the wall. She really liked it. It was three years old.

Nothing different—except for the cactus-green boots. But something else was out of place.

Maybe it had something to do with the boots. Or maybe not. But it appeared him that Helen was out of sorts. She was moody, far moodier than her usual moody self. And she seemed guarded, like she was hiding something.

A fluorescent-green tarp was tacked to the opposite wall. A camera sat beneath it, next to a laptop computer and a cardboard box the size of a bread loaf.

"You taking pictures?"

"None of your damn business."

Dalton picked up the box. His pupils dilated to the size of two Frisbees. A label on the box read, *MR. PLEASURE* in big purple balloon letters. And standing behind the box's plastic window was an anatomically correct sex toy.

"Hey, hey, hey," said Dalton. "What have we here? Mr. Pleasure?"

Helen charged into the living room. "Give me that!"

Dalton hid the box behind his back. "Really? You miss me *that* much?"

"No, I do not. It's for my business!"

"Business? What kind of business needs one of these?"

"I've got to earn a living somehow."

"What the hell are you talking about?"

"Never you mind."

"Come on, just *say* it!"

Helen wearily pinched the bridge of her nose and sighed. "I'm experimenting, okay? I just heard that people make a lot of money doing this kind of Internet stuff."

"Really?"

"Remember Ruby McGonahugh?"

Dalton shrugged.

"You know, that cheerleader who banged the basketball coach and ruined his teaching career. Remember her? Ruby McGonahugh?"

Dalton grimaced and his cheeks flushed.

"Ha-ha. Well, I should have known. But don't be embarrassed, Dalton. She screwed every other guy on the football team for damn near two years. Anyway, she just bought a new Ford F-150 doing the same exact thing I am. It's got heated seats and a roll-bar and everything."

Dalton glared at Helen. "You're an Internet porn star?" He didn't know why he was so angry. If anything it should have helped him get over her. But the thought of Helen taking pornographic pictures infuriated him. For selfish reasons, probably. He was proud of being dumped by her. After all, he had at least dated her. He had gotten *that* far. And not many men in Tomahawk could claim that. But even that consolation prize had been taken away.

"No, dumbass. I'm not porn star. I'm pretending. See, it's not the real thing. Most guys don't think about that, or maybe they don't care. So, I'm not really disgracing myself."

"Then what do you call it?"

She reached around him and snagged the box from Dalton's hand. "I just crop the pictures on the computer. With a close-up, they can't tell if it's the real deal or not. Most guys probably think I'm fondling an actual hoo-ha, which makes me wonder what those men really interested in—me or Mr. Pleasure? Think about it. What's really floating way down in that male brain? But, anyway, they pay good money for it. It's all done on PayPal."

"PayPal?"

"Yes."

"And it's just pretend?"

"It's just pretend. Can't you get a thing through that noggin' of yours?"

"ARE YOU CRAZY?"

"Hey," said Helen, "sometimes I just gotta do what I gotta do. You know how hard it is to get a job in this town."

"What about Jim Bridger County? You said it pays $9.50 an hour."

The bedroom door swung open, and a muscular man with a handlebar mustache stepped into the living room. He lit a cigarette. He wore nothing except for a Stetson hat and plain tighty whities. He stared at Dalton and blew the cigarette smoke from his mouth.

CHAPTER ELEVEN

Helen said, "Zeke, meet Dalton Hawks. Dalton, meet the great Zeke Mueller. Did you know Dalton used to be a world-famous country singer?"

"World famous? Where was he world famous?"

"Right here in Tomahawk."

Zeke took a tug from his cigarette and coughed. "Country singer? I never heard of no singer named Dalton Hawks."

"Dalton was an up-and-comer. But his career, sadly, got cut short."

Zeke stared at Dalton as though he recognized him from somewhere. He rubbed the back of his head and lumbered toward the refrigerator. He opened the door and rummaged toward the back of the fridge until he found a 40-ounce bottle of Budweiser. He twisted off the cap, sat down, and took a chug.

Dalton looked Zeke over, sized him up and down. He was well-built, heavy jaw, caveman brow, broad shoulders and long gorilla-like arms. A guy could probably shovel a lot of dirt with those pipes, thought Dalton.

Zeke was probably into lifting weights and protein drinks.

Probably got one of those ab machines, too. Maybe a Bow Flex.

Somehow, Zeke looked familiar. Dalton had seen the man before. But where? The grocery store? The gas station? The library? Zeke didn't look like the library type. He looked more like the bar type. That was it. Maybe he'd seen Zeke at the Last Straw. Or maybe he'd cooked Zeke a cheeseburger at the Raccoon Bar and Grill.

Zeke looked like the cheeseburger type. A guy who went to bars and ordered cheeseburgers. He probably had a side of fries and some pie afterwards. Banana cream, perhaps. And he probably chased it down with a pitcher of Budweiser and topped it off with a line of cocaine in the bathroom.

"So," said Helen, "how about you two get acquainted? I've got fresh coffee in the pot. Cups are in the dishwasher."

Zeke burped and took another swig of beer.

"That's okay," he said. "I don't want no coffee."

"You sure? I've got Folgers."

Zeke eyeballed Dalton. He lit another cigarette. "What brings you here, country singer?"

"My—"

"You come here to harass my woman?"

"—my guitar. That's all I came for."

"Yeah, I'll bet."

"No, really—"

"Listen, she don't want you around here no more. You failed to satisfy her womanly needs. Don't that sink into your head, numbnuts? Or do I have to beat it into you?"

"Zeke!" shouted Helen from the hall. "This doesn't concern you."

Zeke leered at Dalton, and his face turned red. He stood up. His eyeballs swelled. A vein jutted from his neck. "I ought to kick your ass, coming in here and pestering my woman!"

"Zeke, I'm not your or anybody else's woman. It's the 21st Century. We've progressed."

"We have?"

"Haven't you heard? We live in a bright new age of freedom and justice and enlightenment."

"Who says?"

"It's all because of computers and the Internet."

"Shit, all I do on the Internet is look at porn."

"That's good to know. Mankind's greatest technological game-changer, and that's what you use it for."

"You make money off it."

"Enough!"

Zeke huffed and turned and pressed Dalton's back to the wall. "Listen, country singer, I don't care how much money you make or how many chicks you've banged. You just leave mine alone. She belongs to *me*, understand!"

Dalton stared back at Zeke, his curiosity far outweighing his fear of an ass-beating.

If I didn't see him at the Raccoon Bar and Grill, then where? I'd remember him with a mustache like that—and those boots. I mean, who wears boots like that in this town? This isn't Nashville!

He dug his eyes into Zeke's gaze, and then a bolt of pain surged through his head. His assailant—holding onto the end of a two-by-four—slowly came into focus. Big guy. Cowboy hat. Handlebar mustache. Shiny belt buckle...flashy cowboy boots. Cactus-green.

"Are we clear?" said Zeke. "Or do I need to kick your ass all the way to Ogallala."

Helen's voice shot through the living room. "Goddammit, Zeke, get your hands off him—now!"

Zeke's skin went pale. A wave of fear flickered through his eyes.

Dalton tilted his head, like a confused dog.

Zeke winced and stepped away. It was as though he, too, didn't know where the fear had come from. "Well...let that be a lesson to you, country singer."

Helen stepped back into the living room. "Zeke, get the fuck out of here and go take a shower or something. You smell like you woke up in an alley."

Zeke grabbed his beer and walked into the bathroom.

Dalton looked at the boots by the couch. His mind fumbled for a connection. Nothing. Gears whirled, sparks flew. He'd seen those boots before. In a dream? Had he run into Zeke the night before? And was Zeke wearing those same boots? Did Zeke whack him over the head with a two-by-four?

Impossible!

"Dalton, are you paying attention?"

"Yes."

"No, you are not."

"I am—"

"Look here, in my hand—your gee-tar."

"Oh..."

"You are most welcome!"

"Sorry. Thanks."

"It was here the whole time. And just to think: here I was taking all these questionable pictures, and all the while I could've been practicing up for my country music career."

Dalton grabbed the guitar case and set it down on the dining room table. He opened it and inspected the 1966 Martin D-45 resting on the case's green velvet lining. The guitar's varnish had worn off in spots. The body was scratched. There were burn marks by the low-E tuning peg, supposedly from his daddy's cigarettes. But Dalton didn't know for sure because he didn't know if his father smoked or not. But more than likely he did.

Dalton was one of the few people in Tomahawk who didn't smoke.

The only things Dalton knew about his old man were from what his Uncle Elston had told him. When Dalton was two years old, his daddy hauled a broken RCA TV into the backyard and doused it with gasoline and set it on fire and then he had climbed into his rusty Peterbilt and put it gear and drove away and was never heard from again.

Some say he headed south.

Some say he headed north.

There was a rumor he worked in the Yukon, hauling oil-rig parts over frozen lake beds. Others say, he sold the truck and started hopping freight trains.

But Dalton had shrugged it off. Things like backyard TV fires and errant fathers were normal in Tomahawk. Even the town's fire station had burned down after the fire chief deep-fried a Twinkie in a vat of oil and Everclear.

Dalton lifted the guitar out of the case and strummed an E-chord. A deep full boom rang out the sound hole, a sound that said: *Hello, I'm Johnny Cash.* There was no beating a good Martin. Dalton didn't have too many belongings, but he had a great guitar. A valuable guitar. Probably a collector's item.

But he didn't play it anymore. It brought too many memories of him flopping like a fish on the stage of the Last Straw's open mic nights.

He sighed, put the guitar back inside the case, and snapped it shut .

"I'm done."

"Good," said Helen.

"Fine."

He wasn't used to Helen talking in such short phrases, so he waited for another burst of insults to spray out her mouth.

The toilet flushed and the shower went on.

"What's his deal?" said Dalton. "Is he your new boyfriend?"

"That's none of your business."

"Where did you meet him?"

"None of your business."

"He's sure in a great mood."

"He wasn't looking too hot when he showed up here this morning. He had a lump on his head the size of a baseball. God knows what he was up to last night."

"Must have been a rough one," said Dalton. "Probably those three-for-one beer specials at the Last Straw. A person can do a lot of damage there with five bucks."

"That's a fact."

"You know what, Helen?"

"What?"

"I think you can do much better."

"I really don't care what you think."

"You're pretty, you're smart, you're enterprising, you've got business sense. You're a talented singer."

Helen put her hands on her hips and sighed. "Uhm, Dalton?"

"What?"

"You can leave anytime, you know."

CHAPTER TWELVE

Dalton trudged down the stairs in a daze. He opened the car door. He set the guitar case on the passenger seat and pushed the Buick's key into the ignition.

It didn't turn.

He yanked it out and stared at the key. It was the Buick's key, alright. *Maybe I'm putting it in upside down.*

He tried again. But, still, the key would not turn.

What the—?

But the way the day was going, he wasn't surprised.

He rattled the ignition's lock and then noticed a smell of cigarettes—odd because nobody had smoked in that Buick since 1974, except for Ruby MacGonahugh after she stole his virginity minutes before his nineteenth birthday. And that was over twelve years ago.

———

"Really?" she'd said. "I'm your first? Dalton, I am indeed honored as hell. I can't wait to tell everybody at school!"

Dalton's eighteen-year-old pimpled face had flushed. "Please don't."

She lit a cigarette and blew the smoke out the window and stared at the football field under the lights. The game was long over. And Dalton had not participated because of what had happened at the previous game in Battlesmoke.

The Tomahawk Warriors had won that game. But Coach Roach suspected Dalton had been drinking and so he'd been kicked off the team—ironically after Tomahawk's first and only win of the season, against their biggest rival: the Battlesmoke Gladiators. Coach Roach had found Dalton passed-out on the bench, snoring after scoring an unbelievable touchdown.

And what an unbelievable day it was.

A bolt of lightning had just missed the scoreboard before the end of the fourth quarter. And then Dalton was called from the bench to the field. He rarely played. But another player was out with a case of the clap, which had been running amuck in all three of Jim Bridger County's high schools.

Dalton walked onto the gridiron and put on his helmet, feeling buzzed but somehow energized from the lightning strike.

And then the snap.

Dalton got the ball, and he ran a play so athletic and so stupendous that had there been scouts in Battlesmoke's rickety stands they would have signed him for a four-year college ride on the spot.

But it wasn't to be. Shortly after his touchdown, a whiskey flask was discovered.

Dalton never picked up a football again.

Cut from the team, doing badly in school, and now this...

"It's okay," said Ruby. It'll be our little secret."

She patted him on the knee and smiled.

———

Ruby's voluptuous imaged vanished. Dalton rolled the window down and let the heat out. His knee smacked the steering column. *Strange.* Had the front seat been moved forward?

Has somebody been sitting here? he wondered. *Some short person who chain-smokes? Mrs. O'Leary? Did she drive my car? No, she hasn't driven in years!*

He rubbed his throbbing knee. Geeze, he thought. The Apollo barely ran, and now the key didn't work. The day kept getting weirder and weirder.

What next?

Helen's front door swung open.

"What the hell are you doing?"

Dalton got out the car and looked up, shielding his eyes from the blazing sun. "This piece of shit won't start again. The key won't even turn."

"Of course it won't. You're in Link's car, you idiot. Jesus, no wonder you can't get a job!"

"Link?"

"Yes, Link. My brother...well half-brother, technically."

"Isn't he in jail?"

"He sure is—which is where you'll be if you and your heap aren't out my driveway in the next five minutes."

"You can't throw me in jail for getting in the wrong car."

"I'll find a way."

Dalton remembered that he had parked the Buick Apollo to the right of the Chevy Nova—and not to the left.

I didn't notice that? Am I that hung-over? God, I need a nap...

He examined the two cars and rubbed his head.

But there were more similarities than the color. A slight variation in the shape of the grill and the taillights was all that really stood out. But other than that, despite being different makes, the Apollo and the Nova looked damn near identical.

Helen slammed the apartment door shut, and Dalton moved the guitar out of the Nova. He tossed it into the Buick's back seat. He climbed in, cranked the ignition. This time the key turned. But the results were no better. He turned it six more times. He sighed, popped the hood, and grabbed a screwdriver.

He re-tightened the battery cable and clubbed the starter with screwdriver's yellow handle. But still, the car wouldn't start.

The carburetor? The fuel pump? But the engine would turn if it were one of those things. It might not start, but it would at least turn. Wouldn't it?

He still had no clue how to fix it.

As Dalton's dream of becoming a certified auto-mechanic rolled over and died like a snake-bit prairie dog, he sank into the hot vinyl seat and weighed his options.

Well, I could abandon the car and hit the highway. That would shake things up. I wonder what Kenny Chesney would do? Probably stick out his thumb and head for Nashville, write a hit song, get rich and famous, and then buy a yacht and have a party.

But Dalton wasn't Kenny Chesney. And his guitar wasn't going to make him rich or famous. He could barely play it. He had little sense of song construction and a poor sense of rhythm.

I'm going to have to pawn it.

His throat swelled.

It wasn't losing the guitar that made him that sad. He felt as he was though he losing something else. A future. Or at least the delusion of one.

He looked at his driver's license, which was still sitting on the dashboard. He was too spent to even pick it up and stuff it back in his wallet.

He decided to pay Darnell another visit, get him to come down with his magical socket wrench and resurrect his car. But first, he needed to hide the guitar. At this point the 1966 Martin was worth than the 1973 Buick.

He opened the trunk, but there was too much clutter to squeeze the guitar in. He made room, clearing away an old work jacket, some duct tape, and a six-pack of Olympia...and three bottles of Old Grand-Dad and five bottles of Mad Dog 20/20. He squeezed the guitar in and shut the trunk.

Mad Dog?

He opened the trunk.

Sure enough, there were five flavors of Mad Dog 20/20 staring at him. Blue Raspberry. Red Banana. Grape Wine. Strawberry-Kiwi. A half-empty bottle of Mango-Lime.

Jac Luc had not been lying.

Dalton still didn't remember buying any of that swill and storing it in the trunk. He put the bottle down and something else caught his eye. Two metal arm braces. They had spring-loaded clamps attached to them. Each clamp was mounted in a greased runner that allowed them to slide back-and-forth along the brace. It reminded Dalton of the contraption Travis Bickle used in *Taxi Driver* to conceal his weapons.

You talkin' to me?

Except there were no guns or knives in those clamps. But one of them did have an empty can of Olympia strapped to it. He yanked the can out and slid the clamp back-and-forth on the brace. He tossed the brace back in the trunk, and then something else raised an eyebrow.

A helmet.

He examined it. Part of Darnell's Halloween costume. *So, it was here all along.* He set the helmet down next to a pair of goggles and saw the black jumpsuit.

He pulled it out and looked it over. Exactly as Darnell had described it, complete with a cape and yellow lightning-bolt patches. "Well," he thought, "the case of the missing jumpsuit is solved. It was in the trunk, and I just forgot all about it. Understandable, I guess—Halloween was nearly a year ago."

And then he thought about Mrs. O'Leary's conversation, the part about the guy with the cape with the lightning bolts and the helmet and the goggles—how she thought it had been *him* wearing that garb. Ridiculous.

He shuddered.

Maybe Darnell was playing a trick on me. Maybe we went out boozing together, and he decided he needed some wood for a new homemade table. And then he got dressed up and cut down that tree, and she confused me for Darnell! That's it! Ha-ha...ha....

RIDICULOUS!

His stomach heaved.

His blood iced.

His breathing stopped.

And his mind spun out and crashed—like a motorcycle landing short of the ramp, catching the front wheel on a school bus and hurling him over the handlebars and smashing him onto life's pavement of misery like a rag doll.

Easy, Dalton...

But before he lost complete control, his tiny guardian angel landed on his shoulder. The angel, however, was a different than the ones depicted in books and movies. He didn't wear a gown, nor did he have wings. Instead, the guardian angel wore a helmet and drove a stripped-down 1970 Triumph Bonneville. He was the Evel Angel.

"Just hold her steady, kid," said Evel. "That's it. Just slow her down. Now hit the bottle...I mean, the throttle. Real good. Feeling all right, buddy? You can do it. Lean back a little. Now wheel on down to Darnell's house and get him over here and have him fix this ol' jalopy, and then we'll drive as far from this shithole as we can. Someplace nice...with a good ramp...and plenty of bars..."

Dalton regained his senses.

"Okay," said the angel. "Think. Yes. You're okay. Sun's still up. Birds are in the air. You're not on a motorcycle. And you're not jumping the fountain at Caesar's Palace. Breathe. Good. Okay. Just a step at the time. Keep walking."

The Evel Angel dissipated off of his shoulder. He would be back next time Dalton needed him.

He was sure of it.

Dalton started walking. The sun beat down harder, and he wished he'd put on some lotion. There was no escaping the sun's heat in dry, treeless towns like Tomahawk, towns that sat on the plains like bubbling eggs on a frying pan. He put his hands in pockets and cut through a vacant lot.

He was well acquainted with the lot. When he was seven, he tried to jump his dirt bike over a wooden ramp in that same lot. But the bike chain snapped halfway up the ramp, and he fell off and crashed into a pile of lumber and wound up with three stitches in his left leg.

As he crossed the lot, that same leg was throbbing again. He began to limp. He thought about the bullet in his boot and the wound on his thigh. Getting shot in the leg was becoming easier to believe.

He grit his teeth and rubbed his thigh. It was at least a mile to Darnell's trailer. He would need a ride. No way around that one. Not with that limp.

Maybe Helen could help, he wondered. *Well, she's going to have to.*

CHAPTER THIRTEEN

"I don't know how you convince me into this kind of bullshit," said Helen. She handed Dalton her shoulder bag. It was made of brown canvas and it had a patch, a little parachute, sewn onto the front. She fastened her seatbelt. "You're just lucky I feel just slightly guilty about teasing you about that shitty-ass band of yours."

Dalton fastened the seatbelt. "If you want, I'll just leave the damned thing in your driveway."

"No thanks. Keys?"

"Keys?"

"The car keys are in that bag I gave you."

Dalton raked his fingers around the bottom of bag, fumbling through a mass of receipts, lip balm tubes, pennies and empty cigarette packs. He pulled the keys out along with the latest copy of the *Tomahawk Sentinel*. He gave the keys to Helen and tossed the newspaper on the dashboard. He looked at the dashboard and remembered his license was still in the Buick.

Helen started the Nova and shifted into reverse. "So why's your leg is so sore?"

"I must have fell on a screw or something."

"You can't remember?"

"Nope."

"Were you drinking?"

"Apparently."

"How much?"

"I don't know. I can't remember a thing."

Helen backed out the driveway and headed toward Darnell's trailer park. Both hands on the wheel. Ten o'clock, two o'clock. Two miles below the speed limit.

"Dalton, I really don't know about this. I think we should turn around."

"I just need to get that car back to my apartment. Then I'll never bug you again. Promise."

"Link will murder me if he finds out I'm driving his car. He's a crazy asshole. He destroyed his brain on crystal-meth years ago, and now the smallest things can send him into a rage." She lit a cigarette and rolled down the window. "He loses his mind over the stupidest shit. I mean, his Chuck Taylors will get the tiniest scrape of dirt on them, and he'll carry on like his house had been burned down. And then he'll turn around and completely ignore a steaming pile of wet dog poop on his pillow, and he'll go to sleep right on it."

"Link?"

"You never met him, did you?"

"No."

"This is his car. He bought it after a trip to California a few months ago. Then he was busted for manufacturing methamphetamine. And I'm telling you, he'd kill us."

"But he's your brother."

"Half-brother."

"I saw him while I was visiting my uncle. He's in jail."

Helen adjusted the rearview and glanced at the dusty street behind her. "Not for long. I got a call from him a week ago. He says he worked out a deal with Kovaleski. Jim Bridger County Corrections is letting him out early."

"I doubt he'd care if you drove his car for a day."

"He said he'd kill me. Right before they locked him up, he told me never to drive it."

"Why? Does he have a bunch of drugs stashed in the trunk?"

"That wouldn't surprise me. Nothing that dumbass does surprises me. It astounds me that we even come from the same stock. But then, again, he is only a half-brother. That dipshit Walmart trucker who spawned him must have been a real piece of work."

"Have you ever checked the trunk?"

"No." She signaled left and turned on Enfield. "I can't open it. Lock's busted."

"Maybe he broke it on purpose."

"More than likely."

Helen passed the Stevenson Pharmacy and the Raccoon Bar and Grill. "That place got robbed last night."

"The Raccoon Bar and Grill?" said Dalton.

"No, the pharmacy. They were talking about it on the radio this morning. Nobody knows anything about it though."

"Oh...I remember now. The radio did say there was a witness."

"Probably some wino."

"As a matter of fact, it was."

"I wonder if Zeke had anything to do with it."

"Zeke?"

Helen let out a long sigh. "I wouldn't be shocked. He was acting kind of shifty this morning, and he was gone all night—and he had that big bump on his head. It was like he got smacked on the head with a two-by-four."

A stick of wood materialized in Dalton's brain.

"Well?"

"Well what?"

"*Did* Zeke get hit with a two-by-four?"

"He didn't want to talk about it."

She drove by the Last Straw, Schulz's, and the Tomahawk Pawnshop and Music Emporium. She then passed KJBC-AM and the old hardware store. It had never re-opened after the fire. There was a banner draped over its boarded windows.

DALE KOVALESKI FOR MAYOR
CHANGE YOU CAN COUNT ON

Helen turned her head toward the sign. "He's running for mayor now?"

"My uncle isn't too happy about it, either. Says he'll never get out of jail if Kovaleski wins."

"He'll probably win. Did you know that Mayor Starr just got busted for coke possession? I just read it. It was on page two of the newspaper."

"He probably planted it on her."

"Kovaleski?"

"He's a rat."

Helen turned off Enfield and rumbled over the railroad tracks. Dalton looked back at the charred van. He figured it was left as a grisly reminder for Tomahawk's youth to not race trains at crossing gates.

"Hell of a way to go," said Dalton.

"You're telling me. Looks like the whole thing exploded."

"That'll happen. All that force, that friction, that heat...all that gasoline—"

"Thank you, Stephen Hawking," said Helen.

She crossed the overpass and rumbled down the frontage

road. Dalton rolled the window down and let his arm dangle in the wind. He closed his eyes.

There wasn't much to look at, except for a dried-up cornfield and an occasional cow. And it went on and on like that all the way to the Missouri River. Cows and corn. Occasionally a Pizza Hut or a Waffle House. Or an abandoned gas station. Or a dilapidated farmhouse with some old man, wearing a baseball cap and overalls, sitting on a rocking chair, sipping coffee and throwing rocks. At nothing.

They reached the trailer park's entrance and Helen slowed down. "Ah, the memories," she said. "Which way?"

"Straight ahead. Go two blocks and turn left."

She tapped the gas pedal. "You know, I lived here when I was a kid."

"Oh, yeah? How did you like it?"

"It sucked. If you look to the right, you'll see my sweet ol' childhood home right there. See that dumpy trailer house with the cardboard taped over the windows and the tractor tires on top of the roof? That was ours until mom sold it to get herself out of debt. Supposedly some old drunken hobo is squatting in it now."

"What's with the tractor tires?"

"It makes it harder for a tornado to rip the roof off."

She drove down another block and Dalton waved at a snarling dog behind a chain-link fence. He pointed down the street. "That's it. The green trailer at the end."

"With the big chicken out front?"

"Rooster."

She pulled up closer. "Amazing. Darnell built that?" Helen let the Nova coast to a stop. She cut the engine. "Where's his truck?"

Dalton looked around. No blue pickup. He stepped out the car and opened the gate. He knocked on the door. He knocked again. He looked around the lot. He could hear AC/DC blasting out of one of the trailer homes. *Back in Black.* A screen door opened and a man hollered, "Hey, turn that shit down!"

Dalton saw a wooden apple box. He set it on its side and stood on it. He peered through the window. Nobody home. He got off the apple box and walked back to the car.

"Not there?" said Helen.

"We could wait a few minutes. Maybe he went to get some groceries. He might have run out of cookie dough."

"Cookie dough?"

"He was making snickerdoodles."

"Dalton?"

"What?"

"I need to get back. This isn't my car. I shouldn't be driving it. And, really, this is starting to piss me off."

"Fine," sighed Dalton. "Let's go. I'll see if I can get it running myself. Sometimes that old Apollo just needs a little rest."

"A little rest?" said Helen. "That bucket of bolts needs put to rest."

She drove down the frontage road and crossed the highway overpass. A jake brake rattled the air. Below the overpass, a tractor-trailer barreled down the highway—northeast, toward town of Battlesmoke.

"One day," she muttered.

"One day what?"

"I'm only five-hundred dollars shy from going to truck-driving school."

Truck driving, he thought. *What next?*

A trucking career had never appealed to Dalton. He had seen *Duel* on TV as a child and was convinced that it was his daddy behind the wheel of that demonic Peterbilt, running cars off the road, pushing them onto railroad tracks.

Besides, truckers were not popular with Tomahawk's men-folk, men who were constantly getting dumped for those eighteen-wheeled nomads that lead their wives and girlfriends astray with their cowboy hats, mutton-chop sideburns, steady paychecks, and thrilling tales about jack-knifings on icy mountain passes.

"I want to drive trucks," said Helen. "I think I'd be good at it. An interstate trucker sees a hell of a lot of country. Some of them even got routes through the Yukon. Can you imagine? They drive right over frozen lakes in the middle of winter. I could handle it. You just need a cool head and a steady hand." She raised her hand and flattened it. "See? Like a rock. I could be a brain surgeon with mitts like these."

"Brain surgeon?" said Dalton. "But, gee, what about your porn career?"

Helen stopped and checked the railroad track both ways before giving Dalton the stink-eye. "You don't think girls can be trucker drivers, do you?"

"I thought they were all lesbians."

She drove over the tracks. "With men like you it's a pretty good option."

She turned down Enfield and passed the burned-down hardware store and Schulz's liquors. A white car approached them from the opposite direction. Dalton squinted. As it drove by, he looked over his left shoulder and gazed out the rear window. He noticed a dent on the passing car's bumper.

An unmistakable dent.

"Holy shit," he said.

"Goodness gracious," said Helen. "Did you just swear?"

"Somebody stole my car!"

CHAPTER FOURTEEN

"You sure?" said Helen.

She looked in the rearview and turned on her signal.

"You don't think I'd recognize my own car? It's a '73 Buick Apollo—limited edition, V-8 engine, three-speed transmission, dent on the back bumper. That was my car!"

Helen parked catty-corner to the Stevenson Pharmacy. She reached into her bag and pulled out a pack of Winstons.

"You know, you should really quit smoking," said Dalton.

"You don't think that occurrs to every smoker every minute of the day?"

Dalton looked out the window. The firehouse was still burned down. An old broken pickup truck was still parked on the corner by the pharmacy, rear license plate hanging from one screw, and as it had been for the last five years. And in five more years, thought Dalton, it would still be there, just older and rustier. That was Tomahawk. Getting rustier with every passing year. The old people got older and the kids moved out to cities like Denver or Omaha or some other place with at least the delusion of a future.

He pictured his future self sitting on a rocking chair, staring out at a vacant Enfield Avenue, waiting for an occasional passing car: the husband's hands steady at the wheel; wife in front, drinking bottled water; kids in the backseat, their noses fogging up the windows, awed that anyone could live and waste away in such a godforsaken dump, wondering what people did out there. Maybe go to square dances or shoot bottles off fence posts.

"Well?" said Dalton.

"Well, what?"

"Turn around. We've got to catch up to it!"

"This is crazy, Dalton. I have things to do, and a car chase isn't one of them."

"But it's my car!"

She slapped the steering wheel. "But *this* is not my car. And like I said, Link would kill me. Why can't I get that through your head!"

"The man is behind bars!"

"I bet Kovaleski springs him by next week."

"No way. Link got sentenced for methamphetamine distribution. The laws are tough with stuff like that."

"Those two clowns are like *this*." She crossed her fingers. "They've got some kind of racket going on. And if that bastard wins the election, he'll be able to do whatever he wants. And, anyway, don't you see that sign?"

"The Raccoon Bar and Grill?"

She found a lighter in her purse and flicked it. It barely sparked.

"No, the one attached to the street light. See that large *U* with the big red line across it? That means, *no U turn.*"

Dalton slumped into his seat. He stared down Enfield Avenue. He looked at the bench before the Raccoon Bar and grill. A bottle of Wild Irish Rose flashed through his head. A hobo appeared. He smiled. Dalton blinked, and the bottle and the hobo dissipated.

Vicks?

Got to be. It's made my brain all squirrelly.

"You okay, Dalton? Dalton?"

Dalton scratched his aching head. Helen was stubborn. It would be easier for him to crack a walnut with a Q-tip. Hard-headed as she was attractive, Helen had an answer for everything, no matter how ridiculous her argument. She was so self-assured, even in the midst of horrible decision-making, boyfriends and careers. She had even dated *him*, no-job-Dalton-Hawks. He was an excellent example of her flaws. That Zeke Mueller guy was probably a veritable brain surgeon compared to him. No, that's crazy, he thought. Zeke was a dumbass of epic proportions. She would just never admit to it.

Helen shook his shoulder. "Dalton, Dalton...hey, are you in there?"

Dalton snapped out of his trance. "Listen, if you're afraid of Link, I guess I can understand. He is a pretty tough guy, and I'd be scared of him, too."

"Dalton?"

"What?"

He was beat and he knew it.

"Don't try that reverse psychology shit on me."

But he had to open his mouth and let the words, no matter how lame, flow forth. He had to find the crack that lead to her pride. If he could just get that Q-tip down in there and move it around, break it open.

"I'm just saying that I wouldn't blame you. I mean, who isn't afraid of Link? I know I am. And it's perfectly fine if you're afraid too. The guy is a hardened criminal."

"Shut up," said Helen. "I am not afraid of that turd bucket."

She flicked the lighter and finally got a flame. She then lit the cigarette and jammed the Nova into gear, double-checking the side and rearview mirrors. She hit the gas and cranked the wheel.

A police siren bleeped behind him.

"Oh, shit," said Helen. "Are you fucking happy, Dalton Hawks!"

"But the road was clear!"

She pulled over and cut the engine. "You're paying the ticket, jerk face."

"Me?"

"Don't start with me." She reached into the bag and fumbled for her license. "Christ, I hang around you for barely an hour and already I'm in trouble with the law."

"Come on," said Dalton. "Just explain the situation. Tell him my car was stolen. I'm sure he'll will understand."

"Sheriff Kovaleski? You really think that asshole gives a damn about your car?"

Dalton looked over his shoulder, and he saw that it was Deputy Rhett Harden, not Sheriff Dale Kovaleski, who had pulled them over.

"Harden?" said Dalton. "I thought he just patrolled on weekends."

The deputy marched up to the Nova, his spit-shined boots kicking up a cloud of dust behind his heels. He rapped on the driver-side window, and Helen rolled it down.

"Can I help you, deputy?"

He removed his sunglasses, revealing the eyes of an unyielding man who kept his heart in a bucket of formaldehyde and his emotions in an icebox. "Nice U-turn. Four points, one-hundred dollars."

He stuck his head into the car and sniffed.

"If you're smelling for booze, you're wasting your time," said

Helen. "Last beer I had was for breakfast, and that was over three hours ago."

Deputy Harden pulled a pen from his shirt pocket and tapped it on the ticket pad. "License?"

"Listen, Harden," said Dalton. "We're in a hurry. Somebody just stole my car."

"You don't say."

"Just right now. I just saw it go by. My '73 Buick Apollo."

Deputy Harden yawned. "Description?"

"Two-door, manual transmission, bucket seats, dent on the rear——"

"It's a white beat-up piece of shit," interrupted Helen. She pointed her thumb at Dalton. "Kind of like my ex-boyfriend here."

"Ha, ha," said Dalton. "You know what it looks like, Harden. It's got a big dent on the back bumper. It's got dual exhaust pipes. It's got——"

"Let me guess, four wheels and an engine?"

"If it helps," said Helen, "it looks a lot like this car. Same color and everything."

"Except the hood ornament is probably for a Buick and not a Chevy."

"No," said Dalton, "there's no Buick ornament. It got snapped off years ago."

Deputy Harden filled out the ticket. "Listen, there are legal ways to do this. And an illegal U-turn is not one of them."

"But somebody stole my car!"

"That's no excuse for vigilantism, Mr. Hawks. Rest assured, we, the law enforcement authorities of Jim Bridger County, will do our best to find your automobile. I'll send out an all-points bulletin soon as I can."

"When?" said Dalton. "Christmas?"

Deputy Harden folded the ticket in two and handed it to

Helen. "Have a good day, Miss Wheeler...or should I say, Miss Brandi LaRue." He slapped the ticket pad on his thigh and smiled. "That's some website you've got going on. I was on it all night."

"Great," said Helen. "I hope you enjoyed yourself."

"Hey, Harden," said Dalton. "How come you're working today? I thought you were just a weekend part-timer when it came to patrolling."

"What do you care?"

"How come Kovaleski isn't on patrol? It's Friday. This is his usual day to work, isn't it?"

Deputy Harden slid the pen back in his pocket. "I'm covering for him. He's doing a radio interview."

"Radio interview?"

"Right down the street, at KJBC. Molly Trexler and Don Torrino are talking to him right now about that robbery last night.

"At the pharmacy?"

"Know anything about it?"

"Me?"

"No, your grandma."

"I haven't heard a thing, except for what they said on the radio this morning. Apparently, some old drifter said he saw everything."

"I know. But we need to talk to somebody sober."

"In this town?"

Deputy Harden slapped the Nova's roof. He walked back to the squad car, heels kicking up more Tomahawk dust.

Helen flicked the ticket at Dalton. "My gift to you. Happy early birthday, asshole."

"I guess we're going home now, huh?"

"You guessed right. I'll drop you off."

"But what about my car?"

"What about it?"

"Helen!"

She started the Nova and drove down Enfield and turned by Schulz's Liquors—just in time to catch a glimpse of Dalton's stolen Buick Apollo rolling toward the highway exit.

"There it is!"

"No."

"My guitar is in the trunk!"

"So?"

"I need that guitar."

"Why? You can't play it for shit."

"But I can pawn it." Dalton slumped back into his seat and took a deep breath. "Listen, you were right. I was evicted."

Helen raised her eyebrows.

"Happy?"

She squeezed the steering wheel.

"I have no place to stay."

"I just want to go home, Dalton."

"So do I."

"I'm sorry."

"Please? We can catch right up to it. It'll be easy."

Helen pulled over and crossed her arms. "I said, no."

From the opposite direction, an old black semi lumbered over the railroad tracks. A 1977 Mack. Ten-speed transmission. Sleeper cab. 5,800-gallon tank of gasoline in tow. The driver plainly visible. A woman.

Dalton read Helen's mind.

"I'll give you half," he said. "That guitar is a vintage Martin D-45. It'll fetch at least two grand."

Helen lit a cigarette as the truck cleared the tracks.

"We can catch it. My Buick's a wreck. It's hard to start."

"But it started."

"The needle is damn near on empty. We can catch it at the

nearest gas station. All I have to do is nab the guitar from the trunk." Dalton reached into his pocket. "See, I've still got the keys."

"Just the guitar?"

"Just the guitar. I'm telling you, it's worth more than the Buick."

Dalton leaned forward and watched the Buick turn onto the exit ramp.

"A thousand dollars?" said Helen.

"Truck-driving school. A CDL, if we catch up to it."

"Link said——"

"*Please?*"

"A thousand, huh?"

"Promise."

"This might be the worst decision I've made since I dropped out of high school to go work at the Waffle House."

PART TWO

CHAPTER FIFTEEN

They shot down the highway.

The Nova's tires gummed to the asphalt, already hot and sticky from the sun's infernal blaze. From an airplane, the car probably looked like an ant rolling across the expanse behind a trail of similar ants, traveling over a land that time had forgot.

The Battlesmoke Highway was new, but it too seemed old—like it had always been there since mastodons and saber-toothed tigers trod upon the continent.

Even before that.

Eons ago, in an age before man or even time existed, what was now Jim Bridger County had been a seabed, an inland ocean filled with toothy sharks and gigantic eels. Creatures that swam and ate one another and then died and sank to the bottom.

When the sea receded, the nutrient-rich ocean bed was slowly heaved up and carpeted in snow and ice, and then ground back down into grasslands. And then the Arapaho immigrated into the locale, and behind them French trappers, and then covered wagons, and then soldiers, and then the railroad, which brought in settlers and supplies by the thousands.

And one day after World War II, the Battlesmoke Highway was constructed—by prison labor, sweaty inmates with knife scars and missing teeth who would have rather stayed in their cells like caged animals and smoked cigarettes and drawn artwork on its pitted gray walls.

Instead they, at gunpoint, constructed the Battlesmoke highway. A stretch of road traveled only by the desperate. Zombied gas-station attendants, doll-eyed hitchhikers. An environment of hungry coyotes, spiraling hawks, and greasy diners where waitresses floated about the tables pouring coffee brewed by the Devil himself. Here, in these lonely cafes with broken air-conditioners, truckers filled their paperwork, their gas tanks, their beer bellies. Here Hell merged with the Earth's crust to the point where it was near impossible to tell one from the other. It was the land that even Death avoided, where forgotten souls wandered like lost children in the Walmart at the center of the Earth.

Helen steered between a post-office truck and a dented Trans Am. A plume of oily smoke billowed from the truck's tailpipe, obscuring her view. She punched the accelerator, and the Nova's engine rattled like a blender full of bottle caps. She swerved into the left lane.

"Hurry," said Dalton.

"I'm trying!"

They smoked by a pickup truck and blazed onward. Dalton squinted through the Nova's dirty windshield. No Buick in sight, just a flatbed trailer hauling a load of concrete sewer pipes.

"See it?" said Dalton.

"Nope."

She gunned the engine and a bullet-riddled road sign swished by Dalton's peripheral.

COMANCHE HILLS 26
BATTLESMOKE 95
OGALLALA 107

Dalton peered into the side mirror. The reflection of Tomahawk's water tower shrunk and dipped beneath the prairie. He was at sea, sailing across an ocean of dead wheat fields, dotted with towns sprouting from the grasslands like little dusty islands populated by one or two Robinson Crusoes in the form of old men on rocking chairs staring into the wasteland.

The ancient seabed now had a new form of fish, in the shapes of eagles, cows, coyotes and retired farmers.

And Tomahawk was just one of thousands of inconsequential little towns, whose inhabitants thought of as the center of the universe.

And as Tomahawk disappeared from the mirror, Dalton wondered what the hell ever kept him there for so long. But the answer was easy: Tomahawk, Colorado was all he knew.

————

The only time he had ever left Tomahawk was back in high school. He was traveling on a school bus to Battlesmoke for his final football game. It was the biggest game Tomahawk High would play that year, the annual showdown between the Tomahawk Warriors and the Battlesmoke Gladiators.

Dalton had scored the Warrior's only touchdown on an interception. His picture made the front page of the *Sentinel*, but Dalton had no recollection of his heroics. He had blacked out immediately after diving into the end zone, football in hand.

But he did have some odd recurring dreams regarding that game. Tacklers colliding into one another. Helmets popping into the air. Ruby MacGonahugh flashing her goodies from the stands. A dismayed Battlesmoke QB sitting on the turf, chin strap dangling from his helmet, breath frosting in the brittle autumn air. The ref, whistle in mouth, raising both his arms at the goal line.

However, the strangest dream involved the football itself. It spiraled toward Dalton in slow motion, but when it reached his hand it was no longer a football. It wasn't a Vick's inhaler either.

It was a whiskey flask.

———

Helen raced by a battered tow truck as she hugged the road's centerline. She straightened the wheel and then eased into the right lane. Dalton watched the asphalt rush under the car. He felt like he was in an old Burt Reynolds movie.

"I wish this thing had a working CB," said Dalton, looking at the Nova's dusty dashboard.

"Cell phones ruined that era," said Helen.

"There's no way you could make a movie like Smokey and Bandit with Burt Reynolds ratchet jawing on a cell."

"10-4, Snowman."

"Speaking of which, do you have one?"

"A cell phone? Well, I *had* one, a real old one—QWERTY keyboard, camera, GPS, the whole bit. I dropped it in the toilet. It's a paper-weight now."

Dalton stared through the windshield. Still no Buick—only a semi lumbering in the left lane. *NAVAJO TRUCKING* was written on the trailer door in big orange letters.

Dalton looked at the Navajo maiden, who looked more Western European than Native American, underneath the company logo. Blue head-feather to match her eyes. She was beautiful, an ideal companion for the lonely road ahead. He pictured himself inside the truck's cab, double-clutching that eighteen-wheeler all the way to Texarkana, hauling missiles or Coors beer or whatever truckers carried in those things.

He imagined himself listening to Dave Dudley on the classic-country radio station, *Six Days on the Road.* He imagined himself sporting big sideburns and a cowboy hat; ordering steak-and-eggs at a truck stop off I-76 and writing his handle—something like Bull Goose or Candy Man or Lone Wolf—on the back of bill for any lonely waitress who cared to get in touch with him via CB.

Helen twiddled the radio dial. "This thing work?"

"How would I know," said Dalton as he gazed at the endless prairie surrounding them. He hoped they didn't break down or throw a rod or something like that. The highway was in poor condition, potholed and littered with beer bottles and smut magazines. Abandoned cars lay rotting on the road's shoulder, their good parts (tires, carburetors, fuses, fuel pumps, alternators) long ago scavenged by tow-truck drivers with bib-overalls and bushy beards.

Helen turned on the radio and the opening riff for *Streets of Bakersfield* twanged from the car's blown speakers. "Now, that's what I call country music." She chimed into the chorus, swooping up a perfect fifth, and nailed the harmony.

How many of you that sit and judge me ever walked the streets of Bakersfield?

"The great one himself," said Dalton. "Buck Owens and his Buckaroos."

"I don't mean to brag," said Helen. "But did you hear that harmony?"

"Yes, yes...you're very good."

"You know, it would have behooved you to have put me in the Tomahawk Tornados. Don't you think?"

"Twisters."

"You might have got signed."

"Maybe."

"But you had to have that stage all to yourself."

Dalton squirmed into the seat. He never had Helen's pipes, and his band was too inexperienced to be any good. It was comprised of Jac Lu on guitar, Darnell on drums, and Mrs. O'Leary's husband, Danny, on bass. But they'd been getting the hang of it...slowly but surely.

There was no room for slop in a country band, and the Tomahawk Twisters found that out the hard way. All the parts had to be locked in like Lego pieces. The bass lines had to thump exactly over the kick drum. The guitar had to mimic the bass and then stab short fills between the vocal phrases. The drummer had to be a metronome. Good country bands functioned like Swiss clocks. The Twisters sounded like an old tractor ready for the junk heap.

But the band's sound improved. Except for Dalton. He was too self-conscious. No matter how tiny the venue, his nerves always bested him.

He'd finally quit.

However, Dalton had always believed that it was playing in a band, no matter how crappy, that had attracted Helen to him. After all, he was doing something that she wanted to do. And Dalton figured that by getting friendly with him, Helen had put herself closer to a secret dream of being a performer herself. There was no other explanation. When it came to looks, body and brains, Helen was out of his league.

They passed the Navajo truck from its right, and a white car in front of it appeared. The exit sign for Comanche Hills zipped by.

FOOD, LODGING, GAS

"Comanche Hills, Dalton. You're going to have to kiss your

Buick and that Martin goodbye. Game's over. I'm turning around as soon as we hit that exit."

"I think that's it."

"Your car? Where?"

"Up ahead, in the left lane."

The car drifted into the right lane. Helen hit the accelerator and the Buick's telltale dented bumper came into view.

"Now what?" said Helen.

"We get my guitar."

Helen let off the accelerator. "How?"

Dalton closed his eyes and thought. He thought real hard, as hard as Einstein did when wrote his paper about General Relativity. But nothing came to Dalton because his hangover had turned his brain into peanut butter. Or maybe it was the Vick's inhaler. Maybe it had fried his ability to reason. Maybe that's why he couldn't get a decent job. Or maybe it was because of the mercury fillings he had as a kid. He opened his eyes just as the Buick merged onto the exit ramp.

"I told you," said Dalton. "I bet they need gas."

"So what's the plan?"

"I'm still thinking."

Helen signaled and chased the Buick up the ramp.

CHAPTER SIXTEEN

An old red-and-white metal sign hung from the gas station's awning and it creaked and groaned as it swung back and forth in the hot afternoon breeze.

COMANCHE GAS & GROCERIES
NO CHECKS

Comanche Gas and Groceries: a quiet filling station, where Jim Bridger County's old men came to live out their final days and watch people fill their tanks and spend their change on sunflower seeds or cigarettes or a BJ Thomas cassette and then climb back into their cars and drive off while they listened to *Hey, Won't You Play Another Somebody Done Somebody Wrong Song*, leaving those old men to look out the window and stare at the empty landscape with too much time to think about the girls they'd blown it with, the jobs they could have had, the property they should have snatched up, the talents they should have pursued—pursuits that seemed insignificant at the time, but grew like rainforests in their imaginations, obscuring all the things they really spent their time doing, which was thinking and dreaming about things they'd never done.

The car rumbled into the station. Dalton eyeballed the Buick, trying to get a look at the driver. But the angle of the glaring sun made it impossible. He was sure that this thief, like all thieves, was a person of the lowest order: a drooling ape with a brain swimming in alcohol and drowning in dope.

Car thief? Who would do such a thing? thought Dalton.

A man of no conscience, that was who.

That pesky conscience, he thought, that irritating sense of right and wrong.

How much easier life would be without it. But it was the conscience, he figured, that separated man from beast. It was the conscience that pulled people out of the swamp, the cesspool of existence. It was not intelligence or the lack of it that made a person human. It was that sense of right and wrong.

He stared at the Buick. Despite its age and its poor condition, he felt at one with that car. It had been the one constant in his life. He had seen old photographs of him inside it, as a baby in his car seat. Pictures of him sitting on the hood with Elston. The car barely ran even then, so he didn't drive it much. But he'd wash it from time to time and occasionally change the oil or put air in the tires.

Mostly, he would just sit behind the wheel, with the engine off, when he had time to think about what to do with his life. But he never knew what to do. Some people, he had thought, were just born to ramble until something good happened to them, like winning the lottery or maybe getting drafted.

Dalton ground his teeth and looked at the Buick, still trying to get a glance at the man behind the wheel.

Helen had parked the Nova next to a restroom beside a broken payphone. The receiver was gone, and its cord dangled uselessly. Everything at the gas station seemed to be broken.

The brown field behind the station was filled with junk: refrigerators, tires, broken tractors, and even a tow truck. It had been rusting there for decades and would probably be sitting there for decades to come.

"Now what?" said Dalton.

"You're the one who said it would be easy." Helen reached over Dalton's lap, fished inside the glove box, and found a roadmap. "Hide behind this. You can pretend you're lost."

She grabbed the *Tomahawk Sentinel* from the dash and slouched behind the steering wheel. Dalton unfolded the roadmap. A red hand-drawn line ran across the map from Colorado to California, tracing I-76 to I-70 to I-86, connecting Tomahawk to Fresno. *Or maybe Link bought the map in Fresno and marked his return route Tomahawk*, thought Dalton.

"Look," said Helen, peering over her paper, "he's getting out."

Dalton peaked over the map, shielding his eyes from a glare that reflected from the Buick's rear window. The thief climbed out and shut the car's door. He had a wiry build and was dressed in baggy jeans, a wife-beater shirt, steel-toed boots, and a blue bandana. A tattoo was visible on his shoulder. *86th STREET*. Dalton had seen that tattoo before.

The visiting room at the prison? The guy next to me? Didn't he have a blue bandana?

A pump-action rifle flashed in his head. A bullet. It traveled in slow motion, spiraling toward him like that damn football. It was like there were two people in him, and the other guy had all the information but could only communicate with cryptic daydreams and pictures.

"Recognize him?" said Helen.

Dalton blinked and rubbed his head. The bullet vanished. "I might have seen him at the jail earlier."

"I think it's Lupe Mendocino."

"You know him?"

"Sort of." She folded the newspaper and set it on the dashboard. "He's one of Link's prison buddies. He was part of the Mendocino drug ring, but he got caught after one of their meth labs blew. It wasn't too far from your friend Darnell's place."

"Meth labs..."

"They blow up all the time. Those people who build them really don't know as much about chemistry as they think they do."

"I don't remember an explosion by Darnell's place."

"It was couple of years ago, about the same time the hardware store went up. It was all over the paper. The radio blabbed about it for weeks."

"Huh."

"You should read the newspaper once in a while. You'd be surprised at what goes on in Tomahawk."

"I read it this morning," said Dalton. "Kovaleski's running for mayor, and he wants to oust our current mayor."

"What was wrong with our mayor?"

"She posed for *Hustler*. Apparently, you have to hold yourself to certain standards to be in public office."

"You know, sometimes a girl's go to do what to do what she's got to do, even if it's embarrassing and looked down upon."

"Uncle Elston says she was just flaunting what God gave her, couldn't resist, had to show the world."

"It worked. She's out of debt."

"She might be out of office, too. Sheriff Kovaleski's saying how she's morally unqualified for office, a bad example for young people."

"She's way more qualified than him, probably the most qualified person in Jim Bridger County. She was a social worker once, and she understands how to help people and get their lives turned around, instead of just mocking them."

Dalton stared out the window. Now or never he told himself.

He unfastened the seatbelt and cracked open the door.

"Dalton, what are you doing?"

"We came for my guitar, didn't we?"

"Listen, you don't know Lupe. He's not just any run-of-the-mill car thief. He's a hardened criminal. Link told me that Lupe once ran with a street gang in back LA. He could be seriously violent."

"So what do we do?"

"Call the police."

Dalton looked at the broken payphone, and Helen watched Lupe unscrew the gas cap. He set it on the Buick's roof and began pumping. Dalton figured unless Lupe decided to drive away without paying, he would have to go inside to settle up. He could nab the guitar then.

But then why not just take the whole car while I'm at it? I've got the keys. Hell, what am I thinking?

"Okay, same plan as before," said Dalton. "He's going to have to go inside and pay, right?"

"And?"

"And when he's inside, I'll just run out and snag the guitar from the trunk. Easy."

"Sounds good."

"But, now that I'm thinking of it, I may as well take the whole car while I'm at it."

"And then?"

"And then you just follow me home."

"I don't know, Dalton. I say we just get out of here."

"We've practically got him cornered. Once he's inside the station, it'll be easy."

"Dalton, you don't tangle with people like Lupe. Chalk up your losses, or let the police handle it."

"He's got my guitar—and he's got my car."

"And he's probably got a gun. Don't get yourself killed over a guitar that you can barely play."

"But Helen——"

"No buts."

"But I can take him!"

Dalton had no idea why that thought popped into his head. But the more he studied Lupe, the more convinced he was that he could beat Lupe's ass over the state line and into Ogallala. It was as if the other man sleeping inside of him had told him so. He could feel that man stirring, reaching for a can of proverbial whip-ass, although in his case it resembled a can of Coors.

But then the situation got complicated.

There was a second man in the car.

"The hell?" said Dalton, shielding his eyes against Buick's glare.

A big man with a handlebar mustache climbed out from the Buick's passenger seat. He put on a cowboy hat.

"Zeke?" said Helen.

He pulled a roll of bills from his pocket and strolled toward the store.

"Fuck!" screamed Helen. "Zeke's a car thief?"

"What did you expect? That he was leading a Boy Scout troop in his spare time?"

"He told me he was a truck driver. He told me he'd help me pass my CDL test. He promised to take me on the road with him and show me how to drive. And he——"

"He helped steal my car."

Helen pounded the steering wheel and fought her tears.

Dalton bit his lip and watched Lupe pump the gas. A new imaged flashed into his head: a man with a blue bandanna being hurled into a dumpster. He had a gold tooth.

I must be nuts...or maybe there's something to these weird-ass visions after all. He pushed the door open and stepped out the car.

"Dalton, what are you doing? He's not even in the gas station."

"Stay put. *I'll* handle it."

"Are you crazy?"

"As a matter of fact."

Dalton closed the car door. He squared his shoulders and marched across the pavement. The image of the man being hurled into a dumpster burst back into his brain. *He* had thrown that man into the dumpster.

Dalton kept walking, his footsteps matching the creak and groan of the swinging red-and-white sign.

And then the Evel Angel appeared. "You crazy, kid? You're in no condition for this kind of action. He'll beat the living shit out of you!"

I can take him.

"Not yet. You're not up to it!"

Shut up! He stole my car and my guitar. And I can take him.

"Listen to me, kid. You can still turn around. Even I had more sense than to jump the Grand Canyon. It's okay to change your mind. You've got to pick your battles. Listen to her, goddammit. Get back in that car. You're not primed!"

But Dalton was tired of listening. He had been evicted and his car had got stolen and he couldn't find a job and he was sick of being nice. He stepped under the metal awning and tapped Lupe on the shoulder.

"Sir," he said.

"Yeah, what?" said Lupe.

"I believe this is my car..."

Lupe smiled.

Gold tooth...

Dalton smiled back.

WHAM!

Lupe's fist smashed into Dalton's nose. He stumbled and gasped. *BOFF!* A steel-toed boot between the legs. Dalton winced, wheezed...wobbled, dropped like a sack of cement. Helen scrambled out of the Nova. Lupe jumped inside the Buick and blasted the horn. Zeke ran out from the store.

"What the hell?"

"Zeke. Get in!"

Helen knelt by Dalton's side and rolled him over. His nose was swollen, blood trickled down his chin.

"You're hurt!"

The Buick's doors slammed shut. The tires squealed and the gas cap rolled off the roof. Helen jumped up and Dalton's head smacked against the asphalt. She picked up the gas cap and hurled it at the Buick.

"You bastard, Zeke!" she screamed. "I'll get you for this! Don't think I won't!"

She wiped the tears from her eyes and returned to Dalton. She tugged his shirt and shook him. "Talk to me!"

Dalton's eyes opened. He didn't know where he was, or who he was. He didn't recognize Helen's blurry image.

"Dalton...DALTON!"

"I can take him."

She helped Dalton into the car.

"Lucky punch," groaned Dalton.

"Let me get some paper towels, get that blood off your nose."

Helen ran inside the station. The old man behind the window sold her some paper towels, along with some sunflower seeds and a BJ Thomas cassette.

CHAPTER SEVENTEEN

Helen handed Dalton a wad of paper towels. "Hold these to your nose. Jesus, what were you thinking? He could have killed you!"

"I was—"

"Never mind," she sighed. "Get in the car."

Helen hauled Dalton to his feet just as the cashier walked outside.

"Everything okay?" he hollered.

"Just fine," said Helen. "He got dizzy, that's all."

"Hey, who were those guys in that other car? They peeled off and didn't pay for the gas or the potato chips or the tape cassette or nothing!"

"Couple of assholes," said Helen. "Dipshits who need to be locked up!"

Helen dragged Dalton to the car, strapped him into the seat, started the car, and drove up the exit ramp toward Battlesmoke.

"I think I've had enough," said Dalton. "We probably should go back."

"I'm going to murder that jackass, Dalton. I'll get that

sumbitch if it's the last thing I do. And I don't care if they drive all the way to the North Pole."

She gunned it, and the Nova climbed to seventy miles an hour. They passed a banged-up Dodge Dart and a tractor-trailer hauling a John Deere combine.

Dalton held the paper towels to his nose and wondered what had possessed him to pick a fight with that man.

Vicks?

He had seen an episode on TV about people with multiple personalities when he was a teenager. After a segment about UFOs and cattle abductions, there was a story about a woman—a church-going mother of three named Jonie—who had been indicted for shoplifting cosmetics and attacking her husband with a weed whacker. But Jonie had no memories regarding her doppelganger and what it did after she fell asleep or when she got stressed. Jonie would black out and "Patsy," her evil doppelganger, came out to play and to rob department stores and to chase her husband with gardening tools.

Dalton was becoming convinced that somebody else was living inside him, too—a secret personality who climbed out from the basement of his being while he was asleep. And God knows what that guy was up to, but apparently he liked chopping trees in the middle of the night.

And maybe, just maybe...he liked booze. He thought about all that hooch in the back of the Buick.

...lots and lots of booze.

Helen's hand squeezed his shoulder. His skin tingled, just like old times.

"You sure you're all right, Dalton?"

"I think so."

"Do I need to take you to the hospital? You might have a concussion."

"I'll be okay."

"You might feel okay at first, but then you might start getting and dizzy and forgetful and—"

"No, I'm okay. Really."

She let go of his shoulder. "I don't know what you were thinking, picking a fight with a gangster like that. You're lucky he didn't beat you with a baseball bat, or shoot you." She pushed the cigarette lighter in and then handed Dalton more paper towels. "Here, keep the pressure on. It's still bleeding"

She gunned the engine and swerved into the left lane.

"You can slow down, Helen."

"I'm going to get that bastard!"

"Zeke? He sure turned out to be a real winner."

She pushed the gas pedal to the floor. "Shut up."

Dalton held the towels to his nose and tilted his head back. "So what line did he use?"

"Zeke didn't use any pickup lines."

"Really?"

"I just thought he was nice."

"He didn't reel you in with some insane lie about how great he was?"

They passed the flatbed with the concrete sewer pipes and Dalton looked down the road. No Buick. Just a post office truck and a camper...and a growing thundercloud on the horizon.

"Okay," said Helen. "Zeke told me he was a truck driver. You happy now?"

"Surprise, surprise. Well?"

"Well what?"

"And did he show you his truck? His *big rig?* Did he take you for a *long haul?*"

"None of your business." She pulled a cigarette from her pocket, clenched it between her teeth, and yanked the lighter from the socket. "I'm going to beat that bastard with a tire iron. Car thief...and right out of my own driveway! I'm surprised he didn't try to steal *this* thing, runs a hell of a lot better than yours. What would Zeke want with your shitty-ass car?"

"Maybe because it's vintage piece of American muscle."

"If it's so great, then why are you more worried about the guitar? Why not pawn or sell the car instead?"

"Because that guitar doesn't need thousands of dollars' worth of repairs. It's amazing that it's gone this far without exploding into a ball of flames."

Dalton removed the towel from his nose. The bleeding had stopped. His nose was not broken. But the back of his head hurt like hell. He leaned back and watched the prairie roll by.

A tumbleweed blew over the barbwire fence lining the highway and bounced across the road. Dalton wondered how far the tumbleweed had traveled. Maybe all the way from Oklahoma.

He focused on Helen. The surrounding prairie complimented her soul perfectly. Like Colorado's high plains, she was simple, raw, and seductive. But also just as vast—and as dangerous. Hers was the land of the red-tailed hawk, the sagebrush, the low-hanging harvest moon—an unpredictable prairie environment that could go from serene beauty to tornadoed fury in an instant.

"What are you looking at?" said Helen.

"You."

"Stop."

"Sorry."

Dalton reached for the newspaper on the dashboard. He read the *Sentinel's* headline. *WARRIORS WIN*. A black-and-white picture featured the quarterback flashing a bright all-American smile and pointing his index finger toward the sky. Big news in Tomahawk. They had beaten the Battlesmoke Gladiators for the first time in seventeen years.

The last time they won, it had been Dalton's picture on the

cover. Just a dazed look. And shortly after the game, he had passed out. The *Battlesmoke Bugler* had plenty to say about that. It was discovered that somebody had spiked the Warriors' Gatorade cooler with whiskey. *GLADIATOR'S VICTORY ROBBED IN CHEATING SCANDAL!* screamed the *Bugler* headline. Although, nobody believed it. Liquor is rarely considered to be performance-enhancing, no matter what the activity.

Whiskey, thought Dalton. Who would have done such a thing? Ruby MacGonahugh probably. Probably wanted to get the players drunk so she could love them up in her big-ass pickup truck.

Dalton stared at the brown landscape, broken up by a cluster of gloomy cottonwoods or a junk pile. Occasionally, they'd pass the carcass of an old abandoned farmhouse that seemed poised to collapse with the slightest breeze. Further down the highway, they drove by the large natural gas containers that dotted the sage-brushed landscape. Dalton wondered if the farmers made money off the gas under the land. Maybe they even rented the land to energy companies and collected money from them, too. Then there were cows, lines of cows eating out of feed troughs. And there was just more empty land.

The cloud on the horizon had grown bigger, darker. He switched the radio back on.

Helen read his mind. "Looking for the weather report? That cloud's got tornado written all over it."

Dalton twitched the dial, skipping by an ad for cattle feed, and finally landed on KJBC's signal. Don Torrino and Molly Trexler were recapping the day's headlines.

"—and Jim Bridger County Sheriff Dale Kovaleski has officially put in his bid for mayor of Tomahawk," said Don.

"With the way things are going for Mayor Starr," said Molly, "he's a shoe-in. Dismal times indeed in Tomahawk's mayoral history."

"But hardly the worst," said Don.

"Did you hear she posed for a men's magazine? And please, Don, don't tell me you have that issue."

"I admit, I did see the front cover behind the register at the gas station, and it featured our lovely bikini-clad mayor on a Harley Davidson."

"Yowzah!"

"Hey, when you got it, flaunt it. May as well, right?"

"I disagree, Don. There must be a way for women in this county to achieve their financial goals without debasing themselves. It's the 21st Century!"

"I see your point, Molly. And I promise I did not buy that issue."

"Thank you, Don."

"It's never too late to mend one's ways. Anyway, what else is new in Jim Bridger County?"

"As we reported earlier, Don, the Tomahawk Vigilante has struck again. And this time just down the street from our studio at the Stevenson Pharmacy, where a box containing a hundred packets of cold medicine was stolen."

"You know, Molly, this is sounding more and more like another methamphetamine story to me."

"Indeed it does, Don. And coming up after the break, we'll have an interview with the sheriff——"

Dalton turned off the radio and stared at the billowing cloud, which loomed like an airborne Kraken on the horizon. The cloud flashed. His arm hairs shivered. Bad weather always weirded him out, especially lightning storms. It made him long for his mommy.

Whoever she was.

CHAPTER EIGHTEEN

December 24, 1983

"Uncle Elston, what was my mom like?"

Elston's eyes veered from the Christmas Eve football game on TV (the Denver Broncos were being waxed 31 to 7 in Seattle's Kingdome). He looked at his nine-year-old nephew, who was playing with a toy Evel Knievel Stunt Cycle—an early Christmas gift. A small ramp, made of books and a wooden plank, lay in front of the Christmas tree. A toy train circled the tree and several empty beer cans.

"Well," persisted Dalton, "doesn't anybody know where she lives?"

"Let me show you something," said Elston. He got up from his ratty La-Z-Boy recliner and pulled out a wallet with a chain attached to it. He sat back down, opened the wallet, and produced a faded photograph. The picture was folded in half. "The beautiful Wendy Hawks, one year before you were born, Dalt. We were at a Glen Campbell concert down in Denver when I took this. She loved the hell out of that guy, always used to say to me, 'Elston, I don't give a hoot what you say about

Merle Travis, Glen Campbell is the greatest guitar player ever.' I'm surprised you're not a fan yourself."

Elston suddenly flew out from the La-Z-Boy. "Goddammit, Elway," he said, yelling at the TV. "Throw it to a teammate— just for once!"

"Uncle?"

"What?"

"You showed me this picture before."

Elston sat down and sighed.

"I know what she looks like. I was just wondering what she was like, and where she lives."

Elston emptied a small shooter of Jim Beam into a beer can. "You want the truth, I suppose."

"Yes," said Dalton.

"The truth." He took a chug from the turbo-charged can of Schlitz. "Alright, I'll give it to you—if that's really what you want."

"What happened to her?" asked Dalton, studying the photo. The paper it was printed on was cracked and faded, but he could tell she had sandy hair and inviting blue eyes.

"Your mother," continued Elston, feeling a lump in his throat. "She...uh...boy...well, she went insane shortly after you was born."

"Insane? Is that like, crazy?"

"I hate to put it those terms."

"So what happens when you're crazy?"

"Now that's a question. Well, insanity is sort of like a breakdown of the brain. Her head just kind of conked out, like your Huffy did after the chain busted. Remember that? In a way, a chain in her head snapped and the gears of her brain just went out of control and rolled around and around with nothing to latch on to."

"She had a bike chain in her head?"

Elston rubbed his eyes. "It's a metaphor."

"A metaphor?"

"Yes. It's a mental picture that makes sense out of something you can't see, like God or an atom."

"An *Adam*?"

"What I mean to say is whatever went wrong with your mother's head was like the day when the chain fell off your bike and you couldn't put the brakes on after you went off that ramp and crashed into that pile of lumber and landed on that screw that put a hole in your leg, which subsequently sent you to the doctor for three stitches and me to the bank for a two-hundred-and-forty-three-dollar draining of my savings account."

Dalton rubbed his leg.

"Anyway," continued Elston. "I'm just saying that her head was like that busted chain, and it caused the bicycle of her brain to crash into a pile of lumber...a mental pile of wood, so to speak. And after it crashed into all that wood, it just kept bleeding. Only in her case they couldn't put stitches in it, and there was nothing else they could do. And then they just have to put a person away, before they start drinking too much."

Elston cracked another Schlitz and spiked it with a shooter of Jack Daniels. "Here, let me see that again." He snatched the bent photograph from Dalton and unfolded it. He studied the image of Jack Hawks holding Wendy's hand. "My brother—your daddy—was one lucky asshole. I always wondered what ever happened to ol' Jack."

Dalton pushed his fists into the carpet and stuck to the topic. "If my mom's not dead, then where does she live?"

Elston choked on his beer. "She's in a special place."

"Where?"

"Down the highway, a place called Battle—I mean...a place called Sanitarium City."

"Sanitarium City?"

"That's what I said, Sanitarium City."

"Sounded like you were going to say, Battlesmoke."

"But I meant to say, Sanitarium City. Battlesmoke's full of douchebags."

"What are those?"

Elston handed the picture back. "I'll tell you when you're more grown up."

Dalton set the picture down. He wound the Stunt Cycle's crank and the toy motorcycle zipped from the launcher and down the carpet. It flew up the ramp and flipped over an empty bottle of Old Grand-Dad and sailed over two cans of Olympia and landed solidly on the carpet.

Dalton pumped his fist, and then the Stunt Cycle skidded off a bottle cap and crashed into the train set. He set the train back on the tracks, picked up the Stunt Cycle and packed it into the lunchbox along with the photograph. He looked at Elston again. "So how come we don't go there?"

Elston squirmed into the La-Z-Boy. "Sanitarium City? Are you crazy?" Elston laughed, suddenly getting his own joke. "You never been to Sanitarium City?"

Dalton shook his head.

"Good thing. Those people live like barn animals. But when you're older, maybe we'll pay her a visit. And maybe she'll be better by then. You never know. She might even recognize you, or even me—although for her sake, I hope she don't."

Dalton closed the lunchbox. "So she'll get better?"

"Perhaps. Right now she wouldn't recognize you from Adam."

"Adam...he's a metaphor, right?"

"No, he's an expression. Oh, fer Petesakes, Elway, throw it to the end zone! No-no, not that way! Shit, five million a year and he throws an interception on *first* down?"

"Give him a chance," said Dalton. "It's just a game."

"Oh, really? Just a game. Well, aren't you all grown up all of a sudden? Just a game. If it were only *just* a game!" Elston stared at the ceiling, covered his face with his hands, and moaned. "Why does this shit always happen to me?" He guzzled his last beer and crushed the empty can on his thigh.

"Uncle?"

"What?"

"Does everybody go insane?"

"Of course," said Elston. "Christ, look at *me*. Damn, if I ain't in for a heap of trouble. I'm going crazy just thinking about it."

"Trouble? What kind of trouble?"

Elston pointed at the TV set, an old Zenith perched on four spindly wooden legs. "See that pathetic score there? All I asked for was a ten-point spread. I'll have hell to pay. My damn bookie's going to put me debtor's prison for life."

Dalton smiled. "Elston, only the cops can put you in jail."

"That's the problem," said Elston. "My bookie *is* a cop. And now that bastard's running for County Sheriff. I'm doomed, Dalton. Doomed!"

Dalton stared at Elston.

"I'm sorry, Dalt. You're too young for me to be dumping this kind of grown-up baloney on you. But that's the way the world works: the older and wiser a man gets, the more juvenile and stupid the situations are that he gets himself into. You may as well learn that right now—not that it'll do you one lick of good in the future."

Dalton opened the lunchbox and glanced at the photograph. He noticed an arm next to his mother's side. The arm had a snake tattoo on it, a cobra. He unfolded the picture, wanting to know whom the arm belonged to. He had a pretty good guess. He had seen pictures of that man and his tattoo before.

He didn't need to see the same stony stare, the same crooked smile, the same greasy Peterbilt trucking cap. The same snake tattoo. And although Dalton didn't know much about the man in the photograph, he knew one thing: he was the man who'd driven his mama crazy.

And he was the one who ran away.

He disappeared soon after his mother was sent to the insane asylum. And Dalton, on that Christmas Eve in 1983, decided that when he got big, he was going to lift a bunch of weights and learn kung fu and ride a motorcycle just like Evel Knievel, and he was going to find that man and kung fu the daylights out of him——that mean-eyed dirty dog he was supposed to call, *daddy*.

CHAPTER NINETEEN

A raindrop fell through the cloud and was blown back up again by a windy updraft. The drop froze and fell back down, and another updraft blew it back into the cooler air above. The wind gusts inside the cloud picked up and blew with hurricane force. The icy raindrop continued to bounce up and down inside the cloud's updrafts like a piece of popcorn until it grew to the size of a golf ball.

When it finally became too big and heavy, it plummeted toward the speeding Nova. It smashed down on the windshield and was then followed by millions of its hailstone brethren.

The wind picked up and Helen cleared the smashed hailstone with the windshield wipers. In front of them, a post-office truck and a Greyhound bus pulled over under an overpass near the Battlesmoke exit.

Helen slowed the car and Dalton rolled up the window as another gust shot across the highway. Then the thundercloud opened its floodgates, and suddenly they were driving through a car wash.

"Holy shit," said Helen. "I can't see a thing!"

"Pull over."

Helen eased over to the road's shoulder and stopped. A milk van pulled up behind them and the driver turned on the headlights. The din of hailstones hit the roof like machine-gun fire.

"We'll just have to wait this one out," said Dalton.

"We'll never catch up to that Buick now."

The windshield misted, and Dalton wondered what would happen if he didn't get the guitar back. He contemplated living life on a park bench or in a homeless shelter. Lightning flashed. Dalton's skin tingled.

Dalton looked at a crushed can of Budweiser on the side of the road, and he rubbed his lips. A beer seemed suddenly seemed like a good idea, when...

ZZZ-BAM!

The lightning lit the highway up like a slot machine, and the Nova's roof rattled even more.

"Jesus!" said Helen. "That was way too close, Dalton. Dalton?"

Dalton didn't hear her. He stared out the window, mesmerized by the rain splattering on the Nova's windows—the same way it had during the school-bus ride to Battlesmoke seventeen years earlier.

What a game.

———

There was lightning that day, too. A single strike—rare for October—had struck the scoreboard (Gladiators 3, Warriors 0) and was followed by deafening boom of thunder. And after a timeout, and all declared safe, Coach Roach extinguished his cigarette and turned to the sidelines. He clapped his hands.

"Okay, men," he said, "light show's over. Now let's get out

there and give 'em hell! Think positive. We're only three points down. We can still win this. Hey, Hawks, wake up! This is no time to space out, Dalton. Focus!"

"Yes, coach."

Coach Roach walked up to Dalton and squeezed his shoulder. "You look a little pale, son."

"I'm okay."

"You dehydrated? Need some water?"

Dalton put on his helmet. "No, really. I'm okay."

"Come on, Hawks, it was just a little bit of lightning. You'll be all right."

"I'm fine," insisted Dalton, trying to calm his shaking hands. Lightning always had ignited some primal cavern in his being.

"Good. Now let's show these Gladiators how to play football. You'll remember this game for the rest of your life. Get out there and show these bastards what we're made of!"

"Yes, coach."

"And Dalton."

"Yes?"

"This could be your moment."

Dalton tightened his chin guard and Coach Roach handed him a paper cup.

"What's this?"

"Gatorade, Dalton. Drink up. It's important to stay hydrated. Here, have another."

Dalton remembered gulping down the Gatorade. He remembered that it had an odd taste. He had looked into the stands. About forty-five of the Warriors faithful had shown up. Ruby MacGonahugh, sitting at the topmost bleacher, was looking at him, almost studying him.

And then Dalton got distracted by the girl next to Ruby. His heart leapt. What was she doing here at a football game? Did she come just to see him? But then he noticed the guy next to her and his heart sank.

Of course not. Why would she come to see me of all people? God, I'm a dumbass.

Dalton crushed the Dixie cup and he walked out to the field, searching for his position. It dawned on him he didn't know what position he was playing, or even where to stand.

The rest was a blank.

———

Helen shook Dalton's shoulder. "Dalton? You okay?"

"Huh?"

"You zoned out there for a bit. I was worried."

"I was daydreaming."

"Daydreaming? About what?"

"Football."

"Sure you don't have a concussion?"

He rubbed the back of his head. "Who knows."

"Some weather."

The deluge had calmed, and Helen turned on the car's defrost. The fog lifted from the windshield and Helen pointed at the sky. "Oh my God..."

"What?"

"It just got worse."

Dalton stared at the dark cloud as it descended over the road like a toothy sea monster. Helen gripped the steering wheel and bit her lip. The cloud rotated and turned green. Its mandibles opened, and an angry funnel-shaped tongue slithered down to the highway.

"Oh, shit," said Helen.

The tornado touched down, mauling the roadside as it tore toward the post-office truck. More cars and semis skidded to side of the road. Some people stayed put. Others fled and dove into the ditch. Some hid under the overpass, shielding themselves from flying tumbleweeds and roadside trash.

"Dalton!"

"Hang tight."

More hail piled on the windshield and the twister skirted along the roadside. Dalton hoped it would turn to the field. But no luck. The tornado ripped into the post-office truck and sheered the trailer's roof off. A blizzard of letters, bills, and credit-card applications detonated into the air.

Helen closed her eyes and a swirl of envelopes pounded the windshield. The tornado screamed toward the Nova. The car rocked. Dalton forced Helen down on the seat, used his body for cover as the tornado roared overhead.

"Dalton, we're going to die."

"Hold on."

"Dalton!"

"Hold on!"

The Nova shuddered like a giant paint shaker and the tornado whined overhead. The car's roof buckled with a loud *pop*. Dalton held Helen and closed his eyes. He braced himself and grit his teeth. Another *pop*...and then, suddenly, the shaking stopped. The roar diminished, and everything was still and quiet.

Dalton raised his head.

"Is it gone?" said Helen.

Dalton peaked out the windshield. "I think we're okay."

The tornado weaved through a field, grinding up cornhusks and wheat chaff in a swirling funnel of dirt and debris. It moved behind a grain elevator and shrank and then dissipated.

"That was close," said Dalton.

"Too close," said Helen. Her trembling hands fumbled for a cigarette, but the pack was empty. She turned on the defrost and the wipers and cleared the sheet of hail and letters from the windshield. She blinked. "Am I going nuts? Wasn't that thing behind us?"

"What thing?"

"That milk van. It's in front of us! Wasn't it behind us?"

The windshield cleared and Dalton saw the van's headlights.

Headlights?

There was a knock on the roof. Helen rolled down the window.

"You folks okay?" said a man in a gray work jacket. A patch was sewn onto the jacket's shoulder, *SUNSHINE DAIRY*.

"I think so," said Helen. "Thanks for checking."

"Wow," said the van driver. "I thought I was a goner. I've been driving this here highway for fourteen years, and I never came *that* close to a twister before. Phew! You need help turning your car around?"

"No," said Helen. "I got it."

"I'll back up and give you some room."

Helen rolled the window up. "What the hell, Dalton. That tornado spun us around!"

Helen started the car and carefully turned the car around. "Unbelievable. And we're alive!"

She steered passed the Greyhound bus and the post-office truck. The truck's driver, dazed but unharmed, leaned against the side of his rig, gazing at the envelopes and letters piled like snow around the shredded trailer.

"Look, Dalton. That's it, isn't it?"

"What?"

"Up ahead...isn't that your Buick?"

Dalton wiped the remaining fog off the windshield. "It's got to be."

"Well, it's going up the exit ramp."

"The Battlesmoke exit."

A camper—a nice shiny Airstream—squeezed in front of them, cutting off Dalton's view of the exit ramp.

"Battlesmoke," said Helen. She clicked on the turn signal. "How much weirder can this day get?"

CHAPTER TWENTY

Helen followed the Airstream up the exit ramp. Dalton wondered who owned such a nice shiny vehicle. Maybe it belonged to an old semi-famous country singer, a curmudgeon in a jean jacket who traveled from club to club and across the country, living in the camper with a dog and a banged-up Martin guitar. He wanted to be that guy, the sort of guy without a proper day job. And the more Dalton thought about it, he was that guy, minus the dog. Except, he had no money. Having a secret pile of money was usually the key to being happy while living like a vagrant. He didn't care about owning an Airstream. He just liked the idea of being able to afford one.

The Airstream came to a halt, and Helen hit the brake.

"What the hell?" muttered Dalton.

A clanging sound rang from in front of them.

Helen pressed her head against the hot steering wheel. "Oh, for the love of God."

A whistle blew and a freight train thundered toward a crossing gate in front.

"Dammit," he said, trying to look around the Airstream, which suddenly irritated him along with its driver, who he now pictured in boat shoes and a sweater tied around his shoulders—the kind of guy who had hefty retirement savings and who played a foreign-made guitar with battery powered pickups

"Probably plays a fucking Takamine!" he blurted.

"Takamine? What the hell are you talking about?"

"Nothing."

"Pay attention. We're going to lose them. They probably beat the gate."

"We'll find them. Battlesmoke can't be that big."

"How would you know? When have you ever been to Battlesmoke, or anywhere?"

Dalton was going to remind her that he had been to Battlesmoke, seventeen years ago on that high-school football trip. But he didn't have much to tell, except riding through the town on a school bus, nose pressed against the wet, foggy window. He remembered putting on his cleats. He remembered the lightning strike. He remembered Coach Roach lecturing him and then handing him a cup of Gatorade.

But after that, it was all a blank.

He did recall the *Sentinel's* headline the next day. *WARRIORS CONQUER GLADIATORS!* And a few days later, another headline: *TOMAHAWK HIGH'S BIG WIN QUESTIONED.* And then a week later: *GAME FORFEIT. WARRIORS' GATORADE COOLER SPIKED WITH WHISKEY.*

The train rolled by and the rails groaned and undulated under the tonnage of weight. The clanging and banging stopped and the rear engine chugged by. The engineer peered out the window, probably thankful that he lived somewhere else.

The gate opened.

Helen followed the Airstream over the railroad tracks and onto Battlesmoke's main street, Lanyon Boulevard. Dalton looked at a wooden sign just past the tracks.

WELCOME TO BATTLESMOKE. POP. 1,278

Lanyon Boulevard didn't look too much different than Enfield Avenue in Tomahawk. A Best Western, Super-8, Stucky's truckstop, convenience store, liquor store, vacant furniture store, a Wendy's, pickup trucks parked along the roadside.

"I need cigarettes," said Helen, eyeballing the convenience store. "You need anything?"

"Nope. Be quick."

Helen pulled into the dirt parking lot, sloshing through puddles with floating half-melted hail pellets.

SHORTSTOP GROCERIES, read the sign above the store's glass front door. Shortstop...good name for a convenience store, thought Dalton.

Helen climbed out the car and walked inside. Dalton got out and sat on the hail-dented hood. There was a cardboard notice taped to the store's window.

No kitty litter. No matches. No lighter fluid.
No batteries. No rubbing alcohol. No coffee filters.

He scratched his head.

Who'd think a convenience store would have a run on kitty litter?

He steered his eyes from the notice and looked at the *Battlesmoke Bugler*'s newspaper box. The headline, read:

SIPHILLIS OUTBREAK IN GLADIATOR'S FOOTBALL TEAM
TOMAHAWK CHEERLEADING SQUAD TO BLAME?

Probably not, thought Dalton.

Historically, aside from Ruby McGonahugh, Tomahawk

High's cheerleaders were not that interested in athletes, not even their own, much less Battlesmoke's football players. But truck drivers were another story, even if they were from Battlesmoke. Most of the cheerleading-squad seniors on either team were acquainted with the sleeper cabs of every eighteen-wheeler that ever rolled through town: be they Kenworths, be they Internationals, be they Peterbilts, or be they Macks. As a result, Tomahawk's pimply teenaged boys could care less about becoming doctors or lawyers or ball players or country singers or even movie stars.

Trucks were the stuff dreams were made of. Truckers, they believed, got a lot of action. They earned big checks. Some of them even got benefits and health insurance.

You could be your own boss in a truck: wear a cowboy hat, grow a handle-bar mustache, get tattooed, live in hotels, have a waitress pining for you in every truck stop from Tuscaloosa to Baker City.

Dalton thought about it all the time—not about seductive waitresses, but about becoming a truck driver. However, one thing stopped him from getting behind the wheel and the endless roll of American highway: that old family photo of that man with the cobra tattooed on his arm.

That was why Dalton dug ditches and worked menial jobs in restaurants and took part-time work at insurance agencies. It was why he resented truckers, whether they drove Macks, Peterbilts, or Kenworths, or Internationals. It also was why he resented everything from country singers to people who drove Airstreams and played Takamine guitars.

But he was becoming fed up with that line of thinking.

After all, what had any those people done to him?

His, father most of all, had done nothing to him.

———

Helen walked out the store and smacked a fresh pack of Winstons on her palm. "Why did you open the trunk?"

"Huh?"

"Look behind you. The trunk's open."

Dalton peered around the side of the Nova and saw the trunk was halfway open. He slid off the hood, walked around the car, and opened it all the way. "Didn't you tell me that you couldn't open this?"

"The tornado must have loosened it."

Dalton peered inside, and his eyes widened. A shiver ran from his toes to his head. Inside the trunk was a large cylindrical container, looked like a cardboard oil barrel. He read the label.

KREBS BIOCHEMICAL, NELLORE, INDIA. 55 LBS.

Helen peered over his shoulder. "What the hell?"

Dalton squinted and read the label's fine print. "Must be some kind of chemical. Pseudo—"

Helen's eyes widened. "Pseudo-ephedrine? Don't they use that for cold medicine?"

"They also use it to make methamphetamine."

"Jesus," said Helen.

Dalton closed the trunk.

"Well?"

"Well what?"

"We need to call the cops, or we could both be in trouble. Link...I knew there was a reason he didn't want me to drive this. What now?"

"I don't know."

Helen slammed the trunk closed. "Dalton, this shit could get us both in a heap of trouble. You know that, don't you? We need to turn it in."

"After we find my car."

"Are you crazy?"

"Don't talk to me about crazy."

"What are you talking about?"

"Hey, sometimes *I* just got to do what I go to do. Okay, Mrs. Linda Lovelace?"

Helen handed him the keys. "Then you're driving."

They climbed into the Nova and Dalton drove down Lanyon Boulevard. He passed a John Deere distributor and a bar-and-grill, and another vacant furniture store.

WILKIN'S FURNITURE
NO DEAL WE CAN'T BEAT!
TELL 'EM #29 SENT YOU.

That number stuck in Dalton's mind. Twenty Nine. Dalton drove for another block. He passed the Wendy's and made a right on 11th Avenue, the last street before a frontage road, which followed another set of railroad tracks on the outside of town.

Behind the tracks, loomed a large gray-stoned building. Out of space and out of time. It was though an old stone ruin had transported itself out of the medieval ages and planted itself on the prairie. It stood like Dracula's castle, utterly misplaced.

"What's that?" said Dalton, staring at the wrought-iron fence surrounding the mansion.

"Must be Battlesmoke's old sanitarium."

"*Sanitarium?*"

"Yeah, the old insane asylum. It must be. That place was notorious."

Dalton stared at the decaying building.

Sanitarium City...

It reminded him of a painting he once saw in an art book. *The Scream.* And that building seemed to be screaming, or it had died while it was screaming. Or perhaps it had taken the form of its tenants.

(...*Battle—...but I meant Sanitarium City...*)

"Anyway," continued Helen, "it's been condemned for years. It was big news in Jim Bridger County about five years ago when they closed it."

"Why was it condemned?"

"Look at the place, Dalton. Imagine if somebody you cared about got stuck in a dungeon like that?"

(...*Sanitarium City...do you think I'm crazy?*)

"It was declared an abomination after a government raid. Supposedly, it made Bedlam look like Disneyland."

"What happened to all the people inside?"

"Maybe they just moved in with the general population of Battlesmoke. You know, like zombies. I wouldn't be surprised. The attendant at the Shortstop, she was a sight. Bathrobe and slippers—that's all she had on. Hair still in curlers, the whole bit."

"Was her name Maureen?"

"Who's Maureen?"

"The old lady down the hall from me. Her husband played bass guitar in the Twisters, remember?"

"Oh, Danny." She shook her head. "That was too bad about him."

"Turned his liver into cardboard."

"Well, that'll happen when you drink a handle a day for fifteen years."

"He probably couldn't help it."

"Nobody *wants* to drink like that."

There was a row of bulldozers and earthmovers surrounding the premises. They were probably going to level the place. Maybe turn it into a football field and then pretend this hellhole never existed. He imagined dark and dank halls filled with howling nutcases, ironbound and wallowing in excrement.

"Look at the sign on the gate," said Helen. "Now that just says it all, don't it?"

Dalton's eyes drifted to the far side of the corroding iron fence. A blue sign read:

COMING SOON, A WALMART NEAR YOU

He made a right on Arbor Street. He headed back toward 1st Avenue, checking every driveway for a white Buick Apollo. When he reached 1st Avenue, he headed up Birch Street and back toward 11th. On 11th he turned back down Conifer Street. But still no Buick. Just little wooden houses with flags on their porches and beat-up pickup trucks parked in the driveways. Just like in Tomahawk.

Dalton repeated the pattern, moving west to east all the way to Jasmine Street, Battlesmoke's last residential street. He wearily turned back up to 11th Avenue.

Still no Buick.

"We lost them," said Helen. She sighed and stared blankly through the windshield. "Something's not adding up."

A football bounced in front of the car. Dalton stepped on the brake. The ball tumbled onto the sidewalk and rolled against a nearby mailbox post. A boy ran across the street and grabbed the football and spiraled it to another kid down the block.

"Thanks, mister," said the kid with a quick wave

But Dalton ignored him. His eyes had fixated on the lettering on the mailbox next to the car:

W. HAWKS

Helen waved her hands in front of his dazed eyes. "Dalton? Are you okay?"

Dalton leaned out the window and stared at the name and then at the house.

"Oh, Dalton...you're not thinking of going in there are you? Are you?"

CHAPTER TWENTY-ONE

Dalton walked toward the house.

He opened the gate.

The front yard was in shambles. The fence was about to fall over. A trashcan lay on its side. Empty bean cans, beer bottles, pizza boxes, and egg cartons decorated the yard.

Helen rolled down the window. "Dalton, please, let's go home. I mean it. Something isn't right. I feel it in my bones."

Dalton squared his shoulders and knocked on the home's plywood door. He waited. He knocked again, a little louder. There was a flowerpot full of daisies beside his feet. A cookie jar appeared in his mind. And then an image of him as a kid licking a spoon appeared. It was part of a grainy movie, an old reel that had played in his head since he was a boy. It only happened when he thought about his mother. The movie contained images of her wiping his nose, kissing his forehead, bundling him in scarf and hat, and walking him to school.

He didn't know why or how his mind created those images. There was no way she could have walked him to school. According to his uncle, Wendy Hawks had been carted off to the asylum by the time Dalton was two.

Maybe the visions had come from books, comics, movies, and television reruns—shows like *Little House on the Prairie*, *All in the Family*, and *Leave it to Beaver*. And maybe as fact mixed with fiction, the pictures of all those women had melded into one, and Wendy Hawks became a combination of June Cleaver, Laura Ingalls, Mary Magdalene, Edith Bunker, and Wonder Woman.

He figured the memories of his father were also constructed from TV and movie characters—usually, the bad guys.

While his classmates' fathers were hard at work tarring roads or pumping gas or selling lumber, little Dalton had assumed his daddy was out drinking whiskey, destroying planets, foreclosing homes, betraying Jesus, framing Bo and Luke Duke, or ramming a big ugly semi into cars and pushing them onto railroad tracks. And over the years those TV and movie villains also melded into one entity, turning Jack Hawks into a combination of Darth Vader, Lex Luther, Judas, JR Ewing, and Boss Hogg.

The cookie jar vanished. Dalton knocked a third time, wondering how he ever wound up in Battlesmoke—at this address. Perhaps it was fate, in the form of a 1973 Buick Apollo, answering a subconscious yearning to make sure his mother was alive and well. And perhaps she was well now. And perhaps she would kiss his forehead and make him cookies, and then explain why his daddy ran away.

He knocked again. He sighed and stared at the door. He reached for the knob and his guardian angel materialized on his shoulder.

"Go on," said Evel, revving his little Triumph. "You're a grown man! You scared of seeing your own mother? Just like Coach Roach said, 'this is your moment.' Announce yourself. I am Dalton Hawks. And I am your long-lost son!"

Dalton knocked louder and the Evel Angel dissipated.

"Dalton, get back in the car!" yelled Helen.

Dalton turned the doorknob.

"Dalton!"

It was unlocked. He pushed the door open.

"Dalton!"

He was greeted by the smell of cat urine.

"Hello? Anyone home?"

No answer.

He stepped in. Just a ratty couch, a couple of dried up plants, and a coffee table. There was an old manual typewriter on the table. The typebars were jammed together. He freed them and looked at a blank page on the roller. It read, SCENE 1. Nothing else.

In the corner of the room, the TV was on, but the volume was turned down. A program about Roswell on the History Channel. He took a few more steps into the living room and then heard somebody snoring.

His heart froze.

He peered into an adjacent room and saw a woman. She appeared to be in her mid-fifties. She was wrapped in a tattered bathrobe and sleeping on an unmade bed. A half-empty bottle of vodka was nested on a pillow beside her.

This had to be the wrong house.

Poor woman, he thought. What was I thinking? Hell, Hawks was a common enough name in Jim Bridger County and obviously the *W* on the mailbox could refer to anybody: William, Winona, Wyatt, Wilma.

He stepped back into the living room and he felt something rub against the back of his legs. He spun around and saw a black cat behind him.

Meow...

"Well...hello there," said Dalton. He bent down and stroked the cat's mangy fur. "Aren't you a beauty?"

But the cat wasn't that beautiful. A missing eye, an amputated tail, tattered ears. But for a Battlesmoke cat, thought Dalton, it probably wasn't too bad.

He walked into the kitchen, and his boots scrunched on broken glass. The kitchen window had been blown out. There was glass and dirt all over the floor and the sink.

The tornado, probably. Lucky it didn't take the whole roof off.

He rummaged through the kitchen and found a bag of Friskies. He filled the cat's dish, and the cat gulped it down. He poured more food in the dish and filled an empty water bowl.

"Geeze," said Dalton, "aren't you a hungry one, Mr. Kitty? Does nobody ever feed you?"

He walked back into the living room and turned off the TV. Then he noticed an odd scratching noise. *Shtk-shtk...shtk-shtk...shtk-shkt.* Over and over again.

He turned and saw a record spinning on an old turntable. No music, just a scratching needle. He lifted the needle, put the record back into the sleeve, and shoved it into the cover. He flipped the album over.

Glenn Campbell's Greatest Hits.

The album slipped from his fingers and fell to the floor. The room spun around. His stomached turned. He stumbled to the front door, breath sputtering and sweat beading on his forehead. He looked back into the room and saw the woman on the bed.

Impossible! It can't...it can't be!

He staggered outside. He fell to his knees. He gagged and heaved and then vomited on the daisies.

"What the hell's wrong with you?" shouted Helen.

Dalton lumbered toward the Nova.

"What was that all about, Dalton?"

Dalton climbed into the car.

"Nothing," he said. He cranked the window down and spat

out the remnants of puke from his tongue. "I just stepped on some cat shit...I always get sick when that happens."

"So?"

"So what?"

"So who was in there?"

"Nobody. It was a mistake."

Helen looked at the lettering on the mailbox: W. HAWKS. She sighed and squeezed his shoulder. "I'm sorry, Dalton."

Dalton tried to swallow.

"You know, I doubt you're the only Hawks in Jim Bridger County. And that *letter W on the mailbox?*"

"What about it?"

"Shit, Dalton, that could stand for anything: Walter, Wilbur, Wanda—"

"I already thought of that."

"I'm just trying to help."

The shadows on the street lengthened like long spider legs from the setting sun, which lit up the towering clouds in fiery shades of salmon-pink and blue. Even over a ramshackle town like Battlesmoke, that sunset gave a lot of fine European art a run for its money. But all sunsets in Eastern Colorado did that.

The two boys were still passing the football. One of them went out for a deep pass. Dalton was sure visions of the last Super Bowl were playing in the kid's head as he leapt for the ball that just sailed over his fingertips and bounced down the street. A screen door across the street squeaked open, and a woman called the boys in for dinner. They ignored her and made another attempt and a game-winning catch. Dalton rubbed the sore spot on his leg and tried to keep his mind from driving off a cliff.

(*Easy, kid!*)

(*...let's find some place nice... with plenty of bars...*)

"Helen..."

"Yes? What is it?"

"I..."

A bottle rocket whistled over the car and popped.

"Yes, Dalton?"

"I need a drink."

CHAPTER TWENTY-TWO

Helen and Dalton climbed out the car. A breeze blew across the plains and Dalton's nose filled with the smell of ozone and cow manure. To the west, lay Colorado's beef industry: thousands of cows pooping and peeing while they pushed their heads into feed bunks and guzzled a never-ending supply of corn, wheat and distillery grains, creating a thick smell that traveled for miles. The Greeley Wind, some called it.

It usually signaled a cold front.

Helen and Dalton crossed the dirt parking lot toward a neon sign: *Nonnie's Bar-and-Grill. 2-FER-1 PBR's, 3-7PM.* Helen looked at the setting sun. "Looks like we missed happy hour." They entered the bar and seated themselves in a ratty booth by the window.

Nonnie's Bar-and-Grill was as empty as it was dingy. Dalton assumed the happy-hour people must have gone home. Now it was time for the miserable-hour people.

And even most of them had gone.

Dalton suddenly regretted his decision to get a drink. Bars depressed him as of late, especially this one with its cigarette-burnt carpet, the faint smell of bile. Except for a truck driver chatting up a woman seated at the bar, the place was empty. A Hank Williams song twanged from a dusty jukebox.

> *Your cheatin' heart will pine someday*
> *And crave the love you threw away...*

Song-writing perfection, not a chord or a word out of place. Pure sadness.

The old country classic seemed to have been carved by the hand of God himself into an ancient granite tablet and carried down from mountain by a bearded hermit and then finally hand-delivered to the Hillbilly Shakespeare while he was at death's door, for it was the last song he recorded before dying with his Nudie suit in the back seat of an egg-shell blue Cadillac in January of '53.

Dalton rapped his fingers on the table to the song's ironic bouncy two-step beat. He looked out the window while Helen talked to the waitress. He saw the Best Western across the street. Further down, he saw the exit ramp leading to the highway.

The waitress clicked her ballpoint pen. "Two whiskey sours. Anything else?" She rubbed her rounded belly. Dalton figured she was about six or seven months along. Shouldn't she be taking it easy. Shouldn't her husband be doing the work? Chopping logs, stocking up, preparing the homestead for the baby. But maybe she didn't have a husband. Maybe the father ran off with someone else. Or maybe the father was a soldier, shooting people in the desert while he, Dalton Hawks, sat and decided what to drink. Or maybe the pen-clicking waitress was crazy and in denial that she was even pregnant.

He couldn't judge.

Everything had to be taken in context, even shooting people in the desert.

"On second thought," said Dalton. "Could you scratch one of those whiskies?" He picked at some foam poking through a tear in the booth. "I think I'll just stick to plain old coffee."

The waitress clicked her pen. "One whiskey sour and one coffee. Be right back."

"I thought we came here for a drink."

"I changed my mind," said Dalton.

"Have some fun. I'll buy. I know you don't have any money."

Helen raised her eyebrows, waiting for a response. But Dalton just stared at the exit ramp. It was getting dark, and the odds of spotting his Buick were dwindling.

Helen waved her hand in front of Dalton's face. "Hello?"

"Huh?"

"Are you listening?"

"Yes."

And again, she somehow managed to squeeze out another four syllables. "Bullshit."

"What did you say?"

"Never mind," said Helen.

Dalton stared out the window. *Great, here we go with this shit again.*

The waitress came back with a coffee for him and a whiskey sour for Helen. Dalton stared at Helen's drink, and her question finally registered.

"Drinking screws me up," he said. "That's why."

"So you *were* listening."

"I told you."

"Liar."

Dalton sighed.

"Screws you up?" said Helen. "More like it saps your virility. That's weird. Most guys just get hornier."

"No, I just *act* differently when I'm drunk."

"Alert the Harvard Journal of Medicine. Everybody acts different when they're boozed up. That's the whole point! Hell, look what it does to me!"

No kidding, two beers and you climb on men like they were ladders!

Dalton dumped some creamer into his coffee. "I act *way* different, different than most drunks. And I get the feeling that I'm doing some really weird things."

"Weird? Like you try to pull your underpants over your head?"

"Other things. I just can't remember them the next morning."

He looked out the window. A semi approached the exit ramp and turned on its headlights. A motorcycle sputtered by. But no Buick. He sipped his coffee, and his leg began to throb.

"Well if you can't remember anything, how do you know that you're acting all crazy?"

Dalton reached into his pocket. "I found this in my boot this morning."

"A bullet?"

".22 caliber. I had dreams all night about this, and bats and two-by-fours. I was fighting criminals. I was breaking baseball bats. I was catching bullets out of midair. I was throwing people into dumpsters."

Helen laughed. "You, who just got beat to a pulp at that gas station?"

Dalton rubbed his nose. It was still tender. He stuffed the bullet in his pocket, watched the traffic speeding down the highway. *Long way back to Tomahawk,* he thought. And it was getting longer by the minute. He rubbed his eyes and stared at the Best Western.

The waitress came back. "You folks doing okay?"

Helen pointed at her empty glass. "Can I get another one of

these? Dalton, you sure you don't want something with more kick to it?"

"No."

"No? Like you mean you're *not* sure?"

"I'm not sure."

"Get him a beer, a light one."

"Coors?" asked the waitress.

"Sure. He's worried about his figure."

"Like that'll do any good." She patted her tummy. "I drink that stuff by the gallon every day, and I haven't lost a pound yet!"

Dalton imagined all that beer flooding the waitress's womb. He wondered if that was what had turned his genes inside out, a drunk mother. Something that altered his physical response to alcohol. A bolt of lightning flashed across the sky and illuminated the clouds.

His arm hairs stood on end.

Maybe my mother was drinking and then she got struck by lightning and maybe it scrambled up my genetic code and maybe those dreams are real. Ridiculous. Stop it, Dalton—shit like that only happens in comic books.

"Strange isn't it?" said Helen with a yawn. "I mean, what are we doing here? In Battlesmoke?"

"Looking for my car."

"No, no, no," said Helen. "It's deeper than that. I mean, Zeke shows up to my place early this morning with a lump on his head the size of a baseball. And the next thing you know, he steals your Buick."

"So Zeke's a car thief."

"I'm starting to think that it wasn't *your* car that they were after."

"Whose car were they trying to steal?"

"Well, Link's Chevy Nova and your Buick Apollo—they

look a lot alike, don't they?"

"They do. Buick and Chevy are both owned by General Motors, and I once read that GM used the Nova as a template for the Apollo. Supposedly, the only major difference is in the grill and the taillight design."

Helen knocked back her drink. "And even more obviously, your Buick's white—just like Link's car."

"So?"

"So, I think Lupe and Zeke got the cars mixed up. I think they really meant to hotwire Link's Chevy, not your Buick."

"That's crazy," said Dalton. "Who would make a mistake like that?"

"You did, remember? Just this afternoon."

Dalton picked at the loose foam.

"Anyway," continued Helen. "I bet they were after that barrel of ephedrine in the trunk."

"But that barrel's in the Nova, not the Buick."

"Exactly. They thought they were stealing the Nova because they wanted that ephedrine, and while we drove to Darnell's trailer-home in Link's Chevy, either Zeke or Lupe hotwired the only car in driveway—which was your look-alike Buick."

"No way."

"It makes perfect sense."

"What's Zeke want with a barrel of ephedrine?"

"To make methamphetamine. And you know what else?"

"What?"

"I think Kovaleski's got something to do with it."

"He's a sheriff, sworn to uphold the law."

"Like that means anything. And I think that's why he's springing Link out early."

"You've been doing a lot of thinking."

"I have, while you were mucking around in that stranger's

house."

Dalton picked at the foam.

"And you know what else?"

"What?"

"I think Link told Kovaleski about the ephedrine in the trunk. He probably stole it and then hid it in the trunk. Or somebody he knew hid it there. Anyway, I think Kovaleski and Link worked out some kind of get-out-of-jail-early deal."

"Sounds a little far-fetched," said Dalton.

A battered Honda Accord flashed into his head. It fishtailed out of an alley. Dalton rubbed his eyes and the car dissipated.

"Life is far-fetched," said Helen. "The fact that we're even participating in this cosmic shit-show is far-fetched. And this whole day's been far-fetched since you banged on my door."

The waitress returned with the drinks. "Another whiskey sour for you ma'am. And a delicious Coors Light for you, sir."

"Thanks," said Helen. She rattled the ice and took a sip. "Nice girl, don't you think?"

Dalton nodded as he watched the trucker get up from the barstool. The guy just had that look: malnourished, over-smoked, under-slept, brain addled in white-line fever—but completely confident in himself and his trade all at once.

The trucker paid the tab and left with the woman, who leaned drunkenly to his side. Dalton figured she was a sales rep out on the road and that she had finally found her cowboy, and he was going to take her back to his palatial estate—the sleeper cab in his Peterbilt or Mack or whatever he drove.

Dalton looked at Helen. Really looked at her. Her hair. Her eyes. Her lips. Her shoulders, those same shoulders that he used to caress in happier and better days.

Helen put down her drink. "What are you looking at, buster?"

"You."

"Go ahead. Gawk at me all you want. It's not like anyone else does."

"Everyone stares at you."

"Aw, shucks...well, I suppose they do. I suppose it's in the DNA. My mom modeled in underwear and bras and panties before she had me."

"I did not know that."

"And my old man was quite the handsome devil...before—"

Dalton reached across the table and squeezed her hand. Helen stopped talking. He knew what she was going to say. She was going to say, *before he drank himself to death.* And that made him sad. He let go of her hand and watched the beer bubbles stream in thin lines to the top of the mug.

"Are you going to drink that beer or just stare at it?"

"You can have it."

Helen gulped down the beer, and Dalton could tell she was getting her buzz on. Her eyes were glazed. They seemed to look everywhere and nowhere at the same time. He was both irritated and in love with her at the same time. Damn those eyes. They were magnets.

"Hey, Dalton."

Her voice was louder, and it was beginning to slur.

"What?"

"I'm real sorry about your car. I mean that."

"It's okay."

"And I'm sorry about your guitar, too. I shouldn't have teased you about your music. Takes a lot of guts to get up on stage, especially when you're unsure of yourself. I actually kind of admired you for that. You know, come to think of it, I'm probably just a little jealous. I never had the courage to get up there like you did."

"But you've actually got talent, Helen."

"Talent, schmalent. It's guts that I admire, Dalton. I guess that's why I liked you. You were doing something that I was too scared to do."

Helen leaned back and looked out the window. A neon sign lit up across the street.

BEST WESTERN
$39.95
FREE CABLE
CONTINENTAL BREAKFAST

"Hey, Dalton."

Dalton looked at the empty beer and whiskey glasses on the table. "Yeah?"

Helen leaned toward him and knocked over the empty beer mug with her elbow. Dalton picked up the mug and looked into her glassy eyes.

"It's a long way back to Tomahawk," she said.

A sense of *déjà vu* skirted through him. "Is that a song?"

"No. It's a fact. It's late."

"Maybe it should be a song."

Helen reached across the table and grabbed his hand. "I don't really feel like driving. Do you?"

Dalton yawned. "No, not really."

"What should we do?"

Dalton looked out the window. Best Western...$39.95...Free Cable...breakfast. He wondered if the free cable included HBO, or if it was just the basic package. Maybe Earthquake would be on. Richard Roundtree as Miles Quade, the black Evel Knievel. *The World's Top Motorcycle Daredevil*, said the side of the truck in the movie. And that suit: black leather, yellow lightning bolts. He felt like he really needed to watch that epic disaster movie again...and again and again and again.

Another bolt of lightning flashed and the wind howled.

CHAPTER TWENTY-THREE

Tomahawk, Colorado
September 8, 1974

A thundercloud drifted over the Nebraska state line and flickered above a small house in Colorado.

Inside, Jack Hawks switched on the TV. He collapsed into a tattered chair and smelled the hot dogs cooking in the kitchen.

ABC's *Wild World of Sports* materialized from the TV static.

Jack cracked a beer, blew the foam off the lid.

"C'mon, c'mon, c'mon," he muttered.

The *Wide World of Sports* logo dissolved into a red-white-and-blue rocket, the famous Skycycle X-2.

Jack looked at the RCA logo on the TV set. He adjusted the bill of his greasy Peterbilt trucker cap. "Solid state. No hot tubes," he muttered.

The old black-and-white he had before didn't come with those solid state features. It was an unreliable set that used old-fashioned tubes instead of the new transistor technology. Transistors. That was a big deal to Jack.

The beer tasted nice and cold. He stared at a close-up of the rocket, a virile deathtrap, poised upon its scaffolding, waiting to be hurtled over Idaho's Snake River Canyon.

Jack had been waiting for that moment for weeks and weeks.

"Suicide," said one news anchor.

Suicide? thought Jack. *Brass balls, more like it!*

He rubbed his empty stomach. "Hey, Wendy, hurry up with that hot dog!"

A volley of thunder shook the house. The lights dimmed and then went back on.

Wendy yelled at him from the kitchen. "In a second, Jack! Jesus, give me a break!"

"I'm hungry!"

"Hold your goddamn horses!"

Wendy squirted a line of watery mustard across the steaming hot dog. She opened a kitchen cabinet. Inside, next to a fire extinguisher, was a dusty bottle of wine. It had been sitting there for a long time. She reached for it and popped the cork. She filled a glass and read the bottle's label: PAUL MASSON'S PRIVATE RESERVE.

"One glass," she told herself. "But no more...you never know."

She rubbed her swollen belly. She touched her breasts. They were swollen, too. "Shit," she mumbled, knowing full-well what was happening. "I really should have bought that packet of Trojans. And they were on sale, two for one. God, barely three months hitched. And now this? Well, what the hell did I expect?"

And what did she expect?

A vacation, or something before all this family bullshit. A shot at an education would have been nice.

Oh, well, she thought. *It can't be all bad. Who knows, maybe I'll make manager one day.*

Manager...at Stevenson's little rundown pharmacy. Yeah, that's what she dreamed of when she was a little girl: managing a goddamn pharmacy in the middle of nowhere.

"*Geeze,*" she thought, "*no wonder people become drug dealers.*"

She poured some of the wine into a coffee mug and took a sip. She winced. She looked into the bottle and swore she saw something green dart through the wine, almost like a firefly.

She rubbed her eyes. "Great, now I'm seeing things." She finished the glass of wine and pushed the cork back in the bottle.

More thunder boomed across the prairie. The glasses and coffee mugs clanked against each other in the cabinet. She could smell and taste the ozone in the air. She looked out the window. A dark hissing cloud was coiled above the house like a giant rattlesnake. The tiny hairs on the back of her neck stood on end.

"Wendy, where's that hot dog!"

"It's coming!"

Jack stared the TV, mouth agape like an awestruck chimp. Sure as shit, he thought, the crazy sumbitch was actually going through with it. His eyes widened like two bleary, red Frisbees as the stuntman was lowered by a crane into the red-white-and-blue Skycycle.

———

The Skycycle X-2 was a steam-powered rocket, designed to shoot its pilot from one side of Idaho's Snake River Canyon to the other. None of the test runs had worked, but the famous daredevil was going through with it anyway.

What's an honest stuntman to do? His reputation rested on completing the task, no matter how dangerous.

It was so dangerous that the ABC network was reluctant to air it. But the ratings were too huge to ignore. They'd make a fortune, selling advertising spots for Tide, Coke, Buick, Wheaties, and RCA TVs.

The canyon itself, a rocky chasm that lead to the violent rapids of the Snake River below, was packed with onlookers standing around the perimeter.

And it was hardly a family gathering.

Under a blazing sun, the crowd had turned from curious onlookers into a gang of drunken degenerates, cheering and egging the stuntman on as he shut the canopy and prepared himself—stoically and methodically, like a bullfighter entering the ring—for what were possibly the last moments of his life.

And that's what he was telling himself. So this is how it ends: on a clear, windy September day in Idaho on the edge of the Snake River Canyon.

He had told himself many times that it was better to go out in a blaze of glory than to grow old and die in a hospital bed. Down inside he always knew he'd come out of these stunts okay. But this jump was different. For the first time in his life he really didn't think he was going to make it.

The stuntman fixated on a button next to his thumb. That button would release the two hundred pounds of superheated steam that was squeezed into a titanium tank in the rocket behind him. And then five thousand pounds of thrust would send him from one side of the canyon to other...if everything went as planned.

No problem.

Simple.

Easy.

All he had to do was push the button. Just one button. But

his mind was off-center. The planets or the cosmic waves or whatever the hell it was that normally kept him centered with the task ahead were wildly out of sync.

And he had to squelch that, pretend those feelings didn't exist. Ordinarily, he trusted them, like a cat trusts its whiskers. That's what feelings were to the stuntman: invisible whiskers.

Still, he had to push the button. If he did not hit that button, there would be a riot. And that button was getting larger and heavier with each passing second.

His throat felt like it had crushed glass stuck in it.

He wanted to throw up.

There was only one way to clear those people out of the canyon. He had to make that jump. He had started this—and now he had to end it.

The night before, that same mob of long-haired, jean-jacketed dropouts—imbeciles who had come to witness him get splattered all over the canyon walls—had made bonfires, set up tents, played rock music, popped amphetamines, Quaaludes, cocaine, and God knows what else.

And it had been hot, long night, and their overheated brains—already saturated with alcohol and dope—had reduced them to a gibbering, slobbering band of orangutans beating their chests, boozing, knife fighting, and groping the young women who had so naively trusted them.

Gunshots, screams, and sirens sounded throughout the lawless night.

"Yep...my fans," thought the stuntman.

They pissed him off. He knew what it all was about. He knew what was going through their heads. They would never admit to it. But he knew what that they really wanted.

His *fans* wanted to see him, the world's greatest motorcycle stuntman, get splattered all over the jagged rocks of the canyon.

And there was only one way to clear those shit-nibbling

baboons out of that canyon. He had to go through with it. And he had to, once again like so many times before, stare into eternity's black bottomless eyes.

He had to hit that button.

———

Suddenly, Jack's TV picture went to hell.

"What the——"

Jack flew off the easy chair and banged the top of the TV's faux-walnut cabinet. He was livid. That TV, an RCA Accucolor XL-100, had cost a fortune: his entire four-hundred-and-fifty-dollar nest egg, a good chunk of change for any interstate trucker with crappy credit.

And the man who sold it to him was none other than JD Stevenson himself. On the day Jack walked in, JD wore an aquamarine polyester suit and horned-rimmed glasses. He was a throwback character from a different era, but a trusted name in appliances and pharmaceuticals in Jim Bridger County.

"Four-hundred-and-fifty bucks?" said Jack when he first saw the set.

"It's the best in the RCA line, Jack," said JD. "Solid state."

"Solid state? What's that mean?"

"It means no tubes, Jack."

"No tubes? I think saw that on a commercial."

"It means less repairs. You'll save money in the end."

"That's what the commercial said."

"And that's why you should buy it. If you buy it, you'll save money."

"Really? I never thought of that way."

Jack had seen the commercial for the RCA XL-100 at a roadside bar in Baker City, Oregon. The ad showed a close-up of a football, and then a little announcer popped out of a tiny door at the corner of the screen. Clever camera-trick stuff. Then a miniature announcer took the viewer for a tour inside the TV, like he was in the Fantastic Voyage. But instead of human blood vessels and organs, the announcer was dwarfed by glowing, hot, unreliable chassis tubes—the leading cause of expensive TV repairs.

Chassis tubes.

Terrible invention.

The bane of honest, hard-working Americans everywhere.

The RCA XL-100 was there to save the day. Buying another kind of television was not only unthinkable, it was morally wrong. Jack had to have it.

He worked hard. He hauled a lot of stuff, logged thousands of miles crisscrossing the country in his battered Peterbilt up and down the moonscape of I-80 and I-92. Rain. Sleet. Snow. Hail. Tornadoes. And during all those long hours, he could never get that damn TV out of his head—and those damn chassis tubes.

That's what truck driving did to him, made little ideas roll round and round in his head until they got bigger and bigger like giant dungballs. The truck-driving trade could turn any reasonable man into a full blown conspiracy nut. All those empty miles to fill with out-of-control, ridiculous thoughts. Big Foot, the Warren Commission, the Moon landing, the Bermuda Triangle, pyramid-building aliens, Atlantis, the Loch Ness Monster, and who really ran The United States of America.

And chassis tubes.

Hot, unreliable, expensive, old technology. It was time to catch up to modern times. It was nineteen-seventy-fucking-four, dammit!"

A month later, Jack had walked into Stevenson's and pulled

out his wallet and counted out four one-hundred dollar bills, and then two twenties and a five and three ones. Then he reached into his pocket and produced six quarters, 4 dimes, one nickel, and five pennies.

JD Stevenson shook Jack's hand like he'd just won the presidency, and he said his son-in-law, for a modest charge, would come down to install a TV antenna on Jack's roof, just soon as the kid got out of the Jim Bridger County Corrections Facility.

———

And now this!

No picture!

"What the hell!" said Jack, yelling at the static on the screen. "Goddammit!"

"What now, Jack?"

Jack smacked the top of the television. "This picture. It's all gone to shit!"

"Jesus, have a hot dog, will you?" Wendy came in and set the wine bottle on the bookshelf and handed him the plate. "This'll make you feel better."

"I don't want no damn hot dog!"

"But you just said—"

Jack threw the plate across the room and it smashed against the wall. Mustard splattered all over the room and dripped onto the carpet.

"You asshole!"

"Fuck it, Wendy. Just fuck it!"

Wendy clenched her teeth and picked up the wine bottle. "You're going to clean that shit up!"

Jack peered around her and into the kitchen. He looked at the clock above the oven. He scratched his chin and stared at the ceiling. Another gust of wind rattled the house. He grabbed a half-pint of Jim Beam from his back pocket and took a chug. He gazed at the blizzard of static and wiped his lips, shivering as the raw whiskey cascaded into his belly.

"Dammit," he muttered. "That sumbitch is going to launch into history at any second!"

"Launch? What are you talking about?"

"That piece-of-shit antenna. I bet it blew over!"

Jack stormed through the kitchen and bolted into the back-yard. He found a rotted wooden ladder hidden under a garden hose and an assortment of old shingles and busted fence posts. He kicked off the hose and shingles and grabbed the ladder, nearly tripping over an old ax as he clumsily leaned the ladder against the roof's gutter.

Wendy watched his drunken antics through the kitchen window. "My God," she muttered.

She ran out to the back yard. "Jack Hawks, you are not getting on that roof."

"The hell I ain't!"

"Not in your condition.

"Not in my condition?"

"You're drunk. You'll break your neck."

He pushed her aside and steadied the ladder against the gutter.

Wendy hurled the wine bottle at the back of his head and missed. The bottle smashed on the side of the house, dousing the siding and Jack's head with cheap Merlot.

The green firefly-looking thing shot out of the dripping wine and vanished.

Jack wiped the wine from his face. Wendy gulped. She reached for a metal fence post laying in the weeds by her feet.

"Are you going to beat me with that?"

"You're not getting on that roof!"

"Fine then! *You* fix that antenna!"

She looked up the ladder and at the dust and leaves and twigs blowing over the roof.

Jack looked at her. He tilted his head.

Something was odd.

Despite his wife's rage, she looked beautiful. She was always good-looking, but somehow she just looked exceptionally good...fuller, curvier. She had a glow about her.

He shook his head.

"Fine," said Wendy. She started up the ladder.

"Jesus, Wendy!"

"Just you get back inside and tell me when the picture comes back on."

Jack snarled, his eyes were red, not so much from the Jim Beam but with the rage of molten hellfire burning inside his head. He had paid good money for that TV. He had paid good money for the incompetent seventeen-year-old delinquent who set up the antenna. And this was his reward? A screen full of shit? During the greatest stunt ever broadcast?

Where was the goddamn justice!

He stomped inside the house, unscrewed the cap from the Jim Beam and took swallow. He opened the living room window and yelled toward the roof.

"Can you hear me?"

"I can hear you just fine. Now, sit down and watch the picture, you drunken dipshit!"

Jack sat down, crossed his arms, and stared at the static blowing like the blizzard of '62 across the picture tube.

Meanwhile, Wendy climbed to the ladder's last rung. She tried standing on the roof, but the gale blew her summer dress over her head. She dropped to her hands and knees and inched her way to the antenna.

Jack was right.

The wind had blown the antenna over on its side.

Wendy inched closer, scrapping her knees raw on the shingles. The black hissing thundercloud swirled and billowed above her, glowing from the electrical charge inside it. At this point, it was behaving more like a leaky 1.21 gigawatt power station than a thundercloud.

Wendy gripped the antenna. The hairs on her arm stood on end. She pulled the antenna upward and tightened a loose wingnut on the support plate.

Jack hollered out the window. "That's it, honey. You almost got it!"

The network cut to a commercial, Oscar Meyer hot dogs.

"America's number one wiener," said the narrator. "Every Oscar Meyer wiener is made from the choicest cuts of beef and pork, one-hundred percent US Government inspected!"

Jack rubbed his stomach and immediately regretted that he'd lost his head and sent his Oscar Meyer wiener hurtling to the wall.

"God, I'm an idiot."

And then another ad came on, for a Chevy Nova.

It looked like a great car, real smooth handling. It also looked a lot like his Buick Apollo. But his bucket of bolts needed a new alternator and new brakes and a new gas pump. But still, the Nova was cool. The guy in the commercial had a cute girl sitting next to him.

But not nearly as cute as Wendy.

His heart sank.

"I need to apologize."

The picture cleared up a little more.

"You're getting close," yelled Jack, suddenly forgetting all about the hot dog and his beat-up Buick and how he yelled his wife after she cooked him dinner. "Almost there!"

Wendy moved the antenna to the right.

The picture went back to snow.

"Other way!" hollered Jack.

Wendy moved the antenna back to the left. The picture reappeared. The network was out of the commercial and back to the jump. Steam billowed from the Skycycle's tail while ABC anchorman Jim McKay hemmed and hawed about the possibility of a launch.

"That's it," yelled Jack. "You're getting close, real close!"

Wendy rotated the antenna more to the left. Her hair stood on end. A dust devil swirled across the backyard. She got dizzy and looked back at the antenna, at her own death-defying stunt. Another gust of wind shot across the prairie. Then a hand-grenade sized hailstone detonated on the roof, spewing ice fragments all over her dress and hair.

"Just a little more, Wendy...you almost got it!"

Wendy brushed the ice shards from her face and turned the antenna. But it wouldn't budge. She stood up and grabbed it with both hands. She held on tight and turned it with all her might.

Finally, it swiveled.

The Skycycle's image snapped back.

Perfect clarity.

"That's it! Wendy, you did it!"

ZZZZ——BZZZAAAT!

BANG!

Deep inside the ground, a gopher clawed further into the dirt and covered its ears. And out in the prairie, a coyote bitch yowled under the thunder's report, a Big Bang across the ancient plains.

And then a bolt as bright as the sun shot from the giant hissing cloud and struck the antenna and ran through Wendy and her pregnant belly, at the exact instant when Evel Knievel—the world's greatest stuntman—finally pushed the button and launched the Skycycle X-2 over the Snake River Canyon.

The atomized, supercharged TV waves—carrying the image of the Skycycle, along with Evel Knievel's fierce guts and determination—transploded through the antenna and through Wendy...and through her tiny radioactive-wine-dosed fetus.

CHAPTER TWENTY-FOUR

Helen filled a Styrofoam cup with orange juice.

"You know," she said, "$39.95 is a pretty good deal, especially when you include this breakfast."

Dalton smeared a blob of warm butter onto his hot Eggo. The butter melted and oozed over the waffle. An image flashed through his head. But it wasn't like the usual images. No guns. No baseball bats. No evil-doers being hurled into trashcans. This time, it was a bare leg. Helen's bare leg. Long and glistening.

Shit, Dalton, what the hell did you do this time?

His last recollection of the evening was turning off the motel room's TV. He had been watching *Escape from the Planet of the Apes* while Helen slept. He remembered sitting naked at the foot of the bed, watching the movie's final scene: a baby chimp in a cage saying, "Mama, mama…" He then remembered thinking about his own mother and the talking ape she created.

And he remembered the house he had entered that afternoon. The kitty cat. The Glenn Campbell album. But lots of people owned Glenn Campbell records, especially in these parts. Still, the image of the sleeping woman and the empty vodka bottle persisted. It made him sad. But maybe it really wasn't depressing, maybe she had a party earlier in the day and was just sleeping it off. Maybe it was her birthday and, earlier, she'd been surrounded by friends and family. Or better, yet, maybe she had just sold a screenplay and was tying one on before moving on to the next project. That woman could have been celebrating for all he knew. Hell, there was a typewriter in that house. Wasn't there? And isn't that what writers did? Drank, smoked, typed and slept it off?

Everything needed to be taken in context.

He stared at his waffle and thought about the old woman some more. No, he decided. Just a case of depressing day-drinking.

After all, it was Battlesmoke. And that's what people did there. Same as Tomahawk. They drank, smoked, and slept it off. And if it wasn't his mother, then it was someone else's mother.

Dalton pushed the waffle aside, and Helen reached toward the napkin dispenser—the same hand that had clutched the shaking bedposts the night before.

Dalton steered his eyes to the table next to him. A couple had just sat down. Like Helen and Dalton, they were break-fasting on orange juice and waffles. The couple even reminded Dalton a little bit of himself and Helen. But they had rings on their fingers, and they seemed happy.

Newlyweds, he thought.

The couple smiled and looked into each other's eyes. Helen was watching them, too.

Oh, God, thought Dalton. *She's probably thinking about all her what-ifs.*

He thought about his own what-ifs. What if he had become a truck driver? What if he had saved his money and put a down payment on a house? What if he had had a kid? What if the kid would have become a doctor, or what if the little tyke would have won the lottery when he was all grown up? Dalton paused, sick about thinking of all things that never happened.

It had been an odd couple of days. The daydreams. The bruises. The eviction notice. The stolen car. The tornado. And now here he was: in a motel, eating breakfast after sleeping with his ex-girlfriend.

But why?

He knew *how*. The logistics were there. His Buick had been stolen. And he followed the Buick to Battlesmoke. And then he got lonely. And Helen got drunk. And then they spent the night. And now they were in a motel, eating waffles and drinking orange juice. The mechanics were sound. The math made sense, as far as the little details were concerned.

But the big picture still didn't add up.

Something else was guiding this affair. Like Helen had said, it was deeper than that. Then he heard sobs.

"Hey, what's wrong?"

She wiped her eyes. "Nothing."

"Nothing?"

She sat silent for a minute. Then she trembled. And then tears rolled down her cheeks and plunged into her orange juice.

"Come on, what's wrong?"

She looked at the newlyweds, and Dalton understood.

They were probably on their honeymoon, he thought. They were probably going to Niagara Falls or Yellowstone, before they settled down and planned their careers and bought a house and had kids and watched them dress up as sheep for the school play.

"Oh, why didn't it work," she sobbed. "It'll never work for me!"

"What won't?"

"You know."

"No."

"I'm nearly thirty."

"So?"

"No kids. No proper house. I can't pay rent. I'm making those fucking stupid Internet movies, embarrassing myself in front of the whole world. What the hell was I thinking!" She pounded the table and knocked over her orange juice.

Dalton picked up the cup and soaked up the spilled juice with a napkin. "Helen, it's okay. You just needed the money. I get it."

"You know, it's the second that I think that I'm being the smartest person in the world that I'm just really falling into a dumb pit of stupidity that I'll never crawl out of. Jesus! And I've just slept with a man that I swore I would never have anything to do with again!"

"Helen, it's okay."

"Leave me alone!"

"Helen."

"I want to go home."

"I'm sorry. I—"

"It's not your fault, Dalton. It's mine. I'm the idiot. I guess I was just hoping for something you couldn't deliver."

"What?"

"I don't know, a glimmer of hope."

Dalton wanted to help, but he couldn't. There was no future for a ditch-digger in Tomahawk, especially an unemployed one. Other guys in Tomahawk took jobs they didn't like. They stuck with it. They muscled it out. They soldiered on until retirement.

So why can't I?

"You know, there's still hope for me. I could get a CDL. I could find work as a truck dri—"

"No, Dalton. Please, just be yourself. It's the only thing you're good at.

"Well—"

"Can we go now?"

Dalton bussed the table. He walked into the lobby and handed over the room key.

"Room okay?" said the desk clerk.

He saw the magazine the clerk was reading and smirked. Mayor Starr was on the cover, bikini-clad and straddling her Harley, long hair barely covering her ample breasts.

"You guys need to get HBO," said Dalton. He really didn't like that clerk looking at his mayor that way, the one person who might be able to get his uncle out of the pokey.

The desk clerk licked his finger and turned a page. "Good to know."

"Having HBO will get you way more customers. The sign says cable TV, but it's really not that big a deal. I mean, who doesn't get a basic-cable package in this day and age?"

"That all? Just the HBO?"

"That's about it."

"Nothing else?"

"You could serve your coffee or orange juice in a proper cup. Not Styrofoam. Those tip over too easily."

"Yeah, but we'd have to wash them."

"So? Get a dishwasher. Probably get a used one for a couple hundred bucks."

The clerk thought for a second. "No, people would just run off with cups, like they do with our pens."

"So put the Best Western logo on the side of them. You know, having a bunch of stray Best Western cups all over the country could be good advertising. And people would know they could get Maxwell House in a *real* mug."

The clerk set the magazine down. "Are we done?"

"Yeah, I guess."

"Good," said the clerk. "Come back soon. Have a happy Fourth."

"Fourth?"

"It's the Fourth of July."

"Today?"

"Yes, today."

Dalton thought about all the flags he'd seen on the houses. "Geeze, already? Where's the summer going?"

"It's barely started."

He turned and walked outside. Helen was standing beside the car. He trudged toward her. The dirt was still wet from the night's thundershower.

"Need me to drive?"

"No," said Helen, opening the car door.

They climbed in, and she cranked the engine and backed out. Dalton fastened his seatbelt, realizing he was heading back to Tomahawk poorer than ever. No car. No guitar. No girl. No apartment.

Helen turned down Lanyon Boulevard and followed an old semi toward the exit ramp, a rusty 1955 Model 281 Peterbilt powered by a 270-horsepower Caterpillar engine.

Dalton stared at the truck and rubbed his eyes. He was weary, and he didn't feel like going back to Tomahawk. He felt like hopping out of the car and hitchhiking down the highway just to see where he'd wind up. Ogallala, maybe.

Perhaps I could find work there as a digger of ditches. I bet they've got lots of ditches in Ogallala...

He wondered if that's what happened to his old man. If he just started hitchhiking aimlessly. And suddenly Dalton kind of understood why his father may have taken to the highway and disappeared forever. His old man wasn't evil. He had made some stupid mistake along the line and was unable to forgive himself. Dalton suddenly felt bad for him, and wondered what his father was doing, or if he was even alive. There was no way that old man could have been all bad. If he was all bad, a person like his mother would never have been interested in him. Most everybody had a good side. Suddenly he no longer wanted to kung fu the daylights out of his daddy. Instead, Dalton wanted to find him and give the old man a hug and tell him that it was all okay. He sat back in his seat and just stared out the window. He stared and stared, realizing he needed to forgive himself for all the dumb stuff he had done, too.

"You okay, Dalton?"

He wiped his eye and nodded.

The semi in front of them stopped, signaled left. From the opposite direction, a pickup truck towing a horse trailer drove by. A brown car trailed behind it.

A Honda Accord. Dented side door. The trunk, lashed down with a bungee cord.

Dalton looked over his shoulder. "Kovaleski?"

Helen peered into the side mirror. "He was supposed to be in Denver. Isn't that what Deputy Harden told us?"

"He did."

"I told you," said Helen. "Something is not right."

"Turn around," said Dalton.

PART THREE

CHAPTER TWENTY-FIVE

Helen flipped a U-ey and followed the Honda back down Lanyon Boulevard.

She slapped the top of the steering wheel. "It just keeps getting weirder and weirder. Didn't I tell you Kovaleski's a part of this? I said that very thing last night. I said that Sheriff Kovaleski and my jailbird half-brother Link had worked something out. It makes sense that they'd wind up here at the same time. You know, maybe I should go to detective school instead of trucker school."

"You should," said Dalton, relieved that her mood had picked up. "Don't make it too obvious that we're tailing him."

Helen let off the accelerator and tapped the break.

"So you're really sure that's him, Dalton?"

"There's only one guy in Tomahawk who owns a brown Honda that needs a bungee cord to hold down the trunk."

"You'd just think being sheriff and being in the public eye, Kovaleski would drive something nicer."

"That was all that was left from of his divorce settlement. Before they split up, his wife got mad and backed it into a dumpster."

"How do you know all this stuff?"

"It was on the radio for a week. You should listen to it. KJBC, the voice of Jim Bridger County. They leave no stone unturned."

The Honda stopped at the edge of town before the dirt frontage road by the old sanitarium.

(Sanitarium City...)

Dalton stared at the building, misplaced in space and time, and he wondered if there were still any patients in there. He thought about the Walmart that was going to be built there. Seemed an odd place to put a Walmart.

But what if people were still in there? Down in the basement cellars. What if his mom was still down there? What if she'd been forgotten about? Maybe they would find her, and then she could get a job at the Walmart.

Stop it, Dalton. This is crazy!

Helen pulled over by a Wendy's restaurant across from the asylum and waited for the Honda to turn. She squinted through the dusty windshield. "Do you think he's onto us?"

"Who knows."

"We recognized his car. He could have just as easily recognized this car, especially if he was looking for it. What if he's just setting a trap for us? Maybe he wants his tub of ephedrine back."

"We'll just have to take that chance."

The Honda's right signal blinked, and it turned down the frontage road.

Helen waited until the Honda disappeared behind a bend, and then she followed its dusty trail down the road. She rounded the bend just as the Honda disappeared behind a cluster of trees.

The scenery had changed, some smaller farms with a few

horses and some cows. Lots of hay bales. Nice farm houses, nice big trees. Lots of shade.

He wanted one of those houses. He figured he could sit in a rocking chair and ponder the world and everything in it with that idyllic country quiet. But he figured that it wouldn't work that way. Real farmers, he knew, worked their asses off all day and night.

Probably not a lot of time for pondering.

"I'm impressed," said Helen. "This part of Battlesmoke is not so bad. I think could actually live here."

"Well, that's why traveling is good. It introduces people to new things, new ideas. It expands the mind and soul."

"So how come you never go anywhere?"

He shrugged.

Helen followed the curve in the road. She slowed down, and Dalton saw a dust cloud pluming over a driveway behind a cluster of cottonwoods. And there was an old dilapidated farmhouse and a small shack beside it obscured by another cluster of cottonwoods near a berm alongside the property.

Dalton kept his eyes glued to the farmhouse as they approached the trees. Helen cut the engine and rolled to a stop as quietly as she could. But even the gravel crunching under the wheels seemed as loud as a sonic boom. She put the hazards on and turned off the engine.

Dalton's heart beat like a jackhammer.

"Are you as freaked out as I am?" said Helen.

"Relax," said Dalton, trying to steady his own nerves. "It's probably nothing," he sighed.

They climbed out the car and eased the doors shut.

"Don't lock it," whispered Helen. "The keys are still in the ignition, in case we need to escape."

Dalton made sure the doors were still unlocked and walked to the side of the berm.

It was very quiet. His nose itched. Probably pollen. But besides pollen, a faint but strange odor hung in the air—an ever-so-slight smell of gasoline and chemicals mingling with the hay and cow manure.

He looked up and saw a lone contrail from an airliner jetting across the sky. Dalton had never been in an airplane before, and he wondered what those people by the window seats saw below them. He imagined they wore suits and ties and were flying to places like New York City or Los Angeles. At this point of their journey, they were probably bored out of their skulls. And when they looked out the window, all they would see was an endless sea of brown grass and an occasional forlorn town, and they would probably think to themselves: *What over-population problem? There's hardly anybody down there!*

Dalton boosted Helen up the berm. She clawed her way to the top and hid behind a clump of sagebrush. He crouched behind her. A thorn jabbed him in the knee.

"Ouch."

"Shush."

He rubbed his nose. "Damn this pollen."

"Don't sneeze."

He squeezed his nostrils together until the itch passed. He looked over her shoulder and saw a shack and the old farmhouse behind it.

His battered Buick Apollo was parked in front of the house.

"That's my car!"

"Shush, they'll hear us!"

"I knew I smelled a rat."

"No, *I* smelled the rat."

"Come on, I knew Kovaleski was mixed up in this from the start."

"Dalton?"

"What?"

"You're making my head hurt." Helen leaned over for a better look. "I wonder where the other two are?"

"Zeke and Lupe? I bet they're inside that farmhouse. They're probably talking to Kovaleski."

The old, crumbling farmhouse's white exterior had faded to gray. The door window was broken. Only about half the shingles were still on the roof. The acreage around it had not been maintained for years and was overrun with weeds and gopher holes.

"I'm guessing this place hasn't been lived in for a long, long time," said Dalton.

"Sure looks that way."

Dalton looked at the shack. "I bet we can get a closer look from over there."

They crept toward the shack, ducking behind a feed trough and a wooden barrel. The chemical smell in the air got thicker, a fumy smell of gasoline and rubbing alcohol. And something else that he'd smelled before but couldn't quite place.

"Cats," said Dalton.

"Cats? You see a cat?"

"It smells like cats."

Dalton crept up to the shack and peaked through its broken window.

"What the hell?" he said.

A large flask sat on the stove. It had a ventilated stopper attached to it with a tube that connected the stopper to a distilling apparatus. Six cans of denatured alcohol and three bags of kitty litter sat in the corner of the shack. A pile of surgical tubing and several boxes of matches sat on top of a crude wooden table. A pack of coffee filters and a box of double-D batteries lay next to the alcohol cans.

The cardboard sign from the Shortstop Grocery flashed in Dalton's mind. *NO COFFEE FILTERS, NO BATTERIES, NO CAT LITTER.* Almost everything that the store had run out of was inside the shack.

Helen peaked over his shoulder. "If I didn't know better, I'd think this was a meth lab."

"What do you know about meth labs?"

"I saw a documentary on PBS."

"Check out the size of that glass thingamajig on the stove. What's that?"

"Some kind of huge-ass boiling flask," said Helen. "Looks like it could hold four or five gallons."

"Four or five gallons of what?"

"How the hell would I know?"

"Keep your voice down!"

She looked at the alcohol cans. "Just one spark, and I bet this place would go off like a bomb."

Dalton leaned against the shack. "A meth lab," he whispered. "Can you believe it?"

"Of course. What the hell else do people in places like Battlesmoke do?"

Dalton shook his head. "Only in Battlesmoke."

"I'll bet Tomahawk's got more way more meth labs than this town."

"No way."

"Remember that hardware store that burnt down?"

"Tomahawk Lumber and Supply?"

"Yes," said Helen, "that was a meth explosion. They were cooking it in the back room. Same thing with the fire station."

"I heard that was from a Twinkie."

"A Twinkie? How do you know?"

"They said so on the radio. They were deep frying it."

"Then those firemen were probably on meth."

The front door slammed shut, and Dalton and Helen crawled behind a feed trough.

"It's them," whispered Dalton. "All three of them!"

Kovaleski, Zeke, and Lupe stood beside the Buick's trunk. Zeke still had his hat on, and Lupe looked the same as he had at the Comanche Hills gas station——except now he had a revolver tucked into his belt.

.357 Magnum, thought Dalton. *I wonder if this is a sting operation. Maybe Kovaleski's just fixing to bust somebody and maybe he's just gathering evidence, lining up his ducks.*

Kovaleski picked up a crowbar and wedged it under the Buick's trunk latch. He twisted the crowbar and the trunk popped open. He reached inside and pulled out the guitar case, and Dalton overheard him say:

"Clever...very clever."

Kovaleski open the case and stared at it, dumbfounded.

"What? This is just a guitar!"

He pulled the guitar out the case and dropped to the ground.

KLUNK!

Dalton winced.

Kovaleski frantically raked through the trunk. "Damn, he's got a hell of a lot of booze in here. Kentucky Deluxe, Mogan David, Olympia." He lifted a bottle out. "You want a snort of Night Train, Lupe?"

"I still feel like shit from last night."

Kovaleski examined the label. "I thought *I* was bad!" He pulled out one of the spring-loaded clamps. "What the hell's this?" He slid the clamp across the runner and then threw it back in the trunk.

"So what are you looking for?" said Lupe. "You never did tell us."

Kovaleski stomped his feet. "Dammit! There should be a big barrel in here."

"Maybe check under the spare tire," said Zeke.

"No, it's a barrel that came from Fresno. Link told me it was in the trunk of his car."

Kovaleski took a step back and scratched his head. "You know, I can't quite put my finger on it."

He walked up to the Buick and kicked the front tire. He rubbed his chin. He bent down and examined the manufacturer's emblem on the side of Apollo. "Oh, for fucksakes," he said, dropping to his knees.

"What's the problem?" said Zeke.

Kovaleski walked to the front of the car and opened the door. He looked inside. He reached for the license on the dashboard and studied it.

He stood back up, face red and eyes bulging. "What's the problem? I'll tell you the problem. The problem is that I'm working with morons! This is a Buick Apollo, not a Chevy Nova."

"A Buick?"

"You stole the wrong car!"

"That's the same car that's always parked in her driveway. I should know. I'm practically there all the time."

"Link said that it was a white Chevy *Nova*—not a white Buick Apollo."

"It has to be the same car," said Zeke. "I'm telling you, this is only car that's ever parked in front of her place."

"Don't believe me? Just look at the logo on the side."

Zeke bent down for a look. He shook his head. "Wow..."

"*Wow*. Exactly."

"It could have fooled anyone."

"Do you know whose car you stole?"

Zeke shrugged.

"This belongs to Dalton Hawks. This is his goddamn license. It was on the dashboard. You didn't notice it?"

"Guess not," said Lupe.

"Elston Hawks gave the Buick to Dalton before I carted his sorry ass over to Jim Bridger County. How the hell did you start it?"

"Just jimmied the carburetor a little," said Lupe, smiling and revealing his gold tooth. "It had a bottle cap stuck in it."

Zeke pulled a can of Olympia from the Buick's trunk. "Hmm, Dalton Hawks. You know, I swear I've heard that name before."

Kovaleski rolled his eyes. "Of course you have. Dalton Hawks is Helen's Wheeler's ex-boyfriend."

"Helen?"

"That broad you've been boinking. You were just supposed to steal her car, dumbass!"

Dalton looked at Helen, who was boiling with rage.

"Asshole," she whispered.

"Shush," said Dalton.

He rubbed his nose.

Then he sneezed.

Lupe's head turned toward the shack and Dalton ducked down behind the trough.

"I hope they didn't hear that," said Helen.

Dalton looked up from the trough and watched Zeke crack open the beer can. "I don't think so."

Zeke took a swallow, and stared at the Buick. He set the beer can down and scratched his head.

"I can't believe it!" said Kovaleski. "How could you screw this up?"

"Okay, okay," said Zeke. "I fucked up. We'll just have to drive back to Tomahawk and find it."

"If it's even there. Dalton's probably out looking for you two by now. He could have followed you. Did you think about that?" Kovaleski scanned the surroundings.

Lupe picked the guitar off the ground and strummed an E chord. "Why you so worried about this Dalton guy? We can deal with him."

"Oh, you think?" said Kovaleski.

"Sure," said Lupe. "There's three of us."

"Well, guess what?"

Lupe tuned the guitar's D string. "What?"

"I think it was Dalton Hawks who threw you into that dumpster last night."

The D string snapped.

"You mean that weirdo with the motorcycle helmet? That was Dalton Hawks?"

Kovaleski reached in the trunk and produced a black motorcycle helmet with yellow lightning bolts painted on it.

"Does this ring a bell?"

Zeke let out a slow breath of air.

Lupe leaned the guitar against the car and walked around the farmhouse.

"And just where are you going, Lupe?"

"I need to take a leak, boss."

"Well, put that gun away. You'll shoot your dick off holstering it like that."

Kovaleski rummaged through the trunk and pulled out a bottle of Wild Turkey. He slammed the trunk shut. "Goddammit. Don't you get the magnitude of this?"

"No," said Zeke. "I don't. You never told us what was in that trunk. You just told us to hotwire the car and drive it all the way to here."

Kovaleski leaned against the Buick and uncapped the Wild Turkey bottle. "You really want to know what was in that trunk?"

"Yes."

Kovaleski took a belt of whiskey and grit his teeth. "My early retirement. My future fishing boat. My goddamn beachfront property in the Florida Keys was in that trunk!"

"What are you talking about?"

"There was supposed to be a barrel of ephedrine in that trunk. Link said it was shipped from Canada and that the Feds missed it during the Fresno superlab bust back in '02. It had been lying in a storage shed for damn near five years!"

Zeke took another swallow and threw the empty can into the Buick's open trunk. "Ephedrine?"

"Fifteen gallons, imported straight from India. That translates to at least three-hundred-thousand dollars." Kovaleski took another sip and screwed the cap back on the bottle. "Three-hundred thousand...gone."

He kicked the guitar across the driveway.

Dalton grit his teeth.

"Relax," said Zeke. "We'll find the car."

"Damn right you will."

Kovaleski drew a crude map of Florida in the dirt with the toe of his boot. He turned and looked at the shack. Dalton and Helen ducked back behind the feed trough and kept listening.

"I guess we'll just have to continue do things the old-fashioned way," continued Kovaleski. "Did you at least find some kitty litter?"

"Yeah," said Zeke. "We bought a whole bunch of stuff at the Shortstop. Alcohol, batteries, all that crap."

Dalton hunkered behind the trough.

Tossed him into a dumpster?

Weirdo with the motorcycle helmet?

Dalton looked at the shack. Behind it, clouds were gathering and rising in the distance.

He poked Helen's shoulder.

"What?"

"We're getting in a little deep, don't you think?"

"Yeah, we need to call the cops."

Dalton grabbed Helen's arm. "No, we need to scram!"

And then Dalton heard a metallic click behind his ear.

What the—?

"Well, well, well," said a voice from behind. "Look who's been following us?"

As Dalton looked over his shoulder, the butt of a .357 Magnum bashed into his skull.

Everything went black.

CHAPTER TWENTY-SEVEN

November 1, 1991

Dalton strapped on his helmet and marched toward his position, cornerback—not a position he had much practice with. He wasn't even sure where to line up. But with Wendel Boltman out with a sprained ankle, Dalton had no choice but to fill that spot.

"Hawks, where's your head at?" hollered Coach Roach. "Move to the left, to the left. Other way! More! Come on, Hawks!"

Dalton scooched over left of center and huffed. He hated football. He'd rather sit on the bench and daydream about guitars and tour busses. But since there were only twenty-five males at Tomahawk High School, he had little choice. Tomahawk's tiny population needed every high school boy available to fill that roster or they would have no team.

It was Elston who'd convinced him to join.

"Dalton," he had said, "you'll never meet any girls hanging out in the library."

"I hate football."

"Of course you do. Everybody in Tomahawk hates football. But you have to play. It's the law of the jungle. You're an American male. You're in high school. In America you play football when you're in high school. If you were in Brazil, you'd be playing soccer. And if you were in Cuba you'd be playing baseball.

"Why can't I be from Cuba?"

"Because you're from Tomahawk. And we play football in Tomahawk. It's what we guys do. You don't want everybody to think you're a weirdo, do you?"

"No," sulked Dalton.

So he joined the team.

"Head in the game, Hawks!" screamed Coach Roach. "Focus!"

Dalton took a deep breath. It didn't feel right. He was convinced it was the Gatorade, which didn't exactly taste like Gatorade.

He moved into position at the far left of the defensive line. His mind was racing. His muscles felt achy. He bent down across from his man, Number 29—Battlesmoke High's talented wide receiver, Jamar Wilkins.

Dalton stared at the grass and watched the Gladiators offensive line form across from him. Wilkins's nostrils flared and smoke seem to come out of them.

"Dalton," screamed Coach Roach, "get your head in the game!"

Dalton looked at the stands. Wondering if anyone was there to cheer him on. Sure enough, there was: Ruby McGonahue. She was jumping up and down, and she blew him a kiss. He grimaced and noticed the girl next to Ruby. His heart fluttered. That girl was the love of his life. The girl who made the stars shine brighter and the Earth stand still. The girl who could turn his gray skies to blue. The girl he'd cross a thousand deserts for, scale a thousand mountains for, and hack his way through an alligator-infested Amazonian jungle for. She was girl who made him want to dip a quill into an inkwell as deep as the Pacific and write epic poetry, the kind of poetry that sang out of the page like George Jones did when he sung *He Stopped Loving Her Today*.

That girl was Helen Wheeler.

But she had never paid any attention to him.

Skinny, knocked kneed, dark-eyed, hair blowing across her face, Helen sat on the bleachers chatting to a future insurance salesmen named Wendel Boltman. He was the cornerback who had sprained his ankle on the football field the week before.

He was the guy who Dalton was substituting for.

The irony!

Then should not *he* be *me?* thought Dalton. Should not Wendel be here on the field standing where I'm standing? And should I not be sitting next to Helen? Should I not have my arm around her shoulders? Should I not be taking her to the Waffle House for a milkshake and a hamburger? Should I not be holding her textbooks and walking her home from school? Should I not be knocking on her window at midnight and strumming my guitar in the moonlight?

She was why Dalton really wanted to learn to play that old Martin. Not because he really wanted career in music. He just believed Helen would notice him if he could play guitar.

And he was right.

She had noticed him.

She saw him carrying the guitar case from a lesson and said, "Can you really play that thing?"

And Dalton said, "I'm trying to."

And Helton said, "Are you any good?"

And Dalton stared and the ground and said, "I'm trying."

And Helen said, "I sing a little bit."

And Dalton said...nothing. He just smiled. He tried to force a word out. But his tongue got stuck.

Geeze, Dalton! he screamed at himself. *Dazzle her! Now is your moment!*

He opened his mouth...and grunted.

She had turned him into a baboon!

And Helen had raised an eyebrow and said, "See you later, guitar man."

Dalton looked away from the bleachers. He stared at the turf and listened for the count.

...52, 38, green, 93...

Dalton braced himself, hoping Number 29 didn't bulldoze him into the turf and embarrass him front of his true love.

Then another bolt of lightning struck in the distance.

He looked at the Gatorade bucket.

Suddenly, the chalk line under Dalton's knuckles blurred. He blinked and the line snapped into focus. He didn't feel light-headed anymore. He didn't even feel like himself.

He felt lucid for a change.

Strong.

Fast.

His muscles turned into iron, and an answer to a difficult math problem he had skipped on a test suddenly popped into his head.

What the hell is happening to me?

...blue, 42...hut, hut—HUT!

The ball snapped and Dalton stuck to Number 29, the future USC Trojan of great promise who could outrun a chee-tah. The chase, however, was strangely effortless for Dalton.

The football spiraled toward them. Vectors and parabolas scribbled themselves onto the blackboard of his brain. His forti-fied synapses spat out numbers and functions and differential equations he knew nothing about but, yet, somehow understood. And in a flash, the seventeen-year-old Dalton Hawks knew the football's trajectory was overthrown—by an inch.

A lousy inch.

But in a game of inches, an inch was all he needed.

He lurched forward. The pigskin spiraled over Number 29's fingertips and into Dalton's hands.

"Attaboy!" screamed Coach Roach.

The Battlesmoke Gladiators descended on Dalton like a pride of hungry lions. But go down, Dalton Hawks did not.

He faked left.

He faked right.

He zigged.

He zagged.

The fans in the bleachers roared.

He rocketed to the end zone, a wake of dirt rising from his cleats and across the field.

Coach Roach danced up and down. "Run, Hawks. Run, run, run. Holy shit. RUN, GODDAMMIT!"

Dalton dove into the end zone and somersaulted to his feet. The score was now 6-3. Dalton jogged back to the sidelines, suddenly feeling weary.

Everyone was cheering, even Helen.

"See," said Roach, patting his helmet. "I told you this was our year!" He pointed at the field-goal kicker. "Now let's get that extra point and show these Gladiators what we're made of!"

He looked for his new star. His Adonis. His Joe Namath. His Savior.

"Hawks! Where are you?"

Darnell (eighteen years old and already thinking about creating a giant rooster made of scrap metal) pointed to the bench. "He's over there, coach. He's sleeping."

After the kicker missed the uprights, coach Roach walked over and nudged Dalton. "You okay, Hawks?"

Dalton was fast asleep, dreaming of that beautiful knocked-kneed girl on the bleachers

"I'll be damned." Roach put his ear to Dalton's chest and checked his breathing. It was fine. He sat down and poured himself a Gatorade.

He took a sip and raised a questioning eyebrow.

CHAPTER TWENTY-EIGHT

When Dalton came to, he found himself sitting on a concrete floor. He recognized the smell of chemicals and kitty litter. Where had he smelt that before? How did he wind up here?

Then he remembered.

The events from the previous day unraveled in a series of pictures. Him, driving down the highway and following his own Buick. And then a fight at the gas station. And then a tornado. And then Helen. Battlesmoke. The cardboard drum of ephedrine. A bar. The pregnant waitress. The hotel. Helen again. Helen's lips. Helen's eyes. Helen's naked breasts. The continental breakfast. Following the car, Kovaleski's Honda, down the dirt road. The farm house. The...shack. That chemical smell.

Where's Helen?

His wrists were handcuffed to a pipe behind his back. His head was throbbing. His ears, ringing.

He opened his eyes.

Three blurry people stood around a blurry table. A box sat on the table next to a bottle. Occasionally one of the blurry people would pick up the bottle, drink from it, and laugh. But it wasn't a happy laughter. It was the kind of laughter that came from people who had fallen in love with money.

Dalton's eyes rolled into focus, and he recognized Jim Bridger County Sheriff Dale Kovaleski, gold-toothed Lupe Mendocino, and cactus-green booted Zeke Mueller.

Dalton tugged at the cuffs, and the metal dug into his wrists.

Kovaleski turned and smiled. "What do you know? He's finally come to. If it isn't ol' Dalton Hawks, sticking his nose where it don't belong. I guess curiosity just got the best of you, didn't it?"

"I just came to get my car."

Kovaleski laughed. "And I can see why. Mean machine, isn't she?"

Zeke pulled the cork from the bottle and took a plug. He handed the bottle to Lupe and lit a cigarette.

"Hey, dumbass," shouted Kovaleski. "You trying to blow us *all* sky high?"

Zeke dropped the cigarette and extinguished it with his boot heel.

"I just want my car back. It doesn't belong to you."

"Yes," said Kovaleski, "and technically it doesn't belong to you either. In fact, it's still registered under your long, lost daddy's name. No wait. I've got it wrong. It's currently registered under your uncle Elston's name. You still visit his sorry ass in the county clink?"

"What of it?"

"That'll teach him to bet on the Broncos with money he doesn't have."

Dalton tugged at the handcuffs.

"But as for your car," Kovaleski picked up a piece of surgical tubing and stretched it back and forth. "It seems Lupe really meant to take your girlfriend's car."

"She's not my girlfriend. And that's not her car either."

"That's right, it's Link's car."

Dalton stopped tugging at the handcuffs. They were beginning to cut into his wrists. "So, where is she?"

"We'll just say she's a little tied up at the moment—kind of like you."

"Tied up! What do you mean!"

"I mean, tied up, numbnuts!"

He put down the tubing and poured a shot of whiskey into a Dixie cup. He took a drink and tossed the empty cup into a pile of newspapers.

Dalton looked around the shack. He stared at the stove, the cans of alcohol, the rubber tubing, the kitty litter bags, the stacks of kitchen matches, the coffee filters. He looked at the cardboard box on the table.

An alleyway flashed into his head. A box passed through a broken window. An old man appeared. Gin blossoms on his nose. Wild Irish Rose. The Irish Rose bottle grew larger and larger, and the more Dalton pulled on his handcuffs, the larger the bottle got. He stared at the whiskey bottle on the table.

Wild Turkey.

He was consumed by an overpowering urge for a drink.

Is this what fear does to me? Makes me want to drink? Weak, Dalton. You are WEAK!

Dalton shook the bottle from his mind. He said to Kovaleski, "Leave Helen out of this. She didn't do anything. We just came here for my car."

Kovaleski inched the Wild Turkey toward the center of the table with his index finger. Dalton stared at the bottle. He couldn't stop staring. It was as if that bottle had turned into one of Jac Lu's Bikini-clad beauties, and Dalton was becoming consumed by a powerful desire, a near sexual desire, to get drunk.

"Well," said Kovaleski, "there's really nothing I'd rather do than let you two go. But there's a problem."

"What?"

"You've seen too much. I mean, how can I trust you to keep your trap shut now?"

"I just want my car back. I don't give a shit about what you're up to. Really."

"I can't take that chance, Dalton. Imagine the pickle I'd be in if you spilled the beans. Me, Jim Bridger County's illustrious sheriff, indicted for cooking meth. And you know how unpopular this drug racket is, don't you? Why, the town would turn against me. And what would that do for my chances of becoming mayor?"

"Probably nothing. You're running against a stripper."

"I suppose you could be right. But, still, I can't take that chance. I have to win, Dalton. I *must* win."

"Then why are you all mixed up in this methamphetamine business?"

Kovaleski shrugged. "Doesn't seem too bright does it? But a man's got to earn a living. And God knows being a sheriff in Jim Bridger County doesn't pay the bills."

Dalton tugged at the handcuffs. "You make more money than most people in Tomahawk. And if you become mayor, you'll have two jobs."

"Yes, yes," said Kovaleski, nudging the bottle around on the table. "But it's never enough. No matter how much you make, it's just *never* enough. Three divorces. Two ungrateful kids. One in juvey. You know how it is. Or maybe you don't. Anyway, Dalton, I've made some big sacrifices. And now it's time for my piece of the pie."

"I promise I won't tell anybody."

Kovaleski pulled the cork from the bottle. He bounced it in his hand and then used it to plug the vent on the boiling flask's stopper. He struck a match and turned on the gas underneath the flask.

"Hey, what about Helen?"

"Oh, how noble," said Kovaleski. "Still more concerned about the girl that dumped you rather than saving your own hide."

"She's got nothing to do with this!"

Kovaleski waved a match over the stove and a blue flame ignited under the flask. *WUMPF.* "Don't worry. After I'm done, I'm sure I'll find a way to dispose of her."

"What!"

"You know, I was just thinking the Burlington Northern will be rolling through soon. Could make for a nice, or not so nice, accident."

"You're not serious."

"Oh, I am."

"They'll find out."

"Who? The Battlesmoke PD? Those gimps couldn't find their assholes with a GPS. And even if one of them douchebags did suspect something, they'd never pin it on me."

Kovaleski opened one of the old *Battlesmoke Buglers* and wadded the front page into a ball. "Dalton, in case you don't know, I am an officer of the law. And I do have a way with evidence." He wadded a few more balls of newspaper and tossed them next to the alcohol cans.

Dalton tugged at the handcuffs.

Think...I must THINK!

Kovaleski tossed another newspaper ball onto the pile. "No, they'll never figure it out. They'll just figure you died in a meth lab explosion, like your type always seems to do."

"What about Helen?"

"I've got that all worked out, too. After I'm done, everyone will think Helen, your partner in crime, died trying to beat a train to the tracks after fleeing the scene of the explosion."

"You're crazy."

"No, I'm being completely reasonable. It's not going to be Battlesmoke's first meth lab explosion. They've had five in the last three months. And it won't be Battlesmoke's first collision at a rail crossing-gate either. Gee, Dalton, look on the bright side. When it's all over, the town of Battlesmoke could use you both as poster children for public-safety campaigns. You, for the dangers of methamphetamine addiction. And Helen, for a lesson in crossing-gate safety."

Zeke tipped his hat and Lupe smiled.

"Your burnt and mangled bodies will serve as fine examples for Battlesmoke's reckless youth. You'll leave a lasting impression on them, and maybe they'll make better decisions later in life because of it." Kovaleski paused and rubbed his hands together. "Don't it make you feel good?"

"They'll find out. They'll know you were behind it!"

Kovaleski pulled a lighter from his pocket. He flicked it and touched it to the wadded newspapers. The newspaper caught fire and the flames licked the sides of the alcohol cans.

Zeke hoisted the box of cold medicine over his shoulder. The bottom flap of the box buckled and a cluster of blister packets fell on the floor. He set the box on the table and gathered the packets.

"Jesus, Zeke," said Kovaleski, bending down to help. "Hurry. This is about to go up!"

Dalton wrestled with the handcuffs. It was futile. The cuffs were cutting into his wrists and the pain was too much. He relaxed his arms and looked out the window. Except for the moon, there was nothing to see except for black sky.

Geeze, how long was I out? Five hours? Ten? Days maybe?

He looked through the smoke and saw the whiskey bottle on

the table. Wild Turkey. A baseball bat flashed. It snapped in two against his wrist. He looked at the bottle again. And then back at the flames. Another image appeared.

A football.

It spiraled toward him—and then turned into a bottle. A scoreboard flashed in his head. Tomahawk 6, Battlesmoke 3. Number 9. Vectors and parabolas. That Gatorade. It had been spiked. The newspaper said so! How come he never put the two-and-two together? It was the booze in the Gatorade that did it! No, impossible. C'mon Dalton!

He looked back at the bottle. The flames grew around the alcohol cans and his craving for a drink grew with them. It was as if some entity in a forgotten cave inside his brain knew something that his conscious mind didn't.

He tugged at the cuffs and winced.

Dammit, do something! Say something!

Suddenly the Evel Angel landed on his shoulder. He revved his tiny Triumph motorcycle. "Say something, Dalton. Tell him you want a shot of whiskey."

"Shut-up."

"Whiskey, Dalton. Whiskey. Hurry!"

"Shut up!"

"Dalton, don't screw around. Not now!"

"I said, shut up!"

"DALTON!!!"

Kovaleski picked up the last blister packet and eyeballed Dalton. "Who the fuck are you talking to, Dalton? Yourself?"

Hurry! WHISKEY!

Dalton shot Kovaleski a crazed stare.

"Something on your mind, Dalton—besides dying a grisly death?"

WHISKEY, WHISKEY, WHISKEY!

"Yes," said Dalton.

Kovaleski waved the smoke away from his face. "Okay?"

Dalton coughed. "A last request."

Kovaleski shook his head and sighed. "Make it snappy."

Dalton stared at the bottle.

"Well?" said Kovaleski, stepping toward the door. The flames were lapping the wall and the shack was filling with smoke."

"A drink," said Dalton.

"A drink?"

"Yeah, that's what I said."

Kovaleski picked up the Wild Turkey bottle. He sighed. "Oh hell, what harm could it do?" He smiled and set the bottle on the edge of the table. "Go ahead—if you can reach it!"

Zeke, Lupe, and Kovaleski laughed as they walked out the burning shack. Kovaleski closed the door behind them. A padlock snapped shut from the outside of the door.

Dalton focused on the bottle, and the Evel Angel and his Triumph dissipated from his shoulder.

A two-by-four flashed into Dalton's head. Then a slow-moving bullet. Then the old man. Wild Irish Rose. Those crazy, crazy visions. Was it the Vick's inhaler to blame?

Or the booze?

Dalton thought about the old cottonwood tree outside his apartment window. The axe. *J. HAWKS*. His daddy's axe.

He stared at the bottle on the edge of the table.

Could those dreams possibly be real? Can I really break a baseball bat in half? Can I really stop bullets? Can booze really make me do all those the things I've dreamt about?

Dalton leaned against the pipe, coughing on the smoke as he looked at the table.

Only one way to find out, I guess.

CHAPTER TWENTY-NINE

The shack filled with smoke. Outside, the wind picked up and thunder rolled in the distance.

Dalton stretched his right foot toward the table, but he came up short—just a foot away from the closest table leg.

Come on, Dalton. Think!

He dug at his left heel with his other boot and he loosened the left boot.

Ah, ha!

He slipped the boot off slightly from his heel and, splaying his toes to keep a grip on it, he stretched the extended boot toward the table. Still short.

Jesus!

He slid his hips a few more inches from the wall, wincing as the cuffs cut deeper into his wrists.

Nearly there. Come on, Dalton. Stretch, dammit. Strrrrretch!

This time his boot hooked around the table leg, barely. He tugged at it, pulling the table toward him. The bottle rocked back and forth. He stopped tugging and held his breath.

The rocking stopped, and the bottle steadied.

He let out a sigh of relief. He could not let it fall and hit the floor. What if it broke? Then what? But...if it did fall and he was able to catch it somehow with his feet?

Dalton breathed and then pressed his left foot to the floor, shoving his heel back inside the boot. He raised his foot and aimed for the table leg.

One good whack, he thought. *Just one good...*

—*WHACK!*

Dalton kicked the leg. The table shot back, the bottle toppled forward, and it rolled toward him. Then it stopped.

Come on, come on, come on...

He stomped his foot on the ground.

Roll, dammit...ROLL!

He stomped harder. The bottle rolled until it teeter-tottered on the table's edge. He stomped again. The bottle fell and missed the cradle he created with his boots. Dalton shut his eyes, and he heard a *thud.* He opened his eyes.

The bottle was still intact.

He breathed a sigh of relief and noticed a crack running down the bottle. Some whiskey was also dribbling out of the uncorked neck. There was no time to lose. The smoke grew thicker and he could feel the heat from the flames.

He wrapped his boots around the bottle.

Nuts!

He looked at the crack along the bottle.

He carefully raised his feet, propping the bottle upright on the floor. Then he lifted the bottle and wriggled his boots until it was cradled between his ankles. He pushed his aching back toward the pipe and relieved the pressure from the cuffs. He squeezed his legs together and raised them off the ground at a forty-five-degree angle. The bottle slid down his shins.

He spread his legs slightly and deftly clutched the bottle between his knees. He then drew his knees, along with the bottle, toward his mouth.

He hunched over and clenched the bottle's neck between his teeth. He tilted his head back and balanced it upright in his mouth. Whiskey flooded his gullet and dribbled down his chin. He breathed through his nose and took another chug. Finally, he released his bite and clutched the bottle back between his knees, while coughing and gagging on the whiskey and smoke.

The flames rose in front of him and the flask rattled on the stove. Its stopper was doing a tremendous job of holding back the volatile concoction of ether, ammonium nitrate, and phosphene gas pressurizing inside of it.

Dalton stared at the flask and grit his teeth.

Just a matter of time before that thing blows me and this whole shack all to hell. He stared at the bottle clutched between his knees. *Come on, work, dammit. Work!*

Again, he hunched over and gripped the bottle between his teeth. He tilted his head back. He breathed and swallowed more whiskey with deep, heavy gulps. He bent his head down and cradled the bottle. He took another breath, trying not to cough.

But still nothing happened. No magic. He felt as weak as a used teabag.

Ugh...just crazy dreams, I guess.

...dammit.

The flask rattled again and fire ripped up the wall behind the stove. Dalton did his best to ignore the heat as the flames engulfed the distillation apparatus. He stared at the bottle. At best, there were only a few swallows left.

Hells bells, he thought as he coughed on the smoke. *Oh, come on now. Don't give up yet, Dalton! Not now!*

He leaned over, bit the bottle, and tipped it back. He swallowed every drop he could. Finally, he ran out of air and unclenched his jaw. The bottle fell and shattered on the floor.

The last drops whiskey seeped through a crack in the concrete.

Great...just wonderful.

Oh, well...you did your best, Dalton...you did your best.

He straightened up and took the pressure of the cuffs from his wrists. They still hurt, but not as much as before. At least the whiskey had numbed the pain a little.

He looked through the smoke and out the broken window. He saw the moon. A big, fat yellow moon glowing through a break in the clouds.

Well, if nothing else, it's a nice night, he thought. *That's a good note to go out on...oh, and such a nice moon it is. So noble. So caring. So...round.*

Like God's little nightlight.

And how dull our nights would be without it. How uninspiring. Imagine, the night sky with no moon to keep the coyotes company? Geeze, what am I saying? Coyotes? God's little nightlight? What? Am I a poet now?

Geeze, I must be drunk!

The flask shook violently and a streak of fire shot across the ceiling. Dalton closed his eyes, preparing for the worst. His eyes burned from the smoke. His face burned from the heat. His stomach burned from the whiskey. He wanted to vomit. The Wild Turkey kicked in some more, and he leaned against the pipe. He was lightheaded. He looked at the broken glass on the floor and gagged on the smoke. The broken glass shards grew fuzzy, blurry. The flask cracked. The glass shards popped back into focus. Then he heard a boom. He flinched. But there was no explosion. *What was that? Thunder?* He looked outside the shack's window and saw some heat lightning flash through the clouds.

A can of denatured alcohol blew. He flinched again. Something snapped behind him. Suddenly the pressure from the handcuffs was gone. He pulled his hands in front of him.

What the hell? But how?

The cuffs had broken.

He tore them from his wrists, and a steely sensation ripped through his muscles. Another crack shot across the rattling flask.

Hurry, Dalton. Goddammit, HURRY!

He dove toward the door, ramming it with his shoulder and tearing the padlock off the doorframe. He barreled through and hit the dirt.

KA-BOOM!

The shack's roof blew off, and a purple and orange fireball blasted into the night sky.

Dalton covered his head from the falling wood splinters and roof shingles. He sat up and wiped his brow. All that was left of the shack was a burning pile of lumber. He looked at the starry night. Besides the fireball, fireworks were also bursting from nearby Battlesmoke. He soaked it all in and then stared at the yellow moon.

What a tremendous moon!

He wanted to howl.

And he did.

"Ow-OOOUUUWWW..."

A coyote howled back.

Dalton laughed, and then he got up and walked over to his steed, his trusty Buick Apollo. The Wild Turkey continued to kick in, and he grew a bit more light-headed. And suddenly he wasn't feeling like himself. It was if he were becoming someone else. His clothes also felt strangely uncomfortable. He needed a change.

Huh, I wonder if...

He then walked over to the Buick's open trunk and tossed out the spare tire. In the spare's well, he found Darnell's Halloween jumpsuit. He stripped down to his underwear and put the suit on. He then reached into the back of the trunk and found the helmet. He put that on along with the goggles and then laced his boots back on.

That's more like it, he thought as he adjusted the lightning-bolt cape. *But I think I need some kind of weapon. Anything.*

He walked around the car and reached through the passenger window and into the glove compartment. He retrieved the screwdriver and stuck it into the suit's waistband. He then walked back to the trunk, grabbed a bottle of Kentucky Deluxe, and unscrewed the cap. He took a snort.

He clenched his teeth as the bourbon burned down the back of his throat like warm lava. "Yummers."

He took another swallow and gazed at his fiery shadow. A shadow, created by the remnants of the burning shack, was dancing back and forth on the farmhouse's porch.

Dalton raised the bottle to his lips again. He watched his shadow take a belt from the bottle. He suddenly couldn't distinguish the shadow from himself. He felt as though he had become that shadow.

Is he me? Or am I him? Crazy.

He stared at the ground and saw his driver's license. He picked it up and stared at it.

Yes, he could be two things, he decided. Even more. He felt he was many things: part coyote, part poet, part philosopher, part crime-fighter.

He sniffed the air, and The Shadow took over and he flicked the driver's license into the breeze.

No longer was he Dalton Hawks, unemployable small-town loser.

He was now that that dark shadow of himself—a crime-fighter extraordinaire!

The Shadow stared at the farmhouse. An enticing smell drifted up his nose. *Gunpowder,* he thought. *Maybe from that fireworks show.*

But there was another smell besides the gunpowder. It came from the farmhouse. *A chicken sandwich?* He sniffed again. *Yep, Wendy's. A Number-6 Combo, with a Sprite.* But, still, he detected another smell underneath the sandwich. It was subtle, but it was definitely there. The Shadow paused and smiled. The smell thickened, so thick he could pour it over a stack of pancakes. He felt warm and tingly all over. How he loved that smell. He took a deep breath and filled his lungs with it.

It was the smell of crime.

CHAPTER THIRTY

The Shadow crept up to the farmhouse's rotted porch and peaked through the lit window.

Zeke and Lupe were playing poker. Zeke was drinking the Mad Dog from the Buick's trunk, Lupe just drank a large cup of Sprite. His .357 Magnum lay beside a half-eaten chicken sandwich. A rusty axe leaned against an empty bookcase near the table. The Shadow's eyes honed in on the writing on the axe's handle:

J. HAWKS.

Hmm, what do they want with that axe? I'll have to find out. He pressed the doorbell. No sound. *Then...I guess I'll just have to let myself in.* He took another sip of whiskey, screwed the cap back on and kicked the door in.

Zeke ducked under a large piece of flying doorframe and leapt up from his chair.

"What the—?"

The Shadow looked at the cards on the table and clapped his hands. "Can I play?"

"Who the fuck are you?" said Lupe.

The dust settled, and the Shadow adjusted his goggles. He eyeballed the .357 and inched his hand toward the screwdriver tucked his waistband.

"Who am I?" said the Shadow. "You know, that's a short question with a long answer. Perhaps I'm a ghost. Perhaps we're all ghosts. From an atomic perspective we are mostly empty space." He stared dreamily at the cracked and moldy ceiling. "We're as solid as the morning mist."

But the Shadow didn't really feel like a ghost. And he felt much more solid than the morning mist. His muscles felt like steel cables. His mind was razor sharp. His hearing was bat-eared sensitive. And although Zeke and Lupe tried to hide it, the Shadow heard their hearts pounding like they were scared rabbits.

He also heard a swish of air as Zeke lunged for the Magnum.

The Shadow reached for the screwdriver on his belt, whipped it through the air. The old flathead impaled Zeke's hand to the table. He yelped like a wounded dog. Blood gushed from his palm. It pooled on the table and ran off the edge, dripping onto the floor with a steady *plop, plop, plop.*

The Shadow eyeballed Lupe. He was leaning suspiciously against the bookcase.

"Trying to hide something, Lupe?"

"How do you know my name?"

"I know lots of things about you," said the Shadow. "I'm not a great fan of yours. But I've never been a fan of stupidity. And let me tell you, Lupe, when it comes to stupidity, you are the grand champion."

The Shadow smiled.

Lupe tried to smile back.

The Shadow shook his head.

Lupe grabbed the axe and charged. The Shadow's hand shot up, intercepting the axe in mid-swing. He wrenched it from Lupe's hand and shoved him against the wall.

"Do you fancy yourself as some kind of Lakota warrior? Were you trying to scalp me, Chief Dimwit?"

"No," said Lupe. "Honest...I would never—"

The Shadow swung the axe, pinning Lupe's jacket sleeve to the wall. "Don't move."

Lupe nodded.

The Shadow walked up to Zeke, who was still hunched over the table and writhing in pain. He patted Zeke on the face. "Where's the girl?"

"What girl?"

The Shadow yanked the screwdriver from Zeke's bloodied hand. Zeke howled.

"Shut up," said the Shadow. "Where is she?"

Zeke collapsed to the floor, cradling his hand. "I don't know...really."

The Shadow helped himself to the bottle of Mad Dog. He swished the cheap wine around his mouth. He smacked his lips. *Mmm, real hangover juice.* He dangled the bottle before Zeke.

"Let me warn you, my friend, alcohol does strange things to me—even stranger things than it does to most people. The stuff they *think* it does to them, it actually *does* to me. It really does make me smarter. I can solve differential equations that would have given Einstein a headache. Occasionally, strange words roll off my tongue, words that I never use or normally understand. And before I forget...Zeke, are you listening?"

"What?"

"Booze makes me really strong. I mean, *really* strong." He swirled the Mad Dog bottle. "May I imbibe?"

"Huh?"

"Can I have a drink?"

Zeke nodded.

The Shadow studied the bottle's label. "Mango Lime. Say, this looks like one of my bottles. You know, I paid good money for this."

"Take it," said Zeke. "It's all yours. I just don't want no trouble."

The Shadow shook his head. "That's a double-negative, my good man. You *don't* want *no* trouble. You mean, you don't want any trouble. *Any* trouble."

"No. I mean, yes...I mean—"

"Well, I can hardly believe that. See, if you didn't want any trouble, you would be in church or looking after stray animals. You would be baking cookies or volunteering in the community. And you don't want any trouble. So, what do you do? You commiserate with crooked cops and drug dealers. You prey on the weak. You terrorize the defenseless. You lie. You cheat. You steal. And then you start trafficking dope. And you don't want any trouble? Well, that's too bad. You see, Zeke, you're in for a heap of trouble. People like you order trouble by the truckload." He stared at the Wendy's bag. "Your kind biggie-sizes trouble!"

The Shadow tipped the bottle back and took another gulp. Fifteen more hairs grew on his chest and a random sixty-dollar word sprouted from his brain: *implacable*.

He looked at Zeke and the Mad Dog kicked in. He felt like a mountain lion ready to pounce on a deer.

The Shadow grabbed the Mad Dog bottle by the neck and smashed it over his helmet. He lunged at Zeke's face with the broken end of the bottle.

"Where's the girl?"

"What girl?" said Zeke. "I don't know what you're talking about."

"Zeke," said The Shadow, "you are indeed an implacable asshole."

"Huh?"

The Shadow pressed the bottle under Zeke's nose. "You know damn well what I'm talking about. The girl. Helen. She was with you when I—"

"I don't know!"

He dug the broken neck up Zeke's nostril. "Ever see Chinatown?"

Zeke nodded.

"Good, now I'll say it slower so you can understand. Where. Is. The. Girl?"

Zeke pointed to the bookcase and whimpered. "She's in there, behind that."

Suddenly, Lupe's sleeve tore away from the axe blade. He reached into his jacket, pulled out a knife, and charged. But the Shadow was not fazed. He turned toward Lupe with an expression of a bored grizzly bear. He grabbed Lupe by the arm and twisted the knife until it was before his eyes.

"Hmm," said the Shadow, examining the knife. "I believe I recognize this knife. I've seen it on the TV ads. Tell me, Lupe, is this a Ginsu? Were you planning on sawing a bean can in half?" He twisted Lupe's arm some more, and the knife dropped into the Shadow's free hand. He slid it behind his waistband, lifted Lupe off the floor, and whirled him around like a ceiling fan.

Lupe helicoptered through the air and crashed through the front window.

The Shadow dusted his hands and studied the bookcase. He tugged it away from the wall. Behind it, was a door. He pushed the bookcase over. He turned the knob and pushed the door open. It led to a bedroom.

Except for a bare light bulb swinging above a ratty bare mattress on a bed, the room was empty. Two frayed ropes were tied to the bed's headboard. A dingy curtain covering an open window fluttered in the breeze.

She had been here, thought the Shadow. He could smell her on the mattress, even the Winstons she'd smoked the day before. He could even smell Kovaleski, that unmistakable crooked-cop smell.

"Kovaleski," he mumbled. "You shall pay for this, you duplicitous dumbass."

The Shadow walked toward the window and pulled the curtains back. A car started, followed by the sound of a revving engine and crunching gravel. He recognized the engine's sound immediately.

Unmistakable:

A 1972 Chevy Nova.

CHAPTER THIRTY-ONE

The Shadow charged out of the house.

He bolted around the farmhouse and found Lupe lying on his back and on top of the broken pieces of window glass. He pulled Lupe to his feet. "We've got work to do!"

"Work?"

"Have you been drinking?"

"No."

"Don't lie to me, Lupe!"

"Honest. I just had a Sprite."

The Shadow smelled his breath and was satisfied: just a chicken sandwich, fries and a Sprite.

"Was that the spicy chicken or the regular?"

"Spicy."

"So you are telling the truth, which is good because you and I are going for a drive." The Shadow drug Lupe toward the Buick and shoved him behind the steering wheel. "Now, let's see if we can get this beast to start."

Lupe cranked the ignition key. The engine barely turned.

"Pop the hood, Lupe. We need more juice."

Lupe pulled the hood latch.

"Now," said the Shadow, "this is where things get really interesting."

It was a dangerous situation. Kovaleski had driven off with Helen, probably at gunpoint. He could be anywhere, and the Shadow needed every ounce of his strength, hearing, vision, and animal instincts.

But most of all, he needed his mind.

He walked to the back of the Buick, reached into the trunk, and pulled out a bottle of Night Train and a roll of duct tape. He set the bottle on the roof and found a half-pint of Old Grand-Dad by the spare tire. He held the bottle at eye level, studied the liquid inside, could practically see those amber molecules sizzling and crackling inside the bottle.

Gorgeous stuff.

"Ahh," he muttered, "now here's where my bluebird sings!"

He lashed the Old Grand-Dad bottle to his boot with the duct tape. Then he retrieved the spring-loaded clamps from the trunk and strapped them to his forearms. He snapped a can of Olympia into each clamp. He pulled the clamps back along their runners and locked the release mechanism.

Yes, sir. Locked, loaded, and ready to go.

He took a nip of Night Train and looked at Battlesmoke's bewitching moon. It disappeared behind a cloud, and he felt a breeze and a tug of electricity.

Lightning?

He studied the dark, crackling cumulonimbus swirling overhead, flickering in the dark sky like a broken light bulb.

Yes, perfect conditions for an electrical storm. His arm hairs stood on end. *Let's just hope things don't get too crazy.*

He walked to the front of the Buick and lifted the hood. "Crank it, Lupe."

Lupe obediently turned the key. The engine sputtered and then died.

"Okay," said the Shadow, "hang on."

He hunched over the Buick's four-barrel carburetor and tipped the Night Train bottle over the choke plate. A drop of the wine trickled into the venturi.

That's it. Just one drop. And if I remember correctly, a little goes a long, long way.

"Now try again," he said.

Lupe turned the key. This time, the engine coughed. And then it hiccuped and wheezed. A blue flame blasted out of the carburetor and the engine roared to life. The Shadow closed the hood, snuffing out the flames. He climbed back into the passenger seat.

Lupe clenched the steering wheel with his trembling hands. "Hey, man...wh-why don't you drive?"

"Sorry," said the Shadow. He reached into the glove compartment and found a can of Coors. He popped the top and smelled the crisp Rocky Mountain spring waters that created it, waters that supposedly tumbled all the way down from the ice caps of St. Mary's Glacier and into the brewing kettles in far off Golden, Colorado. He had never been to Golden. But judging by its beer, he figured it was the land of paradise.

He snapped out of his revelry and looked at Lupe. "I'd love to get behind the wheel of this fine automobile, Lupe. Really, I would. But, believe it or not, even *I* don't drink and drive."

"Never?"

"Never."

He scanned the horizon. He saw taillights in the distance. He rolled down the window, cupped his hand to his ear. He detected a distant rumbling sound.

A 1972 Chevy Nova, if I heard one.

"West on that frontage road, Lupe. And no funny stuff."

"Funny stuff?"

"That's right—or I'll turn you into dog chow."

"D-d-d-dog chow?"

"Ow-OOOUUUWWW!"

Lupe pulled out the driveway and onto the road. The wheels dug through the gravel and the Shadow looked at the moon, which had reappeared through the patchy storm cloud and followed him through the cottonwood trees like a giant all-knowing eyeball. The Shadow looked ahead, and the taillights disappeared around a bend.

"Step on it, Lupe."

"I'm trying."

"Try harder."

"This thing won't go any faster!"

"This *thing*, Lupe, happens to be a 1973 Buick Apollo. Its engine is loaded with unadulterated Detroit hellfire. Now step on it!"

"I'm telling you, this is all she's got."

The Shadow craned his neck and looked at Lupe's foot. Sure enough, the accelerator was jammed to the floorboard. "Okay, okay," he said. "We're not done yet."

"We're not?"

"Pull over."

Lupe stomped on the break and the Buick skidded to a stop. The Shadow hopped out while the engine was still running. In the distance, he heard sirens. He looked back at the farmhouse and saw flashing lights.

Hmm, the police must have finally noticed the burning shack. The Battlesmoke PD will be swarming around that place like hornets in no time.

He walked to the back of the car and opened the gas tank's lid. *Huh, what happened to the gas cap?* He scratched his head. *Well, no matter.* He unscrewed the Night Train's cap and dumped the wine into the tank, saving a swallow for himself.

Mmm, good for the nerves…and especially the hearing.

He took another sip, and his eardrums became even more acute. He heard a bat flapping its wings, a spider weaving a web, a cow munching on hay, the dream in a sleeping raccoon. He heard everything. He even heard Lupe's foot shift from the break to the accelerator. The Buick lurched forward.

But the Shadow was too fast.

He grabbed the bumper and lifted the back wheels off the ground. The rear tires spun futilely in midair. Lupe stepped off the gas, and the Shadow let go of the bumper. The rear wheels crashed back to earth. The Shadow climbed into the car and frowned.

"Now, my dear man, what was that about?"

"My foot slipped, honest."

"Lupe, how can I believe you? If you were honest you wouldn't be leading a life of crime. If you were honest, you would be an accountant or a judge or even a bartender. If you were honest, people would trust you with their money."

"My foot, it slipped."

"That wasn't very nice, Lupe."

"I didn't mean to. I—"

"You didn't mean to what?"

"It...it won't happen again. I-I promise."

The Shadow eased back into the seat and took another sip. "Now, kind sir, follow that car."

CHAPTER THIRTY-TWO

Lupe pressed the accelerator, and a fireball shot out the tailpipe. The Buick rocketed down the road.

The Shadow grinned. "Hold her steady." He held his hand out the window, letting the wind jostle it like an airplane wing. "Hoo-wee! I forgot how this bucket of bolts responds to fortified wine. That hooch is jet fuel. Jet fuel, I tell you. Silly me! Ha-ha!"

The mile markers were streaking by like fence posts. The Buick rounded a bend and the Nova's taillights came into view. But they were not the only one on the chase. Behind him, he saw the flashing lights from four Battlesmoke squad cars.

"Looks like your partner in crime underestimated the perseverance of the Battlesmoke's police department. Dedicated bunch, aren't they?"

"Uh-huh."

"Well—step on it, man!"

Lupe hit the gas, and they closed on the Nova's back bumper. The Shadow squinted and looked through the Chevy's rear window. Two people were aboard, a man and a woman. The man was driving, Kovaleski. One hand held the wheel and the other, a magazine-loaded pistol. A Glock 22. In any case, it was pointed at the woman's head.

Helen? he wondered. *It has to be!*

Suddenly a train whistle blasted—the Burlington Northern, on time and on schedule, plowing for the Colorado-Nebraska line.

That bastard! He better not try to beat that train. Even I can't stop a train, not with all the whiskey in the world!

The Nova accelerated, and the Shadow closed his eyes and thought. He thought real hard. Vectors, parabolas, and logarithms shot through his brain like Chinese fireworks. He exhaled slowly. There was only one way to avoid the train. He needed to get inside the Chevy Nova, which would not be easy.

Not easy, he thought. *Virtually impossible!*

But it has to be done!

The Shadow unfastened his seatbelt and faced Lupe. "Listen to me, and listen to me good, Lupe. If you want to see another living day with that gold tooth of yours, you will follow my directions. Got that?"

Lupe nodded.

"I said, GOT THAT?"

"Got it, okay. I got it!"

"Good. Now speed up and pull up to their bumper. And hold her steady, like your life depends on it—because it does."

Lupe advanced the Buick to within a few feet of the Chevy's bumper. The Shadow stuck his arms out the window. He grabbed the top of the door and hoisted himself onto the Buick's roof.

He lay flat, stomach down, and thumped the windshield, motioning Lupe to close in on the Nova. Lupe pressed the gas pedal. They moved another foot closer.

The Shadow slid down the windshield and onto the hood. He stood up, leaning into the onrushing wind, extending his arms for balance. Then he inched his way to the front of the hood. He ducked. A low-lying tree branch whipped over the car.

Come on, concentrate. CONCENTRATE!

He looked up.

Lighting crackled through the clouds, and his neck hairs stood on end. *Must think. I must THINK!* He bent his right arm and then snapped it straight, releasing the clamp on his right forearm. A can of Olympia shot down the runner and into his hand. He popped the top, chugged it, and tossed the empty into a passing mailbox.

The beer vaccinated into the Shadow's bloodstream. His senses sharpened, and he re-examined the vectors and parabolas in his head with the ease of a child analyzing a wooden block.

Ah, hah!

And then he felt the tug.

The Shadow looked up again at the swirling thundercloud. He bit his lip. It looked more like an evil bubble-nosed clown than a cloud. He shivered and the clown laughed, its eyes glowing with a flickering yellow light.

Lightning...

The air's ionic disparity increased, and the Shadow's arm hairs stood straight up like little soldiers at a parade review.

He took his mind off the imminent strike and balanced himself on the Buick's hood while the beer boiled in his brain. He closed his eyes, and the differential equations and force coefficients darted through his mind like fireflies along with the reasoning behind Boltzman's Constant and the Lorentz Transformation, which quickly disappeared from his head like a soap bubble. But in that instant, time-travel suddenly made sense, as did the electron's ability to exist in two places at once. But theoretical physics did not concern the Shadow. Not now, anyway.

He had to save Helen.

And for that he needed his Old Grand-Dad.

He whipped out Lupe's Ginsu and cut through the duct tape strapping the bottle to his boot. He grabbed the bottle and extracted the cork with his teeth. The atmosphere's ionic tug tightened. He closed his eyes and raised the bottle up high, toward the middle of the cloud's electrical vortex.

ZZ-ZZZ-BAM!

A lightning bolt blasted out of the cloud, striking the bottle—dead on.

The Shadow opened his eyes. He was unharmed. But the normally amber-colored whiskey had turned bright purple. Golden flecks of fortified energy darted inside the bottle like radioactive butterflies. The Shadow took a breath and pointed the bottle toward his lips. He ducked another branch, chugged the whiskey, and held his breath, waiting for God-knows-what to happen.

His heart pounded. His breathing deepened. And he trembled as every synapse, sinew, and cell in his body underwent complete metamorphoses. A collage of images flickered through his brain. A bullet. A bat. A football. A flask. His mother. A wine bottle. Lightning. An antenna. A Skycycle. Evel Knievel.

A fetus.

He clenched his eyes shut, and a flame shot out from his chest.

When the smoke cleared, the Shadow patted out the remaining flames on the jumpsuit. He then realized—astonishingly—that Lupe had kept the car on the road during the entire episode.

Geeze, that poor guy must be more scared of me than I thought!

The Shadow took another swig. His biceps bulged. His hands turned to iron. It was good thing. For what the Shadow would have to pull off next, he would need hands of iron.

Now don't mess this up, he thought. *Keep her steady, Lupe. Keep her steady!*

He bent his knees, then leapt from the Buick's hood to the Chevy's trunk. He steadied himself and looked behind him. The Buick skidded to a stop, and Lupe got out, dropped to his knees, and gratefully surrendered to the Battlesmoke PD.

Two of the squad cars, however, stayed on the chase.

Then suddenly, from the opposite direction, a bullet zipped by the Shadow's ear.

The heck? But the cops aren't shooting! Then who—?

The Shadow spun around, and the Nova's driver fired again. The bullet punched a second hole through the Nova's rear window. It zipped toward the Shadow's head. But time had slowed, and the Shadow easily plucked the bullet out of midair.

"Like picking grapes," he mumbled, bouncing the spent bullet in his hand.

But there was little time for gloating. The whistle blasted again, and the train's headlight flickered toward the railroad crossing.

Dammit, what next?

BLAM!

He ducked—dodging a third bullet—and then cartwheeled from the trunk to the Chevy's roof, his booze-senses now fully activated from the electro-shocked whiskey. He blinked twice, and his eyes switched to X-ray vision. He stared right through the Chevy's roof.

Kovaleski, all right—and he's holding the prettiest girl in Tomahawk at gunpoint! His eyes zeroed back on the gun. *Yep, a Glock 22. Or were there two of them? Suddenly he was baffled. Two Glocks? Can't be!* He closed his left eye, and the two pistols melded back into one.

Well, what do you know...double-vision. I guess even I can have one too many!

But no matter, I must act!

He crouched on the Chevy's roof and analyzed the situation. First thing was first: he had to get the gun out of Kovaleski's hand. No way around that one.

The Chevy accelerated as it hit the straightaway toward the train tracks. And the Shadow, with no time to lose, tried to think of a functional plan. *Any plan.* He thought harder, but no matter how hard he tried, he could only come with one workable idea.

And it was crazy. Nuts. But, still, it was all he could think of.

Dammit!

He shook his head. He had no choice.

Well...here goes nothing...

He made a fist and took careful aim. Nothing could go wrong. He was allowed only one shot. He ducked another low-hanging branch, pulled his arm back, and punched through the Nova's roof as if it were aluminum foil, ramming his entire arm through the jagged hole.

He grabbed Kovaleski's wrist, pulling it away from Helen.

The Glock fired twice, but the bullets punched harmlessly through the windshield. He then pulled Kovaleski's wrist through the jagged hole in the roof. Kovaleski fired again, and his last bullet shot through the roof and skidded off the Shadow's helmet.

Good gracious! Was that ever—

The Chevy swerved, lurched. The whistle blasted. The gate swung down. Bells clanged. Lights flashed. And the Burlington Northern's 140-ton engine thundered toward the crossing.

The Shadow X-rayed his vision through the roof. Helen was now fighting for control of the steering wheel. But Kovaleski fought back, pulling the wheel straight with his free hand while hammering the accelerator.

The Shadow leaned toward the passenger door and smashed the window open. He stuck his head through the broken glass.

"Fear not, young lady. Give me your hand!"

Helen stared at the helmeted man with the goggles, dumbfounded.

"Your hand—NOW!"

Helen shrieked.

There was no time for explanations. The Shadow whipped out the Ginsu and slashed Helen's seatbelt. The whistle blared. He grabbed Helen's arm and pulled her from the seat, heaving her through the passenger window and onto the Chevy's roof.

Again, the train whistle blasted—shrill and full of panic.

The Shadow grabbed Helen by the waist.

He jumped.

And they sailed over a barbwire fence and landed onto a stack of hay bales before tumbling into a ditch.

KA-BLAM!

A deafening boom pounded the air, immediately followed by the sounds of screeching and twisting metal, sounds and noises so ugly that the Shadow wished he didn't have ears.

He peeked over the ditch just as the Nova's eighteen-gallon tank exploded, blasting a ball of gasoline-stenched flames into night sky. The two squad cars skidded to a stop, just short of the squealing boxcars.

The Shadow ducked down as the fireball consumed the Chevy like a bag of potato chips. The air reeked of flaming gasoline, burning rubber, and cow manure.

While the two squad cars backed away to a safer distance, the Shadow snuck Helen out from the ditch. She was dazed, borderline unconscious. He hunkered her down behind the three-foot wall of hay bales that they had landed on, out of view from the stunned police officers.

A cow mooed.

Helen came to, slowly sitting up with in a daze. The Shadow sat down and consoled her trembling nerves.

"There, there," he said. "It's all over now."

The cow approached the hay bales, took a nibble. The Shadow scratched the beast on the head. "How are you doing, Missy? Crazy night, huh?"

He bent his left arm and whipped it straight. The second can of Olympia shot out from the runner and into his hand. He snapped the can out of the clamp and glanced over the haybale. He looked at the Chevy's flaming remnants: an engine block and four exposed-metal wheels resting on fuming blobs of melted rubber.

He popped the can's top and turned to Helen. "Want some?"

Helen tried to talk, but no words came out.

She shook her head.

"Good," said the Shadow. He yawned and lifted his goggles and rubbed his eyes. "More for me then." He snapped the goggles back on and took a sip of beer while looking dreamily at the moon, the Creator's nightlight. But no poetry came to him.

He just closed his eyes and passed out.

CHAPTER THIRTY-THREE

One month later...

Dalton looked into the Last Straw's bathroom mirror. He flexed his muscles and rolled up his sleeve and looked at the large bandage on his shoulder. He grit his teeth and pulled the bandage back revealing the tattoo underneath, a spark plug.

It had a banner across the top that read, *CHAMPION.*

He looked at it from a number of different angles and finally pulled his sleeve over his shoulder. The bathroom door opened and Jac Lu walked in toward the urinal.

"Helen is almost ready, Dalton."

"Thanks, Jac," said Dalton. "I'll help her get set up."

He walked out the bathroom and headed toward the small stage in the corner of the bar. He plugged a guitar cord into the beat-up Martin. Feedback squealed through the Last Straw's venomous atmosphere. Dalton backed the guitar away from the monitor and peered through the whiskey fumes. For a Monday night, the crowd wasn't too bad. A handful of truck drivers, a few waitresses, some highway workers—all of them drinking like they were going down with the Titanic.

Helen pulled her fingers out of her ears. "You sure you know what you're doing? Why don't you get one of them feedback busters?"

"What the hell's a feedback buster?"

"Jesus, what kind of soundman are you? It's just one of those rubber lids that you stick in the guitar's sound hole, stops it from squealing in the monitors."

"Never heard of that."

"Even Rascal Flatts uses one."

"Rascal Flatts? Well then..."

"It'd make my job real easy, I'll tell you that right now."

Dalton shrugged and handed the guitar to Helen. She shoved a piece of foam into the guitar's sound hole, which would help reduce the feedback. Dalton stepped off the stage and sat down by the mixing board.

"Play some Billy Ray Cyrus," yelled one of the mutton-chopped truckers."

"Sorry," said Helen, stepping up to the microphone. She put on a pink cowboy hat and took a swig of water to clear her throat. "No, Billy Ray. We're playing nothing but Hank, Merle, and Buck all night long. And if you don't like it, too bad!"

The small crowd hollered in approval, and rest of the band took the stage. Darnell on drums, Jac Lu on lead guitar, and Maureen O'Leary on bass.

After a quick tune up and a half-assed sound check, Darnell cracked the snare and the Tomahawk Twisters launched into an original tune written by Helen.

Dalton listened with a satisfied grin. He loved that song, its steady-rolling beat. And the Twisters were killing it. The sound was balanced and locked in, each player sticking to their part, which fit with the other parts like a jigsaw puzzle.

And then Dalton had an epiphany.

It emerged from the lake of his subconscious, and he caught

it just before the insight submerged back under the water and swam away.

The jigsaw puzzle was kind of like life.

And everyone was a piece of that puzzle, whether they were smart or stupid, sane or insane, employable or unemployable, rich or poor, drunk or sober. Everyone just contributed to a bigger picture.

No piece was more important than the others.

And nobody was the whole puzzle at once.

Dalton honed in on the band. They sounded twice as good as they had the week before. Darnell was right about his train beat. It was very good, sounded like the Burlington Northern running on a new engine and a belly full of coal. Jac Lu's YouTube guitar-lessons were also paying off in thousand-dollar bills. Even Maureen drove her bass lines as if they were Cadillacs. And Helen's confidence was shining like the noonday sun.

Dalton's mind started to work.

Hmm, I bet the entire stretch of I-80 is littered with shitholes like this one. Get me a used fifteen-passenger van and a demo tape, and anything could happen. Anything. But I got to get a photo of the band first, maybe make some kind of press packet. Or do they use websites these days? That's it. I'll make a website. And maybe Elston could help me out with it.

The bartender walked over to Dalton's table. He set a shot of bourbon next to the mixing board.

"On the house," he said.

"What for, Frankie?"

"For a good Monday night, Dalton. It's even busier tonight than it was on Saturday. I got to start booking her on weekends. Maybe put up some flyers."

Dalton picked up the shot glass. He stared at the bourbon like it was a beautiful woman. He licked his lips. But, suddenly, he didn't want to go any further than looking. And like a beautiful woman, that was usually the best thing to do. Just look.

He set the glass back down, and Helen leaned into the microphone for the chorus.

Put yer boots on, boy and get ready to walk

'Cause it's a long way back...to Tomahawk

She's right, he thought, realizing it would have behooved him to put her in the band a long time ago. She had a better voice. She had more stage presence. And of course, she was way sexier.

Hell, even if she sounded like an alley cat, people would still pay money—just to look at her.

"Well?" said the bartender.

"Well, what?"

"It ain't going to drink itself."

Dalton's guardian angel materialized next to the shot glass. He revved his tiny Triumph. "Yeah, Dalton, listen to the man. It's not going to drink itself. Knock it down, why don't you! Hell, I know I would."

Dalton looked at the shot and then back at bartender. "I think I'll save it for Helen."

"Fine by me," said the bartender. "Suit yourself."

"You kidding me?" said Evel.

"See you later."

"I'll be back."

"I know."

"Nice tattoo, by the way."

Dalton rubbed his arm. "Thanks."

The Evel Angel popped a wheelie and evaporated into the bar's whiskey-soaked din.

It had been a good night, thought Dalton. And for a change, it was a night he wanted to remember.

ACKNOWLEDGMENTS

Special thanks to Jonathan Prude who supplied me with the idea for this novel and its title, *Blackout Man*. Many thanks for giving me the football and letting me run with it! Also thanks to Matthew Hunter, my talented song-writing collaborator in Slak-Jaw. He read the first draft ages ago and called it Good. Also many thanks to my wife Kirsten, for supporting me and allowing the dishes to pile up to amazing heights. I love you very much! And many thanks to Gregory Hill and his wife Maureen for reading the manuscript and publishing it. An amazing pair, you two are! And, of course, thanks to my father who always encouraged me to try writing a book because he believed I might be good at it. And also a humble thanks to my mother from whom I more than likely inherited the ability, though it will always pale.

ABOUT THE AUTHOR

Charles Cuthill lives in Denver, Colorado. He has played guitar, bass, kazoo, and jug in every bar in town. When not writing or making music, he stares at the stars and talks to stray cats.